Remember That One Time?

by

Larry Joe Campbell

Finishing Line Press
Georgetown, Kentucky

Remember That One Time?

"Between what is said and not meant,
and what is meant and not said,
most of love is lost."

—Khalil Gibran

ACKNOWLEDGMENTS

I owe a great deal of thanks to Leah Maines for taking a chance on me. Not only did she believe in this book as the publisher, but she also guided me as one of my editors. I'd like to thank my other editor, Christen Kincaid, Elizabeth for the cover layout, Mimi, Jackie, Kevin and the entire staff at Finishing Line Press for their communication and support.

The very first draft I wrote was sent out to those that I knew had a passion for reading. I am grateful to my daughter, Gabriella (who was the very first to read a draft), my brothers, Gary and Danny Campbell (I made them read it twice!), my Godparents, Larry and Becky Musgrave, and my friends, Jason Brett and Megan Grano, for reading the book in its infancy. I would also like to thank those friends of mine that are in the business for taking time out of their busy schedules to read and write a blurb for me: Courtney Thorne-Smith, Kimberly Williams-Paisley, Maribeth Monroe, John D. Beck, Jaime Moyer, and Nancy Hayden. To my dear friends, Jim Belushi, Josh Funk, and Marc Evan Jackson, and to my cousins, Don, Jeremy, and Eric. To my mother and my oldest brother, Billy.

Big thanks to the rest of my family as well. My son, Maxwell, created and designed the cover art. My daughter, Madelyn, designed bookmarks, which I handed out to those who preordered my book at my show. My daughter, Lydia, sent me a song, "Wildfire" by Cautious Clay, which started a playlist that helped inspire part of the journey. My son, Nathan, created a website for me to post information about the book and tour. I love you.

And then there's my wife. Thanks for our journey. I love you, Peggy. Thank you for loving me.

For Peggy, Gabriella, Nathan, Madelyn, Maxwell, and Lydia. Always for the six of you.

…And for me.

Publisher: Leah Huete de Maines
Editors: Leah Huete de Maines and Christen Kincaid
Cover Art: Maxwell Campbell
Author Photo: Joe Funk
Cover Design: Elizabeth Maines McCleavy

Order online: www.finishinglinepress.com
also available on amazon.com

Author inquiries and mail orders:
Finishing Line Press
PO Box 1626
Georgetown, Kentucky 40324
USA

Contents

1

A Log to the Throat

The wind blew the clouds right by me. I was enamored with how fast they were heading east, cruising right over the silver maples that grouped together not far from where I was. The wind had a real crispness to it, and I was grateful that most of my body was submerged in hot water. It was a strange and intense feeling to have my face on fire with what seemed to be an arctic blast, to this transplanted Californian, and the entire rest of my body burning up in 106 degrees of bubbling water.

I was sitting in a hot tub in the back yard at my brother's house. I had been visiting for a handful of days, recovering from a freaky throat injury that left me speechless. Literally. I took a log to the throat, which is such a weird thing to write, but that's exactly what happened when I helped my brother and his two boys cut and chop wood.

My brother, Nate, always seemed to have a big project waiting for me whenever I planned a trip back to see him and his family. One time we demolished an old concrete slab on the side of his house that, I suppose, served as a patio during previous ownership some time long ago. Nate rented a jackhammer, and breaking up the concrete was my job. My hands kept vibrating for three days straight after that. Another time he had visions of having a garage, and we hoisted trusses and set them in place on the other side of the house. That vision didn't last long, and his plans for a garage turned into a guest room, which wasn't so bad, because it turned out to be my room on this trip, and it was essentially new. I think Nate enjoyed seeing me do manual labor. Maybe it was his way of making sure I didn't turn "soft" living as an actor out in Los Angeles. Or maybe he knew I was already soft and got a charge watching me haul and demolish and, well…suffer.

I remember taking a quiz in high school. Our librarian and counselor had a test that helped us see what kind of career a person might want to go into. The idea was to give a "5" for jobs or professions that really caught our attention and a "1" for those we had zero interest in. When I got my results back, sports and entertainment were at the top of the list…jobs like comedian and sports announcer and, believe it or not, clowning. And at the very bottom of the list were mechanic, construction, electrician, and, you got it, general manual labor. My brother constantly teased me about that quiz.

The throat injury was just a crazy accident. Or at least I think it was. Yeah, it was, right? My nephew, Nicholas, was throwing logs that my brother had cut up with his chainsaw, and Nicholas is, after all, thirteen, and he just wasn't looking where he was tossing the wood. In fact, he was doing what thirteen-year-olds often do; he was goofing around. He was swinging his body more and more with every log he threw up into the bed of the trailer. And, from what Nate told me later, Nicholas decided to do a complete 360 and the velocity of the spinning gave the piece of wood some real momentum. And bam, it got me right square in the larynx. I'm surprised it didn't crush my windpipe. I mean, that's what I feared at first, because it really shocked me on impact, and I was a bit out of it. I had to be in the exact right spot for it to happen. 99 times out of 100, the log misses and goes into the trailer bed that was right beside me.

The only reason I sometimes wondered if it truly was a random accident is that four years ago, we were all playing football in the backyard, and I got carried away and dove to knock down a pass that my brother had thrown; and I walloped Nicholas and sent him sprawling across the grass. Oh, the tears. I felt so bad. I didn't even see him, and here I am, a grown ass man and there he was, only nine years old and looking pretty much unconscious. And Shakespearean revenge runs deep in our family genes.

Quick example: My brother had a nasty habit of claiming food even if it was mine. He always liked to take his right index finger, give it a good lick, and then shove it down in the middle of my sandwich. This would, of course, gross me out to no end, and he would wind up eating it. I remember getting so sick of it that I decided to, while he was taking a bath, squeeze my dad's Poligrip all over my brother's back as he was focused on washing his hair and had his eyes closed. Before he realized what was going on, I used all my strength and shoved him against the back of the tub. My hope was that, like my dad's dentures, my brother's back would seal against the tub, and he would be stuck. That didn't happen… but something did. There was some sort of reaction with the Poligrip, and it stuck to my brother's back to the point where it had to wear off. So, in retaliation, Nate decided to take a large amount of Ben Gay, and he held me down and rubbed it on my testicles. Oh, the burn! You can't wipe that stuff off because you inevitably wind up rubbing it in more.

So, this would have been a perfect opportunity for my nephew, Nicholas, to get me back. But judging from his tears when the log hit me, there's no way it was planned. Poor kid. I did write down after I got home from the emergency room "I think we're even." We both smiled and hugged it out. Surgery was deemed unnecessary on my throat, but the brutal contusion was significant and deep enough, I simply could not talk. And I was warned not to even try to speak for at least ten days.

So, I thought I would soak in my brother's Christmas present to himself and his family. He said it was for everyone, but he had been eyeing one for years. I imagine he really needed a hot tub. My brother had put his body through the ringer. He was a really good football player in high school and an even better wrestler. He had separated his shoulder a couple times in football, but his most serious injury in high school came when he tore what seemed to be all his ligaments in his left knee during wrestling. I remember Nate being a terrific wrestler, who had just missed out on qualifying for state his junior year. Then his senior year, he tore up his knee. He was devastated. I imagine he thought wrestling might be his ticket to college and his means to get away from our dad. Plus, we had no money, so going to college meant we would have to take out loans or get grants and scholarships. We were so broke that Nate's physical therapy consisted of putting small heavy objects in our mom's purse and doing leg curls with it.

He made an opportunity for himself to attend college by joining the army out of high school, but the military beat him up as well. In the army, he was a forward observer and, while on maneuvers out in Texas, he took some friendly fire when the artillery they called in came up a little short and one round hit nearby, flipping him, his crew, and their armored personnel carrier. Besides the severe concussion, Nate sustained significant knee and ankle injuries caused by how he landed after being flipped in the air.

I say all this because, while he may have been beaten up, nothing seemed to stop him. And like I wrote before; he was always looking to upgrade his home. He was constantly working on it. I saw him one time (my sister-in-law was FaceTiming Sophie and me) hauling sheets of drywall by himself. Those sheets are so awkward and heavy. Another time we hauled bags of cement from his truck to the back for his new patio. He must've carried twice the amount I did. It's a wonder he had any knees or back left.

So, after he received a Christmas bonus at work, he pulled the trigger on the hot tub...much to his wife's chagrin. She wanted to use the bonus on a trip to somewhere warm. In all honesty I know she thought they would use the money on plane tickets to Florida to see her parents and a trip to Disney World, because that's what they usually did. But my brother and his back had other ideas this year.

So, there I was soaking my throat and the rest of my body in the scorching water, my big ole head—the only body part sticking out—looking like a turtle hanging out in a pond on a hot summer's day, except it was bitterly cold with a fair amount of snow just before Christmas. Nate came outside to see me. I motioned for him to join me, but he hung back and just smiled.

"I've waited my entire life for you to not to be able to speak. God, I remember when we were younger, and you wouldn't shut up."

I smiled, and he silently laughed.

"You were so annoying." He kicked at the ground. I knew he wanted to say something, but I couldn't ask because I couldn't talk, and so he just shimmied awkwardly and gave a sheepish smile. "Anyway, wanted to ask a favor."

My face gestured "Shoot."

"Mara's pissed about the hot tub. Thought she would love it, but she reminded me that she doesn't even like them, and that I was selfish, and, you know."

He swayed back and forth some more, finding the words I suppose.

"Anyway, we're going. We're thinking we'd drive down to Florida for the rest of the break. See her parents. Go to Disney. You know. And I know you came out to see me. And your divorce and all."

It's true. Well, Sophie and I weren't divorced. Separated. Those all usually lead to divorce, I imagine. But it's true, I had come out to see my brother and spend some time away from Los Angeles.

It was quiet, and he didn't know what to say. And I literally couldn't say anything, so it was kind of awkward.

"Yeah…"

So, I smiled and gave him two thumbs up to really sell that I was fine with the new plan.

"Yeah?"

And I nodded, still smiling.

"I mean, you could still stay here. In fact, I would love it. You could look after the house and Chad…if you don't mind."

Chad was their old lab. My brother thought it would be funny to give him a human name. And I gave Nate another, exuberant two-thumbs up.

"Oh great. Terrific. You're helping me out big time. I'm really in the doghouse here. No pun intended."

I didn't think that was a pun, just because he was just talking about his dog and now used the word "doghouse." My brother was one of the smartest people I knew. But sometimes he kind of said somewhat stupid stuff like this. Like when he would say "You get the gist of what I'm saying" and would always use a soft "g" like "go." The word "blatant" had a short "a" like "bat" and "myriad" was pronounced "MY-rid." Weird. Sophie thought that it was because Nate would run off and read for endless hours in an attempt to stay away from our dad, and that he taught himself how to pronounce certain words that he had read long before he heard those words voiced by someone else. Nate was also prone to singing the wrong lyrics to songs and then swore he was right and that I was the idiot. I mean come on. Nate one time sang Journey's "Faithfully" while we were heading into town, and he scream-sang "I'm forever yours…if you leave." *If you leave? If you leave?! The correct line is the damn title of the song!* I could go on and on about my dear brother, Nate.

At that moment, I really wished I had a voice. I would have reminded him that the reason Mara didn't even like hot tubs was because she had a heart condition and wasn't supposed to use them. I'm not even married to her, and I knew this. Again, the truth is Nate wanted the hot tub for himself. Besides his ailments, he wanted to disappear with a beer or two after work and soak his day away. And I imagine he didn't actually forget about his wife's heart condition, but he's always been a salesman in a lot of ways. And truth be told, he's always been terrible at it. Still, I know my brother. And Nate would chalk this up as a win. Mara gets her trip, and he keeps the hot tub. Plus, the idea of being in the doghouse wasn't so bad if it meant hanging out after work in the hot tub with some pops all by himself. In a lot of ways, my brother was a harmless, evil genius.

Nate started to walk away but turned briefly back to me. "The boys are already in the van; so is Mara. So, we'll be seeing you when we get back."

Oh, you're leaving now?

"Love you, buddy."

And I gave him a wave. I couldn't say I love you too, so I just kept waving. And he disappeared back inside and that was that. He was gone, and I was sitting in the hot tub all alone.

There was a time I would have lost sleep over an injury like this. What if I get an audition? What if I get an offer? But there was no work on the horizon. December was always a slow month in my business with everyone heading out of town for the holidays. I've actually only worked one gig in December throughout my entire career. That one was a doozy in that I let my ego get the better of me, and I absolutely hated being there. It was last year around this time, and it was a real trendy show called *The Wild Ones*. Everyone was talking about that show at the time. It focused on a group of teens, all at a prestigious LA private school, all heading to Ivy league colleges, and all completely drunk, drugged out, and highly sexualized. I played a counselor. I was excited for the role because A) I hadn't worked in over five months and was worried about qualifying for health insurance for the family. B) It was a popular show on a popular streaming service, so a lot of folks would be watching. And C) There was the possibility of the role recurring. After all it was a high school counselor, and the show was set primarily in a high school.

I had a couple of scenes to shoot for that episode, and they were scheduled to shoot on the same day. On top of this, my old friend, Danny, his wife, and their two kids were flying over from England the night I was to shoot to spend Christmas with us. Perfect. Get some work in during a traditionally slow month and then see one of my dearest friends whom I hadn't seen in over three years.

The scenes went well. They were fine. I didn't get many takes, so I suppose they got what they needed. They spent most of time getting the stars' singles—take after take with nuanced notes. By the time they turned around and set the cameras up on me, they seemed to be ready to shoot the next scene with the regulars. I got two takes, and the director, who was also the creator, yelled out "Super great. Got it! Let's move." I didn't think it was great, let alone super great. It was fine. But, it was never going to be about me anyway, so I hung out, waiting to shoot my last scene.

I noticed during the four hour break that the cast, the stars of the show, never left the set. They were catching cat naps on the floor of the halls of the high school set. When they were walking around, they looked exhausted, like zombies in search of—whatever it is that zombies go looking for...rest, maybe? We shot my final scene, and I went back to base camp to get my things and sign out. As I signed out, an assistant director said, "Okay, we'll see you tomorrow." This was news to me. I was told I'd just be working one day, even though they contractually had me for more.

"Oh...I thought I was done."

"Nope."

"Did they add a scene?"

"No." She shuffled through some papers. "You still have scene 83. I'll text you later on with your call time." And off she went, walking away hurriedly to put out a fire.

Before changing in my trailer, I grabbed my script and found scene 83. I didn't see Counselor Jones anywhere in the scene. It was a scene with a lead teenager, parents, the principal, and a detective...but no Counselor Jones. One my way back to my car, I saw the assistant director who signed me out.

"Sorry to bother you; I know you're really busy."

"No, it's cool." And I believed her.

"I'm not seeing my character in that scene you mentioned."

"Show me."

I rummaged through the script and showed her. She scanned it, and stopped, pointing to a stage direction that read "An OFFICE AID cracks open the door and hands a note to Principal Adams. Hustle and bustle from the OFFICE STAFF outside. After handing the note, she—"

I looked at the assistant director. "Oh, I assumed that the office aid was a woman because it says—"

"No, no, you're part of the hustle and bustle...the office staff."

"Oh."

"I'll text you with your call time."

"Okay...Thanks."

"No problem," she threw back to me as she was walking away.

This sucked. And it was, probably, entirely my ego. Well, more like fifty percent my ego, and fifty percent the industry changing in a way that was becoming completely impersonal.

They could've gotten anyone in the pool of extras to play the office staff while the door is cracked open. Later, I read an article in which the director considered himself some sort of auteur who needed everything precise and accurate—almost method-like. He would use the cast as extras instead of regular extras in order to keep his vision authentic. He wouldn't use stunt drivers on drone shots. He wanted the actors for those scenes even if you didn't see their faces.

It was completely my ego.

And my expectations.

Once I realized that my scenes could be in the can before my friend, Danny, flew over, I got excited and turned that into reality. I expected to be wrapped on the project because my scenes had been shot, but the truth is, they contractually had me until the episode was wrapped. And to be honest, if the director decided to give me another scene in which I could work my craft, I would have been delighted. That's where my ego got me in trouble. All they wanted me for was to have my big head in the background…and maybe it would be on camera, and maybe not… probably not. And that pissed me off.

I had also rented a Sprinter van for mine and Danny's family. We rented a big house in the mountains for the weekend, so that we could all be together. Danny's step kids were around the same age as Graeme and Bree, and they all got on well. Jessica and Sophie had a great time together. And considering that things felt off between Sophie and me, I really put all my eggs in this basket. Looking back, I hoped that Sophie would cut loose and have fun. She had been working more and more hours on a job she said she hated, and I rarely saw her. I was really looking forward to laughing and drinking wine and playing games. I even kept daydreaming about it while I was in my trailer, thinking about the fire popping in the cabin's fireplace, while Danny made us laugh with his offbeat sense of humor. "May I interest you in champagne? Champagne of Beers?" And he would pull out a can of Miller High Life that he had purchased. I must've heard him use that stupid joke a couple dozen times, and he laughed harder every time he said it…and we laughed too.

And now, I would have to drive up by myself Saturday morning. Sophie and I were already at the point where our patience with one another was shaky at best. I was hoping for a little sympathy but should have known that she would wind up getting upset at me for even planning the getaway trip.

"Oh great, Max. That means I have to drive."

"Danny and Jessica can help out."

"I'm exhausted."

"I didn't think they'd need me back."

"Why are we even going if you can't get up there?"

"I'll be up as soon as I'm done."

"It's just so much money."

"I might probably be up Friday night."

"Max." She sighed.

"I'll basically be right behind you."

"So expensive."

This was starting to get to me. Sophie had no idea what the cost was. I was the one who researched the house cabin and the van rental. I did all the leg work. It was during these times that I felt like I was fighting with myself. Meaning, I kept pulling back on the things I wanted to say, and it seemed she got to say anything that came to mind. I think it was because the moment I started to speak my mind, she got really defensive and accused me of attacking her and being irrational. So...I always tried to keep my cool...and the anger pent up inside of me.

And now we're separated. Damn.

I was hoping to get an early call for the school office scene and arrive up in the mountains Friday evening. But, as it turned out, my call wasn't until noon. They then fell behind on shooting and didn't get to the office scene until after dinner. The first shot for that scene wasn't until 6pm. We shot until 11pm that night. What's funny is that they decided to let everyone in the background go just after they started filming the scene...except me. They wanted me to walk past the small rectangular window in the door at a certain point late in the scene. We rehearsed it at six and then shot a master with me walking by. When I walked by what they call "video village"—an area on the sound stage where the director could watch on a monitor what the camera was filming—I saw a playback of the master. It was a wide shot that included almost everyone in the entire room. I just shook my head, because you couldn't even tell it was me that walked by the window. They then told me to hang out for when they got tighter coverage of an actor who was by the door. When I heard the first AD yell out "That's a wrap, everybody. Have a great weekend," I approached him because they never wound up using me after that initial shot. When our eyes met, all he could muster was an "Oh shit. Well, we got you in the master. Have a good one."

This business that I fell in love with, that I dedicated my life to…it changed. And I guess I was too desperate to see that it was changing until it had already changed, if that makes sense. What started out as a passion and something so personal, where real human connection was made in scenes and on sets with others getting to practice their craft had changed into something less than…human. The romance was gone…and I felt like a number.

2

Another Big Difference

I was lost in thought, thinking about that short weekend in the mountains. It wound up being a nice day and a half. By the time I had arrived, Sophie and the kids and most everyone else were already out, hitting the slopes for some snowboarding. I wasn't sad to have missed that, actually. Sophie was damn good on a board. She had dated a professional snowboarder before we met—he was legit, placing in a number of Winter X Games. Sophie had made it a point to teach the kids. And me? Well, ski rentals were way too expensive growing up, and I just never learned how to do it. I've tried it a few times with the fam, but I just ended up crashing and straining muscles. When I got to the rental, Danny was the only one there…limping about.

"How was it?"

"Ah, there he is!" Danny's face brightened whenever he laid eyes on me. And I never doubted his authenticity. I loved seeing his face light up.

"You look like you took a couple of spills."

"Ha! Ya think? I couldn't stay on the bloody thing. Never could." And somehow, I have no idea how, he had two cocktails at the ready and placed one in my hand.

"C'mon. The Jacuzzi outside is burning up."

Have you ever taken Advil before getting together with someone, because you know you're going to laugh so hard your head will start hurting? I had to do that with Danny…a lot. And the cool thing was…I made him laugh too.

By the time Sophie and the rest got back, Danny and I were a few drinks in and feeling great. Sophie, who rarely drank by then, saw Danny making another round and yelled out, "You got one of those for me?"

"I'm in!" Jessica crept up from behind Sophie's shoulder, and we spent the rest of that Saturday hanging out, playing games, grilling in the snow, and, of course…laughing. It wound up being a great hang.

It was then that I locked in on Sophie's face…*in my mind*. I was still in my brother's hot tub, and I could only see that face of hers. Her big eyes that took up so much room on her small head. Her eyes that revealed so much compassion and worry and dread and hope. And her lips.

A Hapsburg lip they call it where the bottom one is larger than the top and hangs, almost droops…pouting…those beautiful, succulent lips. Graeme had the same lip, but Brianna had mine. In fact, Bree had a lot of my features, while Graeme largely took after Sophie.

Sitting there, thinking about Sophie and the kids, hurt. It made me somber, and honestly, a little angry, so I tried to shake away those thoughts. I looked out and saw the edge of the forest. It was bare, of course, this time of year, but just seeing the naked hardwoods made me miss how deciduous it was back here—I loved the spring buds and blossoms and how they transitioned into such a dense green in the summer, only to acquiesce to the vibrant colors of autumn. I also loved the vast emptiness of the forest in these winter months as well. My brother and I grew up north of here, and my mom still lived a couple hours north of my brother, although she was spending the winter out in Arizona with my Aunt Rosemary, her sister-in-law. My brother had managed to get himself through school, like I did, but he settled here in Greenville, and oddly so did more than a few former high school classmates of mine. I guess I would call Greenville a rural hub. It has a big enough population to have different kinds of restaurants and a few shopping centers, but you're in and out of town before you know it: so, it's still pretty small…comparatively.

Then I started to think about how different the Midwest was from Los Angeles. It dawned on me that I spent the first twenty-three years of my life in Michigan, and, as I sat there and did the math, twenty-two years in California. Basically, half my life in both places, and they seemed very different to me. Living in California, you see a lot of small shopping plazas, and you could always count on certain businesses being in each one, at least around where I lived—A dentist office, a massage place, and a nail salon. Why are there so many dental offices? And massage parlors? They're everywhere. Of course, in LA, they call themselves "spas," but they still offer cheap, hourly massages. And in other, more posh areas, storefronts shifted to "Noninvasive Fat Reduction Centers," Pilates/juice bars, and luxury pet motels...though those were, to anyone else/anywhere else, just expensive kennels.

In Michigan, the offerings seemed a little different, and it always made me laugh. I remember driving up from Detroit, when I lived there after college for a short spell doing theatre, and I would visit my mom. I would see the same sort of billboards on the three-hour drive. There were billboards advertising gun shops, alcohol, and plenty asking, "Are you on the right road?"—religious advertisements warning about the threat of eternity in hell. There was a particular billboard I remember near Saginaw that read "Repent before it's too late, and your bones burn in hell's fire...Join us Sunday's 8:30 Bible study, 9:30 worship! We'd love to have ya!" But the strangest ones were the adult stores with a picture of a large sex toy that advertised on I-75 and then read "Take M46, then turn left at the second light, drive 14 miles take a right at the stop sign" or something weird like that. And there were plenty of those billboards as well. It made me laugh thinking *I guess there are only so many things you can do in Michigan...drink, hunt, and have sex...oh, and then go to church and repent.*

Another big difference was just how important plans were in Michigan. Parties were a big, big deal back here. Folks really looked forward to them...and, if there was a special occasion, like a wedding or anniversary or graduation...well, those were on the books for several months. But even just your typical Saturday night party seemed like a momentous happening. I imagine that midwestern folk, who seemed to work so hard, jumped at the chance to do something out of their normal routine. So, RSVPs varied greatly in Michigan compared to California.

In Michigan, "Yes" meant "Hell yes!" "Maybe" meant exactly that... "Maybe. I'll check with my spouse, and I'll be sure to let you know before the deadline." And "No" was a very apologetic midwestern "No"—"I'm so sorry, we already have plans, and we are so sad to miss out." I think that was people's way of ensuring they got invited to the next party. Or it would be something like "Sorry, my aunt died, and we have to attend her funeral..." But it was still loaded with Midwestern remorse... at missing the party, not about the funeral.

In LA, "Yes" means "Maybe." "Maybe" means "No." And "No" means "Hell no." Actually, no one ever replies "No." They just don't answer. And that's typical in LA. People just don't respond. I think they're always looking for a better invite or opportunity. Sophie and I have had get-togethers where we thought a dozen people were coming and three dozen showed up. On the flip side, we invited around 25 people for Thanksgiving one year. We had three turkeys—one brined, one deep fried, and one roasted…and, of course, a Tofurkey for the vegetarians. Well, eight people showed up. I ate turkey sandwiches for two weeks.

But the biggest difference, at least when I first moved out to LA, was the physical appearance of people. More specifically, women. When I first got out to LA, I couldn't believe all the fake boobs. I mean, it seemed when a woman wanted bigger breasts growing up in Michigan, she just put on weight. But in LA, you had these super slender women with enormous chests. Then I started noticing Botox, long before you saw commercials for it. I would work with female actors and kept wondering what was going on with their foreheads. And in the beginning of Botox, it seemed like doctors were still getting a feel for it, and maybe injecting a bit too much, because these actors were losing their facial expressions. And don't get me started about the botched facelifts where they look like they were in trouble with their opened eyes super wide and their faces pulled taut, or the lip injections where they looked like they had just been punched. But then it seemed, like everything else, they started to get really good at Botox, and everyone was doing it…including men. The last few gigs I worked on had their fair share of men with absolutely no wrinkles around their eyes or on their foreheads. I had read just before flying to Michigan where twenty-year-old women were getting Botox as a way to "prevent" wrinkles. Seems like a sales job to me. I also had neighbors who bought their daughter breast implants for her graduation present…her high school graduation present. I won't even start to go into butt lifts and rib removals. Let's just say LA seemed a long way from here. But what do I know? I'm just an out of work actor with huge trenches in my forehead and sun damaged skin.

3

It's Like a Funeral Home There

I sat on the couch (pretty sure it was my brother's "side"). He and Mara definitely had "sides." In fact, the more I looked around, I was certain I was sitting on his side. The end table right beside me had markings of coffee cup rings. It also had pipe paraphernalia. Like a legitimate old-timey pipe—not something for weed. I had forgotten my brother mentioned he was "enjoying a nice pipe these days" and we started riffing on dick jokes. On the table next to Mara's side lay coasters (that my brother should have been using) and some embroidery kit. I feigned polite concern momentarily thinking that she had forgotten her kit, but then I figured she had multiple sets—one in the car, one at work, one down at her parents' place in Florida…that's how Mara rolled. Jealousy started to rain down over me. Nate and Mara seemed to really just…accept one another. Mara was particular about how things were to be done around the house. Shoes off and stored in the mud room, dishes not only washed at night, but also put away…things like that. My brother was way more freewheeling. He was bawdy and crude; he had the best dirty jokes I've ever heard. Oh, and the best stories.

He told me this story a couple of Christmases ago:

"Oh man, Max, I gotta tell ya…I just love this time of year. Mara, me and the boys were out shopping, and I stumbled across this Rudolph playset. I mean, this thing had everything…Yukon Cornelius, Hermey, Clarice…the abominable snow monster, oh, uh, what's his name… Bumble! It even had the talking snowman, you know, that looks like Burl Ives. And we get it home, and I set it up, and the boys asked, 'Can we play with it, dad?'

And I was like, 'Of course, that's why we got it.' And I just stood there watching them. I couldn't take my eyes off Nicholas and Zachary... and Mara lights some candles, turned on the lights on the tree, and poured herself a glass of wine. And she comes up and stands next to me, and I'm enjoying a cup of mulled cider, just watching the boys, you know?..And Max, Mara's wearing this, like, sundress and that's it. And of course, I start rubbing her back and taking it all in...how beautiful it all was, and how grateful I was...and I slowly move down to her ass...and I'm just rubbing, you know...and I pull up her dress, ever so slowly...and I...I...I stick my finger in her butt. God, I just love this time of year!"

He was open with Mara about how often he wanted sex. And she laughed it off. Here they were in their early fifties...well, I think Mara was about to turn fifty, and they seemed to be at peace with the idea of who each other was and that they'd be spending the rest of their lives together.

One time when Nate and I were working on one of his home renovation projects he said, "You have to find a balance between passion and comfort. Adventure and safety. And I may be stereotyping here, but I think I'm on to something. As we get older, Max, I think it's fair to say that women typically slow down sexually, and men, for the most part, not always, but for the most part are still filled with desire. Look at those dudes in their seventies who become new fathers with women in their thirties. Happens all the time.

(I questioned in my mind if it happened ALL the time, but I smiled and kept listening.)

"Mara and me...Our biggest fights are when there's a breach in the balance of those two things—passion and comfort. Mara is fine with every other week, hell, once a month. I still want it every week, sometimes twice. But...But, I can't expect that from her, but it can't go all the way over to her side either. So...you gotta talk it out. And, truthfully, Max, it's usually me, who reminds Mara—that the agreement was being threatened and then...most of the time...not always, but most of the time she meets me halfway and..."

He didn't finish but instead smiled a big shit eating grin. "B...7... BINGO!" And he gave a wink.

Nate and Mara were still raising their boys, who were both thirteen, so maybe in some ways they knew they had to stick it out...at least for the twins. But honestly, I do think it was more than potentially feeling "stuck." I feel like they genuinely enjoyed one another's company.

I can't say the same for Sophie and myself. As time went on and the kids got older, Sophie just seemed annoyed when I wanted to have sex. Looking back, I think she was exhausted, but she didn't laugh it off like Mara could with Nate. I even remember one time getting real flirty—I tried a little sexy dance like John Travolta in "Pulp Fiction" and asked her "You here alone?"—and Sophie said point blank, "You look like a perv." God, that hurt. She seemed annoyed, and I not only "seemed" resentful…I was resentful. And…this is going back a handful of years now…we just started hanging out less and less.

I think Sophie thought I was just going to always steer it back to sex. I think. I mean, I don't know. We never really could get to the heart of any problem because we're both sensitive and would get defensive. And then, just a couple of weeks ago, she said she wanted to separate and gather her thoughts. I admit, I started spinning when she told me that.

"God, I just love this time of year." I heard my brother's voice in my head once again.

And he truly did. The sex stuff not withstanding; my brother went all out at Christmas. And as I looked around the house, I took in all of the cedar boughs he had cut down from his woods out back and hung around the top of the various doorways. He put lights up everywhere and set up a really nice nativity scene that I guessed Mara had made in her ceramics class. She was a real "crafty" one.

Nate and I both really enjoyed the holidays. To put it bluntly we did not have a good childhood. Our dad was erratic, and a narcissist, and completely unpredictable. He would be gregarious and the life of the party when he had friends over, but when it was just him and us and my mom…He was, at best, brooding, and at worst, he would fly off the handle with these fits of terrifying rage. I have this memory of when I was probably seven, and our dad had Nate paint a flagpole that he had fashioned out of the trunk of a small tree. While Nate, who would've been fourteen, painted the flagpole, our dad dug the hole. Well, Nate painted it from top to bottom, and our dad completely lost it, because he wanted it painted from bottom to top, so that when Nate had finished painting, the bottom would have dried, and the pole could have been set in the hole. It's one of the most disturbing images I have from my childhood. He grabbed Nate by the back of the head and smashed his forehead into the side of our house…Because Nate painted a flagpole "incorrectly"…Because Nate was slow to learn—what—"efficiency?" But Christmas…that was off limits.

There was some sort of unspoken truce around Christmas. And it was amazing.

So, when Sophie told me, just before Christmas, that she was heading to her parents, I was furious. How could she do this...right around Christmas? I mean, what about Graeme?

"Graeme has an opportunity to spend Christmas in Dublin. He's not coming back this year."

What about Bree?

"She was invited to go snowboarding in Vail."

Over Christmas?!

Truth is Bree and Graeme could see the writing on the wall. Graeme was a junior at DePaul studying philosophy and religion. And Bree was in Boulder studying "partying," I think. Actually, she hadn't figured it out yet. She was a freshman, and I guess, she thought she had some time. I don't worry about Bree, to be honest. I mean, we always worry about our kids. I always love to know where they are...not to be nosy really; just to be safe. I'm amazed they agreed to share their locations on Snapchat. I told them that I didn't care if they were out at parties or out on a date. I just liked to pull up Snapchat at night and see where they were and say "Sweet dreams. I love you." Every night.

Graeme is quiet and driven. He's going to apply to law school next year. That guy is really on a mission. Bree is flamboyant and a smart ass, to be frank. Prior to the separation, I asked her about coming home for the holidays, and she looked at me like I was an idiot and just said "Dad... really? It's like a funeral home there." So even though I was furious with Sophie and complaining about us all not being together...anyone of us could see this coming. I think I was just in denial.

So...I just sat there on my brother's couch...sullen...and alone. It appeared Chad could feel my energy and found something better to do. He was going to town on a chew toy while lying on his floor pillow.

I pulled up the guide on the television and couldn't find anything interesting. Hundreds of channels now and all they seem to have are shows about morbid obesity and teenage pregnancies. I'll admit, I went to the Playboy channels, but my brother hadn't subscribed. Damn. Just for a moment, I longed for the days where those channels were scrambled, and if you were lucky, every now and then you could see a nipple or the crack of an ass.

That's when my phone buzzed. And it was a text from...Bree:

hey pops figured you were getting annoyed at only hearing
Christmas songs so I made you a playlist...
I call moody winter vibes love ya bear

That's what I called her...Bear. My little Pooh Bear. God, I love her.

There was some sort of link that I hit, and it sent me to Spotify. I started scanning the songs.

"Wildfire" by Cautious Clay,

"The Woods—Acoustic" by Hollow Coves

"Beige" by Yoke Lore,

"Blindsided" by Bon Iver,

"Old Pine" by Ben Howard,

"4:38am" by ford. and Barrie,

"A Different Age" by Current Joys,

"Stockholmsvy" by Hannes, waterbaby...

I didn't recognize any of the songs. I was more of a classic rock kind of guy, so I stopped scanning and jumped up. I even startled Chad. I took this as a sign from heaven that I needed to get off the couch and... well...live. I was gonna jump in my brother's car, play Bear's playlist, and head into town. Heck, it was five days before Christmas. Might as well soak in the local holiday spirit.

I "hearted" her message and wrote:
Thank you. I needed this. I love you.

4

Days Long Since Past

I saw a man running in pants. Jeans if I'm honest. They were definitely jeans. When you see someone running in jeans, your first thought is *What are they running from?* You don't choose to exercise in jeans, right? Although growing up in these parts, I did see a handful of guys play slo-pitch softball in jeans; but I just assumed that they couldn't afford the team uniform or the team didn't care, because it is just slo-pitch softball so…whatever. From my experience playing, men's slo-pitch softball is more of a drinking game than an actual sport.

Although, I do remember things going from "just having a good time" to super-serious when I played with my friends, and we would enter tournaments during our college days. We were so excited to put our athleticism to good use. We were all former athletes, having played some sort of team sport in high school; and early on we won a handful of league titles and tournament championships. We had an absolute blast. But then it simply got too intense.

Some guys took it way too seriously and fights would break out. And I'm talking about within our own team. Some were there, like I said, to keep the athletic juices flowing. Winning is always fun for everybody, but those guys could let a loss go fairly easily. Some guys were there to party. They enjoyed the drinks afterwards way more than playing, but they knew they had to pull their weight and "earn" the postgame cocktails by giving it their all during the games…kind of like my golf game. I'm at best a double-bogey golfer; I mean, I'm bad, and so obviously my favorite part of being out on the links is when the beer cart lady drives up.

Then there were a couple of guys, Tom Keller and Andy Nelson, old high school classmates of mine, that just took it way too seriously. Their identity became slo-pitch softball. (That's a funny thing to write.) They obsessed. They started calling team meetings, and they would start criticizing some of the guys' effort and play. They would read aloud team leaders' batting averages and home runs, and things like that. I remember one time Bob Peterson, one of the partiers on the team and one of the guys on the bottom of the ole stat sheet, got up and told Tom and Andy to kiss his ass. And he just stood there, Bob that is. Like, to this day, I think he genuinely wanted them to walk up to him and kiss his ass. They called him a loser, to which he violently laughed. I remember him saying "I'm gonna hit the bar and then get laid. You two are gonna work on line-ups for fuckin' slo-pitch softball all night…and I'm the loser? Got it." A lot of friendships were lost playing this silly sport.

I recall the last of my playing days. We were in the last tournament we would ever play together. This was after college, and I think it was one last attempt to reclaim some of the early "glory" we felt when we first started and seemingly just played for the fun of it. We made a promise to just "enjoy it." But that was never Tom and Andy's plan. They brought in a few guys I had never met before—real athletic looking dudes. And I found myself no longer playing my normal left field position and was relegated to catcher. I mean, if you know the game of slo-pitch softball, catcher is not a vital position. I remember playing Little League and the worse players were usually stuck in right field, but in slo-pitch softball, a batter can pretty much hit wherever they want—the good ones, that is— so you need athletes all over the outfield. And catching in Little League is critical because base runners can steal, and the coach is signaling to the catcher what kinds of pitches he wants. The catcher in baseball is like a quarterback in football, in my opinion. But not in men's slo-pitch softball. There's no stealing. The pitcher basically is just lobbing a high-arcing ball and trying to hit just behind the plate, so there are no signs and all that nonsense. And so there I was playing catcher and get this…hitting last. Hitting dead last in the lineup. I was pissed. I was hurt. These were my friends, right? And they wanted to win more than…well…me. By which I mean, they wanted to win more than they cared about our friendship.

It all didn't matter much. We got killed the first game and were sent to the losers' bracket of the double elimination tourney. And during the second game, in which we were about to get mercied (I mean, it was already, something like 12-2 in the third inning) the team we were playing had a guy just absolutely jack the ball over the center fielder's head and smack the wall with such an enormous THUD that I remember thinking the ball was going to go through the wooden structure. There were two guys on, and they scored easily, and the batter was trying for an inside the park homer. The relay was late, and I never had a chance to make a play at home…BUT…but I remember getting down in a crouched position as if the ball was about to hit my glove. This, of course, forced the batter to slide unnecessarily and the opposing teams' dug out was livid.

"That's bullshit!"

"That's so bush league, asshole!"

"Hey, dipshit, you can hurt someone doing that!"

And their entire team rushed me. The umpire quickly got in front of me, and I suppose those guys knew that if they actually started an altercation, they'd be disqualified from the tournament. So, the tension started to slowly subside…but not without some more name calling. Looking back, it really was bush league of me, and making a guy slide unnecessarily was stupid. I guess I was just upset at how the whole tournament played out. But the biggest thing I remember is that the new dudes, and more importantly, Tom and Andy, did absolutely nothing to protect me. There was Daryl, who was one of the original guys from when we first started, who came running in from first base and told their team to "fuck right off." But absolutely nothing from Tom and Andy. They simply did not have my back. It was then that I retired from slo-pitch softball…and lost a couple of guys that I thought were my friends.

But back to the guy running in jeans. I do remember a "ringer" wearing jeans in a big tournament in a small town just north of my brother's. Nobody took the dude seriously…because of the jeans, and he could absolutely crush the ball. Plus, he looked nothing like an athlete. He actually looked like a stoner who dropped out of high school, skinny as hell and proudly sporting a mullet. He even had one of those cheesy, skinny mustaches. (He may have been wearing an Iron Maiden shirt if memory serves me right.) Actually, come to think of it, he probably was a stoner. Where I grew up, there really was no definitive line amongst the cliques. There weren't enough people for cliques. At my high school, athletes were partiers, and stoners were also kind of nerdy. A lot of them got good grades.

Still, it was odd seeing this man run in jeans. My first inclination was to roll down my window and ask if he needed help. I mean, if he wasn't running FROM something, then he must have been running TO something. Maybe he got word his house caught on fire. People still heated with wood in this area, so it wasn't uncommon. Or maybe his wife went into labor and his car broke down somewhere. But you would assume almost everyone has some sort of cell phone now, right? I mean, he would have gotten in touch with someone by now if that were the case.

I didn't roll down my window. The thought did cross my mind (several thoughts constantly cross my mind) that if he is indeed running FROM something, then I really have no business picking him up. I mean, he isn't running from a bear. I would see a bear. There was no bear. He could be up to no good and running from getting caught. But that's not the reason I didn't roll down my window. I didn't roll down my window because I still couldn't speak. So, what good was it going to do? Besides, he wasn't really running that fast, so it didn't seem too urgent.

I soon ended up near town. I was driving my brother's Jeep, and I got all sorts of waves from the locals. My brother and I are certainly not twins, and he is seven years older than me, but we look enough alike that I'm sure everyone thought that I was him. As I was getting closer to town, a patrol car passed and made a very quick u-turn to follow me. I hate, absolutely hate, when cops follow me, and my mind started racing to figure out what I had done wrong. The speed limit in town was 35, and I was going around 30. I mean, I wasn't in a hurry; I was just taking in the sites and reminiscing about days long since passed. That is until this cop started following me.

1. Police cars following me and 2. Being wrongfully accused of something and being sent to prison are my two biggest fears. Mind you, I've never been arrested. I've been pulled over here and there for speeding or not coming to a full stop, but nothing more than a citation and a trip to internet jail to take a class in order for the points not to get the attention of my insurance company. I think it's the threat of the injustice that worries me. Whenever I see news of someone who was jailed for several years and was finally set free, because he was wrongfully incarcerated, I get sick. All those years spent in prison, for what? Why? Because someone wanted a pat on the back for the conviction, or they wanted to win reelection, or someone was lazy in their investigation? It really is the worst feeling in the world to me.

Strangely enough, the cop car didn't start flashing its lights to signal for me to pull over. And when I slowed down hoping it might pass and pursue someone else, it didn't. This sort of thing, believe it or not, happened to me when I was living in Detroit, just before moving out to Los Angeles.

Some of my friends and I were at a newly "found" bar in Hamtramck having a few beers.

The place we discovered would become our hang. It had a pool table, a dart board, and a jukebox loaded with all sorts of great Motown and soul CDs.

I had a ritual of throwing in two bucks and picking 10 songs.

"I'd Rather Go Blind" by Etta James

"I've Been Loving You Too Long" by Otis Redding

"For the Night" by Robert Bradley

"Wish Someone Would Care" by Irma Thomas

"I Wish it Would Rain" by The Temptations

"If You Need Me" by Solomon Burke

"Try Me" by James Brown

"I Miss You" by Harold Melvin & the Blue Notes

"Love TKO" by Teddy Pendergrass

"Sail On" by The Commodores...

And the best part, it had the coolest owner...the coolest human really...that I would ever come to know—George. He was an old Macedonian immigrant who played on a professional soccer team in Australia during his younger years. I mean, that right there says it all, yeah? He went from being a pro athlete to owning basically a dive bar in a city inside Detroit. He was an adventurer, and I admired him instantly. I would tease George about not having Marvin Gaye in the Motown inspired jukebox. "How can you not have Marvin Gaye, one of the greatest voices God ever created?" I think George's stubbornness was his way of teasing me back, because he refused to put any Marvin Gaye in the jukebox until my going away party, which was my last night there. That night I picked eleven songs and finished my set with "What's Going On?"

Anyway, I was on my way back to my apartment from the bar when a patrol car started following me. I was more nervous than usual because I had had a few beers. I know guys always say, "a couple" when they get pulled over, but I, in fact, had "a few." And "a few" means three. I had three Skopskos, a wonderful Macedonian brew. I felt okay to drive, but here I was being followed by the fuzz ever since I got off I-75 and hit Mack Avenue. That was the longest two mile stretch of my life. They followed me the entire way, and when I say "entire," I mean it. The parking lot in the back of my apartment was accessible only through a long alley, and the police even went down the alley all the way to the gated parking area. And just like now—driving in Greenville—they never turned their lights on. So, I just kept driving until I pulled into my designated space, and the cop car pulled up right outside the gate. I took a deep breath, gave myself a quick lecture on walking straight, and got out of the car. One of the cops flashed a light on my face as soon as I stepped out from my ride.

Oh Shit!

The lamp they shined was so bright, I squinted and raised a hand up as a visor. The entire area around me and my vehicle suddenly brightened into an artificial, white sunlight.

But then the patrol car pulled away. That's it. No questions, no waiting to see how I walked, no...nothing. I promised myself at that moment that I would never drive if I ever had any alcohol.

"They were seeing if you were black," I remember my friend, Brandon, telling me when I told him the story backstage the next night. We were getting ready to close "Twelfth Night." He was a really good Andrew Aguecheek. I was an okay Toby Belch.

"They were profiling," he continued.

"Really? Wow."

"If it was me, they probably would've put me through the tests and given me a breathalyzer."

"Wait—why?"

"Why do you think?"

"They didn't do it to me."

"C'mon, man. You're not new here."

"Maybe they would've let you go inside like they did me," I said.

"Then let me ask you this. Why were they doing it in the first place?"

I wasn't sure what to say. Brandon had shared stories before about his experiences as a black man, and I knew what he was getting at...it was making me depressed, so I sat there quietly.

"I mean, you thought the whole thing was strange, right?" Brandon asked.

"Definitely."

"Strange enough to tell me the story tonight."

"Yeah."

"And they let you go, right?"

"Yeah."

"Then why were they doing it…like, at all?"

I didn't know what to say…or rather I didn't want to say what I thought.

"They were making sure a black dude knew his place and didn't dare try to break the law."

Man, that bummed me out. My Uncle Don was a cop. And I always thought he was a good one. I couldn't imagine him doing something like this. In fact, he would tell me stories when I was little where he knew a guy was drunk, pulled him over, and then would drive the drunk guy home…told him to get his car in the morning. I would like to think that my Uncle Don did that no matter what the person looked like.

"That's why I don't drive," Brandon added.

"I thought you don't drive because of insurance."

"Insurance is a racket!"

I laughed.

"It is. But the big reason I don't drive is so I don't put myself in situations outside my control."

"Man…" I didn't know what else to say.

"I could get pulled over at any time, and they can just make up a reason. And then…everything else is out of my control." Then he finished putting on his makeup and got ready for the show.

Well, back on the road in Greenville, I finally pulled into the parking lot of Missy's Waffle House, and of course, the patrol car pulled in right behind me. I parked my brother's car and got out.

"Hey Nate!" A voice came from the police cruiser. I stopped and looked to see who was calling me by my brother's name.

"Whoa, Max?" The same voice asked. I was still trying to figure out who it was.

Andy?

"It's me, Andy. Nelson."

My old classmate was a cop in Greenville? My face brightened at the realization, and I smiled. Not that I was excited to see Andy. It was more of the coincidence that I was thinking about him and how life can be like that sometimes. I gave a wave and approached the vehicle.

"I thought you were your brother. I follow him all the time. It really pisses him off," Andy laughed. "What the hell are you doing in town?"

All I could manage to do was to point to my throat, then give a slashing motion in front of it, hoping he would understand that I couldn't talk. Instead, he looked confused, and I shrugged. Just then, his walkie blurted out about some incident happening somewhere…it was all pretty much garbled to me, and Andy seemed to spring into action.

"Oap, gotta go. Hey, it's been too long, man. I've been thinking about you and your career and those police roles you've had. Thought maybe you'd enjoy going on a ride-along with me sometime."

Really? Was this the same Andy from our softball days? And the walkie barked again. I gave him a facetious "thumbs up." I immediately worried that he interpreted my sarcasm as enthusiasm.

"Okie dokie, I'll be talking to you." And he drove off.

Oh, well. That might actually be an interesting ride with Andy, I thought. Not just to see how the real officers do it…I've been on my share of ride-alongs with LAPD and LA County deputies to research roles I've had in the past…but I thought this ride-along might be interesting to see how people change, namely Andy…or maybe me.

5

Don't Ever Do That Again

I was standing in the parking lot of the restaurant but wasn't really that hungry. So, I decided to just take a stroll through downtown and see what folks were up to. Since there were a few "Tow-away" signs in the parking lot, I wondered briefly if I should move my brother's car but decided that employees didn't really monitor the parking situation. I don't think they really care if you wind up going into their establishment. I guess maybe there's someone inside who cares, but I was willing to take my chances.

Walking the sidewalks was actually a real treat. It was slower here than in LA. And it was cold. So, I don't know, seeing Christmas decorations hanging from streetlights felt a lot more authentic. In LA, they had decorations on streetlights, but it was 68 degrees and not a snowflake to be seen.

I was also surprised by how different people looked. Not racially, of course. This area was very white...but more so in how they dressed. I saw my fair share of guys my age with big, hairy beards to match their big, burly bodies, and those bodies were cloaked in bright orange and camouflage hunting gear. And it was every kind of camouflage you could think of—forest camo, winter camo, and even a sort of desert, digital camo. (Though I'm not sure how useful that would be in these parts.) But they weren't coming back from a hunt or going out on one. These were their shopping outfits. These jackets and hats were what they wore, I assumed, pretty much all the time. These guys tended to be hopping out of large trucks. I thought maybe they were unnecessarily large, but not in these parts. In LA, yes, I see dudes jumping out of jacked up F350s, and it's not like they work construction or are hauling heavy shit. Their trucks are usually clean as a whistle. I think those guys in LA just want to drive around like that. Also, California has some weird law about needing a special permit to have a ball trailer hitch on the back bumper. So, those guys that drive their monster trucks sometimes have some sort of metal testicles hanging where the ball hitch would go. I always think they're trying too hard. What's the phrase…"Small dick energy?"

But here? Here, they seem to need these big trucks. Most of the ones I saw were beat up, and they hadn't seen a car wash in months. There were salt lines running along the bottom of the trucks from where the plows laid the salt to clean up the snowy roads. There were some with rust and miscellaneous crap in the beds of the pickups.

It made me think back to a time when we had an old Chevy Silverado pickup that my brother and I used to haul wood from the forest out in the back of our house growing up. Our dad insisted we get in twenty cord of wood every August, or we couldn't play football. This affected my brother way more than me, because he was so much older than I was. When he was heading into his junior year of high school, I was playing junior pee wee ball. Hell, Nate did all the work. I just helped stack a little and basically kept him company. And mind you, the forest in the back wasn't ours, which meant we were trespassing and cutting down trees that belonged to other people. But that didn't seem to concern my dad. Plus, it wasn't him out there doing it, and if Nate and I got caught, you can be sure that our dad would sell us down the river, even if we were minors.

My brother once asked my dad why he didn't get out there and help us. I remember thinking that Nate was about to get thrown across the room. It had happened before. My dad didn't like to be challenged like that, but my brother started to learn to bend the way he said things. And he bent the heck out of this one. He said it more like "I'm curious" or "I'm sure you have a lot on your plate" rather than "Why the hell aren't you out there helping us?" Anyway, our dad didn't seem put off by the question. He put out his cigarette and simply said "Sometimes thinking and planning is harder than actual physical labor." He then popped two Dexatrim and took a huge gulp of his coffee; then he lit another cigarette. (Our dad was far from overweight. He was just addicted to the amphetamine-like compound in the pills.) And that was the end of that. My brother was smart…and smart enough to know he better not push his luck with a follow up question.

Well, one time when Nate and I were loading wood in the bed of the Chevy, we had a heck of a time getting this big ass log up into the bed. Nate was tired by this point. He usually cut the logs down into pieces, and then we would chop them up when we got back to the shed by the house. He just wanted to be done. But the log was too big for me to help lift, and Nate was getting frustrated. He told me to get the hell out of the way and then proceeded to lift the log by himself and threw it into the bed of the truck. God, he was strong. Unfortunately, the log went further than Nate anticipated and smashed through the rear window of the Silverado. Yeah, he was frustrated alright.

That was a quiet ride back to the house. Nate knew he was in for it. Our dad was not only going to have to get that fixed with money we didn't have, but he was also going to be inconvenienced…and would have to drive around with the rear window taped up with Visqueen plastic sheeting and duct tape, because we couldn't afford to get it fixed anytime soon. But, and my brother and I never talked about this (but we knew somewhere deep down in our consciousness), my dad would be embarrassed…and this is the worst for a raging narcissist. You see, it's true, we didn't have money. Our mom was the only one who consistently worked, and the jobs our dad would get wouldn't last long, because he thought they were beneath him. But our father really looked down on, well, people like us. They were "white trash," and he used that phrase all the time talking about so many people in our community. But that was us. We were no different. However, my dad worked so hard to present a much different picture than reality.

So, yeah, this rear window/log incident thing was a huge deal, and we both knew my brother was going to get the hell beat out of him.

When we got back to the house, our dad was sitting at the kitchen table with his coffee and cigarettes, looking out the kitchen window. Nate was trembling…

"D-dad?"

"Yes." He didn't turn to look at us.

"Um…"

It was uncomfortably silent, which would also aggravate my dad. If you had something to say, you better say it clearly and confidently.

"What?" Now he turned to us.

"Uh, well—"

"I broke the rear window of the truck!" I blurted out and started crying. "I'm really sorry."

I don't know if Nate was looking at me or not. I don't know if my dad was looking at me.

I couldn't see through the tears, and I was trying to wipe them away. Were the tears from the fear that Nate was about to get hurt again? Were they because I was scared that I was in for it? Or did I just hate that there was always a cloud of fear and tension hanging over our family whenever our dad was around?

"How?"

"Dad?" Nate chimed in but was immediately shut down.

"I'm asking Max."

"I was carrying too big a piece of wood, and I threw it on the bed of the pickup, but it was barely on there, and so I crawled up in the truck and threw it again, but didn't go far enough, and so I got mad, and really threw it, and...and—"

"And what?"

I was doing that panting talk/cry thing that kids do when it's hard to catch their breath.

But what a lie, huh? And looking back, it was so articulate. Like Shakespeare couldn't have written it better and Brando couldn't have delivered it like I did.

"And I...I...I broke the window!"

I could feel Nate tense up in the silence as my dad pondered my punishment.

I knew Nate wasn't about to let me take a bullet for him. But I grabbed his hand to signal to keep quiet. I saw my dad's eyes move down to the hand holding, and I guess it must have softened him. (He did have his moments, I suppose.)

"Well...accidents happen."

I was shocked. I'm sure Nate was too.

"But...you're going to have to work it off. To pay for the window. You're going to have to take over Nate's chores...mowing...raking when it's time."

"Okay."

"On top of your own chores."

"Okay."

"You still better take out the garbage now, or I swear to God..."

"I will. I promise."

And my dad slowly turned his head back to staring out the window as he lit his cigarette.

My brother and I lingered for a moment and then slowly walked back outside to chop the wood. When we got to the shed, Nate grabbed me, and to this day, it's the biggest hug I've ever gotten. And it was long. But while he was holding me, he said, "Don't ever do that again."

And I cried again, because I loved my brother.

I continued to walk the main drag of Greenville's downtown and saw other kinds of people as well. There were slender, older people out and about, but not too many. They looked as if they were professors at some university, but of course, there were no nearby colleges. I found that a bit peculiar.

There weren't many younger adults at this time, and I wondered if they would be out and about like this at any time. Or was that uncool? Did they do all of their shopping from their phones, like my kids do? There were some moms with toddlers, and the kiddos were walking as opposed to being pushed in strollers. Maybe this just wasn't stroller weather. I couldn't figure that one out. A stroller, to me, seemed easier on the parent. Maybe one would need snow tires on their strollers…an all-terrain type of deal.

The sound of a long honk turned my head towards its direction, and I saw a square of a man, not terribly old from my vantage point, but certainly not young, wearing a bright red stocking cap with a poofy ball on the top, which seemed like it could fall off at any moment because it was too small for his big head. He was carrying a full, reusable shopping bag and walking against traffic on Washington. He was walking across the busy, main drag when it wasn't his turn. Other cars joined in with different honks of their own, as the man shuffled through the crosswalk, while the stopped vehicles had the green light. For every honk that rang out, the guy would hold his hand up to them as if to either say "Sorry," or "I'm walking here. Deal with it." His shuffle was slow. So slow, in fact, that by the time he got to the sidewalk on the other side, the light turned red for the waiting cars, and they were unable to drive through the intersection. And wouldn't you know it, he then walked across the intersecting street, Lafayette, just as the light was turning green for that group of vehicles. And, of course, they started honking as well, and the man, once again, held up his hand after each honk. He made it across the side street and slowly disappeared out of view with his bag of goods.

I couldn't help but think about a few things. I wondered if the man had an intellectual disability of some sort. Perhaps he had some ailment in which he had to get back to his home as soon as possible, or he didn't have a sense of direction or rules. Maybe he had a severe case of anxiety or really hated to be out in public. Maybe there was dementia at play. And then I pondered *What if it's none of that*, and he just decided to do what he wanted to do. Maybe he didn't want to wait. He was tired of waiting, and decided this day would be different.

I mean, those are two very different scenarios, right? The latter means the guy is just selfish and being a dick, while you must lend patience to the former, or you're the dick.

Then I started to think that this sort of scenario is what's dividing the country these days. If the man can't help himself, we all have a responsibility to help him out…and in this case, that means taking a deep breath and waiting or even jumping out of your car and helping him cross the road. But if he can help himself, that means HE decided to not be responsible and figured he had the right to do whatever he wanted… which wound up affecting a bunch of other people. And, what if someone else saw the man, and said "The hell with it; I'm gonna do that too. Why should I have to wait?" We would wind up with anarchy and chaos. Thankfully the vast majority of us still feel a responsibility to follow the rules, but I keep feeling that percentage is shrinking every day with the swelling of entitlement.

Rights versus responsibilities. Of course, all of that played out in my head for a brief moment in time. Regarding the man crossing the street…I have no idea what the truth was.

I ended up at a grocery store and figured I would get something to take home for the evening.

"My cart!"

I didn't hear it at first, or, actually, what I heard was just loud incomprehensible gibberish.

"My cart!"

I looked around and saw an older, tiny man, with an odd sort of waddle, quickly approaching me. Well, not quickly. He wasn't fast at all, but he was intense-looking and moving as fast as he could.

"Thank you! My cart!"

I had no clue who he was talking to until he got up next to me and grabbed hold of a shopping cart just to my right.

"Thank you! My cart!"

And off he went. I watched as he headed down an aisle, and I so wanted to tell him that I had zero intention of taking his cart. Hell, I was headed towards the stack of hand baskets since I didn't need much in the way of food, but he was gone, and I couldn't speak.

I picked up a few things. Nothing important, but I was struck at the selections in this part of the country versus out west. They had fewer gluten-free options and vegan offerings and, well, fresh produce. And where the hell was the sushi? (Man, I had turned into such a Californian.) I wondered if the Midwest was behind on these sorts of things, or if people didn't care about that kind of food, or if it was just this little grocery store. Maybe Meijer, the big grocer in the area, had that stuff. Or maybe there were stores that specialized in those sorts of items, but I didn't see them around this town. I'm sure Grand Rapids has something like that.

What they did have was beef, a lot of beef…and pork…and a great cheese selection. I hadn't had beef or pork in a long time, but I did grab some cheeses. Grabbing some smoked Gouda and Brie made me want to also grab a bottle of wine. I turned and saw a basket of airplane-size bottles of dill pickle vodka, and I immediately lost my desire to drink.

I bought a few other items and checked out. The tiny old man was finishing up around the same time, and we wound up converging near the exit.

"Next time, leave a man's cart alone!" He really emphasized ALONE and walked away. I watched him waddle to his old, little S-10 pickup truck, and I could still hear him talking about touching another man's cart, and how you just don't do that. I even heard the word "disrespectful" a few times. I smiled to myself and watched him drive away. He saw me watching him, and so he flipped me off, and I let out a silent laugh. I actually couldn't stop laughing to myself for a while. You just don't get this kind of interaction in Los Angeles. So many people, millions of people packed together in one place, and yet everyone seems to be shopping online or having food delivered. These moments when you run into an eccentric fellow like this were rare, and yet LA is full of eccentric people.

While I was still in town, I wanted to buy something to expedite the healing in my throat, so I walked down the block to a drug store. There I found a wrap that I could freeze or heat and then apply to my neck. After finding what I wanted, I stood behind an older couple at the register. I would guess they were in their mid-seventies, maybe older. The cashier, a disinterested woman in, what imagined her to be her mid-forties, began to ring up the few items that were on the counter.

"Where's your stool softener?" The wife asked her husband.

"I decided against it."

"Oh no. Go get it."

"I don't—"

"You'll get all cramped up."

"I don't—"

"You know you will."

"I've been okay."

"Harold...go get the damn softener." And Harold started to slumber away. "And hurry up! People are waiting."

But Harold seemed to have forgotten which aisle had what he needed. I watched him start to head down aisle five but then back up and start down aisle four. He disappeared for a bit, only to reappear and try five again.

The cashier asked, "Can I get your Value Aid Number?"

"What was that?"

"Do you have a Value Aid Number?" And the wife gave her a phone number. While the cashier typed in the number, the wife called out "Hurry up, Harold!"

"Would it be under a different number?"

"What's that?"

"The number you gave me didn't work. Would you like to try a different number?"

I couldn't blame the older woman for not hearing well. The cashier seemed so bored, she couldn't even be motivated to articulate, and so she mumbled through the entire interchange.

"Oh, for God's sakes. Um...my husband's, um..." The wife's face angled up to the ceiling of the drug store in an effort to remember. "These damn cell phones. You just hit a name, doncha? HAROLD?! Who remembers numbers anymore?"

Harold reappeared, and I didn't see a box of stool softener. Just a magazine rolled up in his hand.

"There you are. What's your cell number?"

"My what?"

"Your phone number!" And he said it out loud.

"Start again," The cashier mumbled.

"What?"

"What's the number?"

"What'd she say?"

"She wants your number again."

"6165555904."

And a handful of taps were heard from the keyboard.

"Where's the stool softener?"

"I couldn't find it."

"Harold!"

"Do you wanna try a different number?"

"What?"

"That number didn't work."

"What the hell?!"

"Just forget it, Candace."

"Absolutely not. I'm not paying full price for my eye drops. They're thirty dollars a bottle."

There was this sort of standoff for what seemed to be a minute in which the cashier just looked back and forth between Harold and Candace, and Harold and Candace looking at one another.

"Just pay the lady."

"Try 6165552834. That's our home phone. You think I'd remember that one. We've had it for forty odd years...I don't believe you." Candace turned her attention back to Harold.

"What?"

"We came here for stool softener."

"I didn't want to come in the first place."

"Do you have another number?"

"What?"

"A Value Aid number?"

"Does anyone ever understand what you say?" Harold finally asked the cashier, and Candace was visibly embarrassed.

"Harold!"

"Oh come on, I have no idea what she's saying."

"I'm sorry," Candace said to the cashier, who gave an *I don't really give a shit* shrug.

"She wants our phone number for the discount."

"6165557341" Harold yelled out and Candace looked at him in

disbelief.

"That worked," The cashier slurred.

"What's that number?" Candace asked Harold.

"My old one."

"You're something else, you know that?"

"What?"

"I asked you for the Value Aid number."

"No, you asked me for my phone number."

"Harold!"

"What?"

"Sorry about him." Candace apologized to the cashier.

"You want that as well?" The cashier asked.

"What?"

And the cashier pointed to the rolled-up magazine in Harold's hand.

"Give that to her."

Harold handed it over, and the cashier unrolled the magazine in search of a barcode. I couldn't make out the title but there was a scantily clad woman with a long line of cleavage on the cover giving her best sexy eyes in a micro bikini. It didn't look pornographic (more like Maxim or FHM.)

Attaway, Harold.

"Oh, Harold."

The cashier managed her first smile, albeit just the right side of her lip raised the slightest bit.

"You're something else, you know that?"

"What?"

"What. What?! What the hell am I gonna do with you is what."

The cashier gave them the total. One of them asked "What" again, payment was exchanged, and the couple made their way to the exit. Candace led the way, muttering something, and Harold threw his hands slightly up in the air as he shrugged his shoulders, walking behind her.

As I made my way out of the store I thought about Sophie. The older woman reminded me of her. Somewhere along the way, as our relationship progressed, Sophie would, and I don't know how else to say it…demean. Mind you, she would always tell me I was dumb, ever since we started dating, when I would do or say something funny. But she did that with everyone.

That was her thing, and she meant it affectionately actually. I would make her laugh, and she would shake her head and say, "You are so dumb, Max" and laugh some more. But as the relationship went on, the way she talked to me, especially around others, didn't sit right.

I remember one time at a party with a bunch of football parents (some fundraising get-together for Graeme's high school football team), Sophie and I were standing in a circle making small talk with a few other couples. It was just some get-to-know-you banter. I have no idea how it came up or what they were talking about, but I remember one of the guys saying, "It's hard to get that thing in there." And I replied, "Have you seen that movie?" I used to say that instead of the ole "That's what she said." Some people didn't get it. One of the wives laughed hysterically and said, "I didn't see the first one, but I saw 'It's Hard to Get that Thing in There Three'." And I laughed…and loved…that she got my humor. One of the couples didn't get that we were alluding to fake adult film titles and just stood there quietly, sipping their cocktails. Sophie then said, "You teach them how to behave in public, but then…" and she made a face—a grimace—as she looked at me. I never knew why she said that. She had heard that stupid game of mine a thousand times during the course of our relationship. Hell, she used to laugh at it. Maybe she felt I had made the quiet couple uncomfortable. Maybe she didn't like the one wife laughing so hard. Maybe Sophie didn't even want to be at the party in the first place. I don't know. I asked her on the way home why she said that, but she just said that she didn't know what I was talking about. She said she didn't remember saying anything.

It's kind of like how commercials are written anymore. The easiest way to write an ad is to have an expert and a novice, and the expert introduces the novice to the product being advertised and it's life changing. And, for a little pop, they try to add some humor. So, whenever you see a married couple, it's usually the wife that's the expert, and she winds up educating the husband, but not before treating him like he's a complete idiot.

There was a phone app commercial a long time ago, and the app allowed you to talk to the phone to set a reminder so that you didn't forget anything important. In the commercial, the wife tells the husband to not be late for the pediatric appointment for their child. The husband sits in his recliner, watching sports highlights, and mutters an affirmative "uh-huh." The wife then grabs his phone and says "1pm. Dr. Katrina."

"Oh wow, what's that?" The husband asks, suddenly super interested. And the wife shakes her head, like this is just one of a hundred things during the course of a day she has to explain to this knucklehead, and then proceeds to sell the feature of the phone app.

The commercial then cuts to later in the day to the husband pulling up to the doctor's office as the wife waits on the sidewalk. He gets out of the car, and she says, "Oh wow, you remembered."

"Of course!" And he references the phone that's in his hand. She looks at him for a moment and then asks, "Where's the baby?"

With a terrified look that washes over his face, he whispers, "I'll be right back."

And she shakes her head again.

I get it. It's a commercial, and it's not like you're going to sell many products with the husband telling his wife that she's stupid. A) It's not funny, and B) Research shows that women do most of the shopping. So, I don't imagine corporations would sell a whole lot of what they're marketing. But to have someone in a couple treated like they're dumber than the other, to me, that's just lazy writing, and it's how a lot of commercials are written anymore. And anytime I see a commercial like that, it reminds me of Sophie. And my heart breaks a little more each time.

Maybe Sophie and the old woman at the drug store just get embarrassed or start feeling insecure and their response is to project some superiority over their husbands in a way that helps them get out from under feeling small. I don't know.

I decided I had seen enough of town for the day and went back to my brother's house.

6

Those Long Islands

Back in town the next day I felt peckish and found a local diner. The host inside had a unique impediment when he spoke. His THs were Vs. I had heard THs as Fs. My friend, Danny, from England would say "Fanks." And when he counted, he managed to say "One, two, free." But this guy definitely had a V going.

When he approached me at the entrance to Jack's Cafe, he asked "Are you two togever?" It caused me to look over my shoulder, and to my surprise, there was quite an attractive woman standing next to me. She had cheekbones. Most of the women I had seen in this area didn't. They're faces were too full for that. It was the climate, I imagine. Living in LA, there are cheekbones everywhere as people, not just women, starve themselves. But here, the winters don't need cheekbones, they need layers.

"No. We are not." The woman chimed in a little too quickly, just as I was about to mutter, "I wish." But the way she stated, quite firmly, "No. We are not," killed the opportunity for the joke, which made me grimace. Also, once again, I couldn't speak. So, it wouldn't have been much of a joke anyway with me muttering something incoherent like I imagine a rabbit would talk.

She swooped in front of me, and the host led her to her table. I waited for the host to return, but the attractive woman was picky about where she sat. She waved off a booth that seemed to still have a few old dishes that weren't bussed properly, and then she took off her long black winter coat and sat at a stand-alone table in the middle of the room. However, when she placed her hand on the table to support her sitting in her chair, the table moved. She then wobbled it back and forth to her dismay and immediately got up. She then grabbed her coat, reached in her purse, pulled out her phone, dialed, and scooted past me back into the foyer of the diner and left the restaurant. I gave her a little wave and smile, but she didn't seem to notice. The host soon came back with an expression on his face as if he had just been scolded.

"Right vis way, sir."

Gosh, she was really pretty…even angry, she was quite attractive. But I did wonder on my way into the dining room why someone would be picky in the cafés and diners that populated this area. I mean, they had specials on three eggs, three strips of bacon, three links of sausage, three slices of ham, with an extra bonus of biscuits and gravy or a stack of pancakes for $9.99. This was not a fine dining experience. Their main concern was filling guts, not wobbly tables.

I took my seat at a booth with my back towards a pair of middle-aged women in turtlenecks underneath flannel shirts. As I sat down, I took a quick scan of the two ladies. I would guess they were somewhere in their late forties…like they could have sex with their husbands but probably don't. I imagined they were teachers of some sort…maybe elementary school. So, even if their husbands were into sex, these two would complain about being too tired, at least on weekdays. Which, even though Friday would probably not be considered a weeknight, they would be exhausted come Friday night as well, because of all the things teachers have to do during the week. I imagined they probably fall asleep around 7:30 on a Friday evening. So that would leave Saturday as "sex" day. I also thought that what they wore looked new. Like they both just went to Old Navy or somewhere like that, picked out an outfit together and then wore it out of the dressing room. And even though it was a brief glance as I took my seat, they also had similar hair styles, short around the sides and back and a poofy top with flared blonde highlights. I only caught a glimpse of one of the lady's fingernails—alternating red and green with the opposite color Christmas tree on each nail—but I guessed that the other one had the same set.

"Your server will be wiv you shortly. But first, let me tell you about our specials. We have vree today. The one-pound, double decker burger wiv fries and tots, rack of ribs wiv corn on the cob and slaw, and our world famous, mouv watering lasagna wiv your choice of vree sides. Here's our main menu, a drinks menu, and our healvy menu. And remember, always let us know if it's your birvday and you'll get a free banana split on top of our homemade monster brownie."

He said it with a rote, monotone voice at what seemed to be double-speed and then walked away. I then began to wonder how something becomes "world famous." Is there another location in Germany? Did they enter an international food competition? Did someone's relatives from Canada, in town for a visit, pay a compliment on the lasagna, and the owner ran with it? The more I thought about it though, the more I was convinced that they just made it up. My attention then returned to the two women next to me. They were in the midst of a heavy discussion.

"But who on earth would give the go ahead to build a mosque around here?"

"I'm telling you, Pat, these people are moving everywhere."

"Why can't they just hang around Grand Rapids?"

"I don't know."

"I mean, they must know they wouldn't be welcomed here."

"You don't mean—"

"I mean, I'm not saying 'not welcomed'—"

"I know what you mean…"

"It just seems like they're making waves is all."

"It does, doesn't it?"

"It really does, Sue."

"It does."

"Like okay, you want to live here—"

"Mmm-hmmm."

"Fine. God loves everybody."

"Right."

"But do you need a mosque?"

"I know."

"Just make the drive to GR—"

"And everyone can be happy."

"Exactly."

"Ladies doing alright?" The younger, male voice behind me asked, and I assumed it was their server. Who coincidentally hadn't come to my table yet to make my acquaintance, but I assumed I was his next stop.

"Oh, you know…"

Fargo, that's it! I kept thinking *Where have I heard those voices before?* And it was from the movie "Fargo." It was the "Oh, you know" that made me think of it. Actually, these two made it sound like a bad scene from an acting class the way they were laying on the accents…but it was real. Go figure.

"We're fine thanks."

"Okie dokie."

"Maybe a refill on the coffee."

"You got it."

And suddenly the young man was at my table.

"Hello, sir. You doin' all right?"

I couldn't tell if he was unaware that I had just recently arrived and needed my order taken or if he was asking a sort of "how is your day going" general life question. Like, "you doing all right today?" Needless to say, I couldn't answer because of my throat, but I had taken the time to fashion a sign before I came for such an occasion.

HELLO GOOD HUMAN. I HAVE INJURED MY THROAT AND HAVE NO VOICE.

The young man took way too long to read such a short note.

This lunch is going to be a challenge.

But it wasn't like I had anywhere to be, so I just waited for him to finish reading it. While he was reading it, I was able to smile and give him a good look. I didn't want to stare, so I kept looking at him and then the paper I typed up and back up at him.

I mean, for the love of God what is taking him so long? I typed the thing in a large font for crying out loud. It's not like I wrote it in my awful handwriting.

I couldn't help noticing that the poor chap could have used a prescription of Accutane. One of my many faults is that I'm secretly judgmental, and I thought all that acne is really going to leave some deep marks on his face. Then I felt bad for thinking it.

"Injured your throat, huh? How?"

I smiled, hoping he'd understand that I really couldn't go into detail…but he didn't. He waited for a response. So, I pointed at my throat and shrugged, still smiling.

"Oh, oh right. You can't speak. Welp, would you like anything to drink to start you off?" And I pointed to a tea on the menu. They didn't have an herbal tea in these parts, so I just went for the Lipton and made a squeezing motion with my thumb and index finger over an imaginary cup.

"Tea with some lemon?"

I smiled and nodded.

"Coming right up."

I was happy with the interchange but soon realized that I was missing out on the lady friends' gossip next to me.

"Oh, it was quite a scene."

Shoot, did I miss a juicy part?

"You don't say. Wow. Who started it? Kirk or Janice?"

Wait a minute. I knew those names. Kirk and Janice. Not only did I have dinner next to them the other night, but I also knew of them from my brother, Nate, and Mara. Mara in particular had some issues with the couple. Kirk was their boys' youth football coach. Nate talked about what a good coach Kirk was, even if he was arrogant, and how Kirk and Janice spoiled the entire team with barbeques and pool parties after games. Mara was more critical, even insinuating that the two were swingers and certain parents were invited back to the house when they hosted these pool parties as a way of interviewing them and getting to know the new couple.

"Now, c'mon, you don't know that," Nate shook his head.

"It's what Michelle told me."

Michelle was Mara's co-worker; they worked in some sort of lab together—drawing and testing blood...that type of thing. And Michelle was there, the other night, when I saw Kirk and Janice. She and her husband, Gary, were having dinner with Kirk and Janice at the Red Lion. It seemed everyone knew everyone else in this town. More accurately, everyone thought they knew everyone else in this town, but really, they did not...at least on a deeper level.

"You and I go to these parties all the time." Nate said to Mara.

"And do you notice there's a new couple there when they host?"

"No."

"Well, there is."

"It's just new parents, you know, new to the team...or area. Kirk and Janice are just being nice."

"Sure they are."

"What if they're not actually swingers?" My brother asked Mara. "I mean, you don't have actual proof, do ya?"

"Was I under the bed? No. Thank God."

"See..."

"But more than one person has brought it up."

"So? That's just more than one person who should be minding their own business."

"You've seen them." Mara waited for Nate to respond, but I suppose he didn't feel the need to. "Nate, look at how toned they are. And they keep getting work done. And they're constantly working out—"

"They own a gym."

"Yeah, but it's too much."

"They're selling a product, Mara. They have to look the part."

"Nobody spends that much time on themselves."

Mara needed to spend more time in LA. She would see it everywhere…gym memberships, spinning classes, hot yoga, day spas, treatments, outpatient surgeries.

Nate talked quite a bit about Kirk and Janice in the past. I think he considered Kirk a friend. They coached together, although as Nate put it, "It was Kirk's ship. I'm just there to help and be with my boys." I think for Nate, Kirk kept him feeling young. Kirk was probably ten years younger than my brother, and they both had sons on the team. Nate had kids later than most in this area. Given how we were raised, I think Nate debated on how good of a dad he would be, considering the one we had had. It's sort of strange to think about, and not something that was discussed much, but I was seven years younger than Nate, and my kids were in college… his were in middle school.

From what Nate often told me, Kirk was, how do I put it, well, in 1880's terms…a scoundrel; and in 1980's terms…a horndog. And what my daughter, Bree, would call "having rizz." Kirk loved talking to the moms after practice. Someone was in charge of providing a team snack afterwards, and the moms, according to Nate, seemed enthusiastic to talk to Kirk. Kirk was also a winker. He'd say something he thought was funny or punny as he flirted with the moms, and then he'd give Nate a wink, who was standing nearby. My brother thought it all harmless and got a big charge out of it. Mara, on the other hand, did not.

"Janice practically falls out of her bikini at those parties. Our twins talk about it."

"Why wouldn't they? They're seventh graders."

"Does he still send you porn?"

"Mara."

"See?"

"It's not porn. And no, he doesn't."

"Max, Nate got in trouble for opening one of Kirk's texts at a meeting."

I looked at Nate, who shrugged guiltily.

"He opened the text—"

"It was some TikTok thingy—"

"And this woman was moaning."

"It wasn't porn."

"Loudly."

"It was a practical joke."

"Were your bosses laughing?"

Again, Nate shrunk with a look of guilt.

"Pretty good get," Nate whispered to me, and I smiled.

"And you still defend that pervert."

"Oh Mara. He's just havin' fun."

That's a little background on Kirk and Janice. Anyway, back at Jack's Café' with Pat and Sue...

"Oh, it was definitely Kirk."

"I guess guys think it's okay if they cheat but not the misses, huh?"

"Oh, c'mon, Pat, there's always been a double standard."

"Well, I tell ya, Sue, I just don't get it."

"Well, Janice was, well, evidently, because I wasn't there now, but evidently, she let him have it."

"I always thought those two were really into each other."

"Mmm-hmm. Me too. But apparently Kirk had slept with a trainer at the gym."

"Hard Bodies?"

"It's the only gym I'm aware of."

"Oh, I wonder if it was Jesse..."

"Someone named 'Brittany,' I think. She's, I guess, not only a trainer there at the gym but an aspiring fitness model. She's half his age and, apparently, has..." Sue's voice trailed off.

"Has what?" Pat asked.

Well, you didn't hear it from me, but she apparently, has an..." And, once again, Sue didn't finish her sentence.

"Sorry, I'm not understanding what you're mouthing there," Pat confessed.

There was more silence, and I assumed Sue was determined to be discreet about what she wanted to say.

"Still not getting it, Sue."

And Sue frustratingly whispered, "Only Fans. She apparently has an Only Fans."

"Oh, definitely not Jesse then. She's a bit of a roly-poly if you ask me. Not even sure how you get a job at a gym looking like that."

"Jesse Hagstrom?"

"Yeah."

"Oh, you think Jesse's a big girl?"

"Well—not if she was working at a check out aisle or—

"I think Jesse's a pretty girl."

"But for a gym, Sue, for a gym? C'mon."

I was really hoping they'd get back to the point of the story. Plus, if you saw Pat and Sue, they really had no room to talk about how heavy someone else was.

"Well, anyway—"

"Yeah, go on...sorry—"

"Not at all. Anyway...from what I heard, and again I wasn't there...but from what I heard, Janice knew about this Brittany lady."

"Oh, yeah? Wow."

"Yeah. But I guess she just went along with it, you know, because of the kids, I suppose."

"Oh right, they have a bunch, yeah?"

"Four."

"Wow."

"Yeah. Anyway, Kirk was drunk—"

"Sure…"

"He had a few Long Islands—"

"Good Lord."

"Right?"

"Those things, Sue, my word."

"Pretty potent."

"Well, I guess! I mean, how many shots are in one of those?"

"Too many if you ask me."

"I'll say. Gee whiz."

For the love of God, please get back to the story.

"What can I get ya to eat?" The server was once again at my table dropping off my tea. I hurriedly scanned the menu and pointed to a club sandwich…wanting desperately to get back to Pat and Sue's story.

"Super salad?"

And I nodded.

"Which one?"

I looked at the server, confused."

"Super salad?"

"And I nodded again.

"Sir?" The pimpled dude asked, and I waited. I was so lost. A nice, big salad sounded great.

"Soup…or…salad," he overly articulated.

OH!

And I looked at the menu, found the soup section and pointed to the word "soup."

"Beef vegetable, clam chowder with bacon, chicken noodle, or our homemade chili?"

I stared at him.

He stared at me.

I pointed to my throat and shrugged.

"Oh, right! Um, let me see…Beef vegetable?"

I shook my head.

"Clam chowder with bacon?"

I shook my head again.

"Chicken noodle?"

I nodded with a big smile.

Coming right up." And the server left. And I was agitated, knowing I missed a big chunk of gossip.

"And that was the last time I ever had a Long Island Iced Tea!"

Oh, thank God.

"Well, so…Kirk starts grilling Janice. Something about his brother. And he just keeps asking her about him. 'I knew you two teaching together was a bad F'n idea!' 'My own F'n brother!'

"Wait! Kirk's brother, Ray?"

"Yeah."

"The varsity football coach?"

"Yeah."

"Whoa."

"Yeah. And Janice seems surprised and even tries to laugh it off, but Kirk is persistent.

Then she's looking around the pub because Kirk's getting louder."

"Oh dear."

"And so, Janice starts to get annoyed and tells him that he doesn't know what he's talking about. But Kirk won't let up. And he just keeps saying 'I know what you did...I know.'"

"Oh, I so wish I was there."

"Right? Me too. But get this. Janice finally had enough and says something like 'I think someone's feeling guilty.' And well, of course, Kirk has this indignant look on his face, and get this...get this...I swear to God, well, evidently...Janice leans in and whispers...loud enough for folks to hear...she says, 'If you try to deny anything, I promise you, I will make a scene.'"

"Really?"

"And she waits. She leans back in her side of the booth and waits."

"And?"

"And, wouldn't you know it, Pat, Kirk smiles and says, 'I don't know what you're talking about.'"

"No?!."

"Yep. And Janice let him have it. She starts raising her voice talking Brittany this and Brittany that, and 'fitness model, my ass'!" The word "ass" voiced under Sue's breath.

"Oh my." And Pat clapped her hands a little.

"Janice says 'I know all about how you've been f'ing Brittany at the gym. God, Kirk, everyone knows.' Well, that, of course, shut Kirk right up. Now it's Kirk who's looking around. And of course, everyone is looking at them, so Kirk goes 'We should go. We'll talk about this—' and wouldn't you know, Janice stops him and says, "We'll talk about it NOW!""

Pat laughed, utterly captivated by the story.

"'We'll deal with it all, now!' That's what she says."

"All?"

"Yep. And she says 'You can't keep your big 'A' 'D' in those pants of yours. Like super loud."

"Big 'A' 'D'?"

"Pat."

There was a pause. I'm assuming it was taking Pat a bit of time to understand what Sue was referring to. Then, suddenly, there was a large gasp from Pat.

"Ohhhh! Got it. Got it…Wow."

"Janice actually used the 'A' word and 'D' word—"

"Of course."

"But the whole restaurant is staring at this point."

"Oh, dear lord."

"I mean, apparently. At least that was what Dottie told me."

"Oh, Dottie was the one, huh?"

"She was there."

"She's always…THERE, you know?"

"Oh yeah, that Dottie. Anyway. Janice basically tore into Kirk saying that it was guilt that was making him all suspicious, and that…get this…She says 'But I wish I had slept with your brother! From what I hear Ray's twice the man you are!'"

"Ohhhh, ouch, wow."

"And the place is silent…pin drop, ya know?"

"Oh, I'm sure."

"Yeah, and Dottie said you could see that that really hurt Kirk."

"Oh, I bet."

"So. Kirk gets up from the booth, just nodding his head, taking in what Janice just said," Sue recalled. "And by this time, everyone is staring at him. Now you know Kirk."

"Sort of."

"Well, you know what he looks like?"

"Oh sure."

"Still fit."

"Oh, how fun would that be?"

"Pat!"

"Oh, come on, Sue. I mean…come on."

"Yeah, he's really nice."

"Isn't he though?"

"So, Kirk sees that everyone is looking at him. And he's drunk—"

"Those Long Islands…"

"They'll get ya."

"My lord…"

"And he screams out 'Who wouldn't want to sleep with this?!' And as God as my witness, well Dottie, I mean. Dottie tells me that Kirk…he then drops his pants revealing…you know…and apparently there's a lot down there…"

That last line was spoken as if out of the side of Sue's mouth.

"Really? I mean, I've heard." Pat seemed super intrigued.

"Well…It's true…according to Dottie. And he just slowly waddles out of the restaurant. Dottie said his butt's nice too." And Sue giggled. They both giggled.

"Wow."

"Yeah."

"In December?"

"Yep."

"With the snow?"

"It's not about the weather, Pat."

"But that would be cold on his you-know-what."

"It's more about him showing his you-know-what to the entire town."

"Those Long Islands."

"Mmm-hmm."

"I don't know what else to say."

"What else can you say?"

"Just, wow."

"Mmm-hmm."

"Well, I don't know if you can come back from that."

"That's not all."

"Oh. Stop."

"Just one last thing."

"Stop it now."

"When Kirk got to the door, he turned back to Janice, and said 'Do you know how I knew about you and my brother'?"

"Oh, so he still believed it?"

"Get this…he says… 'Gary told me.'"

Oh shit.

"Gary?"

"Gary Stephenson."

"The band teacher?"

"Yep."

"At the school?"

"There's only one band teacher, Pat."

"Huh."

And that's the same Gary of Gary and Michelle, who's my sister-in-law's co-worker, from the Red Lion the other night.

7

It's Just a Hypothetical

The night of my throat incident, Nate and Mara were obligated to attend Nate's Christmas party at work. I figured I'd play some *Madden* or *Call of Duty* with my nephews, but they wound up heading over to a neighbor's house to do, well, the exact same thing…just not with their injured, mute uncle. I wasn't offended. They told me that their friend had a high definition 156" projection screen down in this cool ass basement, so to them, it seemed like a no brainer. I sat in my brother's living room, and got a hankering for some soup, figuring it would speed up the healing process for my throat. In previous trips to see my brother, we always had a pretty good time at the Red Lion in town, so I headed there.

"I don't know what I would do if I was with a really attractive man."

That's sort of where I entered the conversation that night where the two couples faced each other. And it was Michelle who said it. I remember because Gary, who was sitting next to her, seemed visibly hurt by what Michelle just said, even though, I'm sorry, but Gary didn't seem to be a catch. He looked like, well, me. Not bad looking, but certainly not stunning.

"I mean, I would feel so intimidated. Like, we would have to do it in the dark," Michelle finished.

"Then you'd miss out on how hot he was," replied Janice.

"Oh god," Michelle said embarrassingly.

Gary went from being engaged in the conversation to looking away. He just sat there with his wife, Kirk, and Janice in silence, half-listening to the other three laugh and giggle and explore the hypothetical presented to Michelle about being with an good looking dude.

Mara had brought up Gary several times when I would visit, and we would be sitting around the living room catching up. Working with Michelle so intimately gave Mara some insight, however biased, as to who Gary was. Gary was the high school band teacher, and from Mara's perspective was a little stuck up. He seemed unsettled in this small town and wanted more. Big fish, small pond, but maybe only in Gary's mind. Maybe it was because Mara was content with her life, and from listening to her talk about Gary and Michelle, I gathered that Michelle was satisfied with the life she was living as well. But, according to Mara, she did bring up conflicts, arguments that Gary and Michelle would have. Of course, this was all from Michelle's perspective—Gary was unhappy, and Michelle couldn't seem to fill that hole any longer.

"You don't know." My brother would constantly chime in. Or "But you can't be certain."

Mara seemed to side with Michelle, because Michelle was the only one who had the ability to affect mood and morale at work. I mean, Gary's not ultimately important to Mara's well-being, only Michelle is, because the two work so closely together. So, it seems natural that Mara would have a bias towards Michelle's point of view, because Mara's trying to navigate a healthy work environment.

Gary, from my brother's perspective, was a decent man. A bit of an oddball, sure. Full of himself? Nate never got that sense. Gary was just…different. He was an easy target, in my brother's opinion, because he always wore polo shirts tucked into his pants and a sweater draped over his shoulders…("Tennis, anyone?") He constantly led the high school orchestra to regional and state accolades, but the size of the orchestra kept dwindling over the years, because kids thought it was nerdy…or they thought Gary was.

To me, that night at the Red Lion, Gary looked…"okay." I mean, he was no slouch. He looked like he may have been an athlete back in the day. Not a star; nothing all-league. My brother told me that they had golfed together. I imagined he tried sports as a teen, but didn't stand out, but he didn't just sit the bench either. He was a music man, and playing an instrument doesn't burn many calories, leaving him with a dad bod and a bit of a beer gut.

Maybe he was thinking of something else, but still he seemed hurt by Michelle's comments. Was I the only one who noticed? I scanned the table. Janice seemed to be checking in with Gary but managed to stay involved in the conversation. It definitely seemed to me that Gary had a different energy compared to the rest of the group. He just sat there, not saying much of anything really. An occasional head nod or a courteous chuckle, but he didn't add anything to the conversation. He just sat there seemingly lost in what Michelle had just said, while the others laughed about sex.

"If he had a six pack, wouldn't you want to run your fingers up and down those crevasses?" Janice pressed.

Michelle put her head in her hands, trying to hide, her smile peaking through her fingers. "Stop. You're crazy, Janice."

Kirk was laughing right along with the ladies.

"Gar? Gar. Gary?"

Gary looked up; a smile ran across his face seemingly trying to hide the fact that he was someplace else.

"Yeah?"

Kirk continued. "What say you?"

"I'm sorry, I was thinking about something—work. Don't know why. We have that competition coming up, ha! Yeah, thinking about work. For a minute. There."

Michelle looked at him with what I thought was concern.

"What were you guys saying?" Gary asked.

Kirk repeated, "Would you enjoy a woman with ripped abs?"

Gary glanced at Michelle, who waited, like the others, for his reply.

"Michelle has a great stomach."

"Yeah, right," Michelle interjected a little too quickly.

"I'm serious."

"Gary, I don't have abs...let alone ripped ones."

"You have a stomach that bears the markings of motherhood."

"Gee, thanks."

"Michelle's the only woman I would ever want to be with."

The room went quiet for a moment as that last comment sank in.

"Jesus Christ, Gar, now you're making me look like an asshole!" Kirk broke the tension, as he called the waiter and motioned to his near-empty cocktail glass and then twirled his finger around signaling "drinks for the whole table."

"You are an asshole," Janice said to Kirk with a laugh.

"Why? What?" Gary asked.

"Kirk, said he'd, what was the word, Kirk, 'bed'—"

"Bang," Kirk blurted.

"Bang, yeah, a ripped-abbed chick in a heartbeat."

And Janice and Kirk laughed, but it seemed uncomfortable between Gary and Michelle. Mind you, I don't know any of these people… just some brief stories from my brother and sister-in-law. And, not that Nate and Mara would lie, but when people retell tales, there's not only bias but hyperbole, if only to make stories more interesting. There was, though, a palatable tension at the table. The laughter faded as Kirk went for a pull of the last of his drink. He jumped in to end the silence.

"No. Wait, I'm calling bullshit, Gar." And everyone looked at Kirk. "What are you some fuckin' saint? Nah. C'mon, we're not being for real, you know. This ain't a documentary, bud. We won't hold you to it."

It was quiet. The four seemed to be looking at one another at different times…eyes dancing around the table to see who was going to add anything.

"Well?" Kirk persisted.

"What…I find my wife sexy."

"Yeah, sure, we all do. Michelle, you know I think you're hot…but we're just talking here, buddy. Like 'I Never,' and 'Who Would you Kick Out of Bed'." Kirk, and maybe he was drunk…or maybe he sensed the tension that I had felt, would not let up. "I mean, it's just a hypothetical, Gar."

"You want to know what I think?" Gary asked.

"Uh, yeah…That's what I've been talking about."

Janice looked around, "Where are those drinks?"

Instead of answering, Gary took a swig of his beer.

"You seem to like them on Instagram," Michelle said ever so softly.

Gary gave her an incredulous look. "What?"

"Fitness models type of thing."

"What do you mean?"

"I don't know. At night, when we're lying in bed, and you think I'm asleep."

"Busted!" Kirk jumped in.

"That's…That?…That's nothing."

"Or the porn." Michelle seemed to be over sharing now…And the rest were there for it.

"Porn?!" Gary seemed indignant.

Kirk seemed content to watch his friend drown in the deep water, while Janice waved the server over, who was landing at their table with a fresh round of drinks.

"When you think I'm asleep. Or, or, or when you think you have your earbuds in, but you don't…I can hear—I don't know—moaning."

Gary was visibly embarrassed, and quite frankly, I wasn't sure what was going on now. Kirk started howling with laughter, and Gary gave him an angry look. Janice took a huge gulp to finish off her old cocktail, and Michelle seemed to fidget in her seat.

"I'm sorry," Michelle whispered.

"Excuse me." Gary was now trying to leave the table, but he was inside next to the wall.

"Gar, it's no big deal." Kirk jumped in.

"I'm sorry," Michelle said it again but a little louder. Kirk simultaneously chimed in again, "Who doesn't watch porn?"

"Yeah," Janice added.

"Hell, we watch it together." Kirk added, gesturing to Janice.

"We used to," Michelle muttered and then finished what seemed to be a vodka cranberry. She then went right for the fresh one.

"I need to use the bathroom," Gary was still trying to work his way past Michelle who was now trying to let him out.

"What you going to do?" Kirk asked Gary, but winked at Michelle, and immediately laughed hysterically.

"Kirk," Janice blurted out.

What? It's a jack off joke."

"Oh, really?" Janice retorted sarcastically.

"Would everyone just relax? We're here—" Kirk began to lecture.

"May I please get the fuck out?!"

Michelle, Kirk, and Janice froze. Kirk was the only one who looked at the frustrated Gary.

"Dude, chill."

But Michelle moved, and Gary awkwardly stormed off. Kirk then looked at Janice, who took another long swig from her drink.

And me? I just sat there like I saw the best play in years. What the hell just happened?

The table was quiet for more than a moment, then Janice asked if

Michelle was okay.

Michelle dabbed her eyes with her napkin and nodded.

"What the hell was that?"

Kirk's question went unanswered. Michelle's eyes veered towards my table, and I quickly looked down at my plate and quickly slurped my now lukewarm bisque. I didn't want anyone to think I was prying, though I certainly was. My hope was that Michelle was glancing around the entire area to see if Gary had caused a scene, and not wondering if I, alone, was eavesdropping.

"He's been a little weird at work as well," Janice added to break the silence once again.

"What do you mean?" But when Kirk asked that question, Janice only shrugged as she reached for her cocktail and took a swig.

Michelle just sat there. And so did Kirk and Janice, though they kept hitting their drinks. I have no idea how much time had passed, but it was substantial. And Gary never came back.

"I have no idea what I've done wrong." Michelle finally spoke.

Kirk drank some more, but Janice quickly added, "You've done nothing wrong."

"Obviously, I have."

"No."

And then Michelle went silent again.

It's my fault," suggested Kirk. "Stupid hypotheticals. I was just playing."

"No," Michelle whispered. "It's something else."

"What do you mean?" Janice asked, but Michelle only shook her head and whispered, "I don't know."

Janice and Kirk looked at one another, and Michelle started to slide out from her seat at the booth.

"I've gotta go."

"But you haven't touched your drink," Kirk blurted…a little too hastily.

Michelle poked around in her purse and pulled out her wallet, but Janice motioned with her hand that that was unnecessary. "We've got this."

"Let us at least give you a ride."

"I drove, remember?"

"Oh. Right, right."

"Sorry about tonight."

"Don't be."

Michelle was now about to head out, and Kirk gave her a slight wave goodbye. Janice slapped his arm, a clear indicator to let her out so that she could hug Michelle, and Kirk got up quickly. Janice shimmied out of the booth and embraced Michelle.

"Call me." Janice said inches away from Michelle's face. Michelle nodded and walked away.

"Fuckin' wild, huh?" Kirk asked rhetorically and grabbed Michelle's drink. He gave it a healthy pull.

"We should go," Janice responded.

"Yeah, yeah. For sure. I'll find the waitress and get the check."

"I need to use the restroom," and Janice disappeared.

Kirk shook his head, and then proceeded to drain all the unfinished cocktails. He then walked away as well.

So that's the story from the other night. And now to hear that Kirk found out about Janice sleeping with his brother from Gary, well, that made me think of a few scenarios as I took a bite of a corner of my club sandwich back at Jack's Café sitting next to Pat and Sue.

First, was that Gary's wife, Michelle, must have told him. Right? I was trying to piece it all together in my head, like I was some private investigator for some gossip rag. I wondered why Gary would tell Kirk. I get why Michelle would tell Gary. Gary's her husband, and sometimes you feel you just need to unload that kind of secret on your spouse. Plus, she could have told him when they met up back home as a means to deflect whatever it was that just happened at the restaurant.

Second, what if Gary didn't hear it from Michelle? That might explain Gary's behavior. What if that whole time, Gary knew about Janice, and now he had to sit there, feeling trapped—not wanting to be there, or be around Janice, wanting to tell Kirk, but feeling it was the wrong time. I mean, what if Michelle didn't even know. I guess I initially assumed Janice and Michelle were tight, and so Janice confided in Michelle, but that would be poor detective work to just assume that. I don't know these people.

But, and, thirdly, what if Gary made it up? What if Gary told Kirk as a different kind of deflection: one that saved Gary some face from his embarrassment at dinner that night...from his wife hearing him masturbate to iPhone pornography when he thought that she was asleep.

And (Now my brain was on fire.) not only that, but Michelle said, "We used to." As in, we used to watch porn together. That seemed to indicate that Gary seemed to have drifted away from his wife. What if he was engaging in illicit, adulterous activities and was just trying to get the spotlight off himself?

I stopped myself. I didn't have any concrete details to go on…I was just letting my mind wander. I was entertaining myself, basically. Again, I didn't know these people, and yet I was adding color and story to their lives, that I didn't even know was factual. So…why was I spending so much time thinking about them? I was no different than Pat and Sue. It's fun, I suppose. There was a time when I would have been so judgmental of small-town folks talking about other small-town folks, and here I was totally obsessed with this entire situation.

But one thing was for sure…Kirk and Janice were having fun a few nights ago while I was sitting next to them. And then, a few nights later, the proverbial shit hit the fan, and they were shouting at one another as Dottie, Pat and Sue's friend, observed.

Just then Pat and Sue squirmed out of their booth at the cafe. It was quite an effort. Like, for a moment, I wondered if they were stuck and needed help. The plastic, pleather seating was making loud ripping and warping sounds as the two shimmied out of their seats. I couldn't help but turn my head to watch. I mean, it was pretty loud. And I had to laugh to myself watching Sue's belly shove into the table, which smashed into Pat's belly as Sue tried to get out; but then Pat's belly shoved into the table, and the table thrusted back into Sue. "Look at us." Sue laughed.

And Pat laughed too. Well, at least they had a sense of humor about it and seemed to enjoy one another's company.

8

You Always Hope That One Gig
Will Lead to Another

I've noticed that about the Midwest. They don't seem to take themselves too seriously. I never really thought about it when I was young and lived here. But ever since I lived out in Los Angeles and would come back for a visit, I noticed that Midwesterners were, seemingly, way more laid back.

In LA there just seems to be a cloud of anxiety over the entire city. First of all, it's expensive. And of course, everyone's on edge with the traffic. But there are even more reasons for the stress.

I'll start with dating. I haven't dated in LA since meeting Sophie over twenty years ago. Yes, it's true, I am separated from my wife, but this is a recent event, and there hasn't been any time, nor desire, to look around. We're supposed to be working on our marriage. We're not. We're currently absent from one another's lives…but we're suppose to be. I'm certainly not looking to date anyone. I suppose I wonder if she is. Wow… I've never really given it any thought. I mean, we haven't been happy for some time, but I never thought about being with someone else. I wonder if she has. God, I wonder if she has already seen someone else. Well, now I'm spinning, and that's not the point.

The point is is that it's stressful to date in LA, and I know this because of my friend, Keiren. He was an actor out there, just like me.

I should add here that some of the best times in my life were with Keiren and Danny—Danny, the English friend I mentioned earlier. When the three of us hung out, it seemed like all we did was chortle and guffaw. And we could turn anything into a game. We would mute the television and add our own dialogue. I think the Brits get away with it more, because of their accent, but Danny could say the most vulgar things, and you couldn't help but cackle to the point where your ribs hurt. He even made Sophie laugh. Don't get me wrong, Sophie liked to have a good time. But when I was dirty, she would make a face and called me "gross" or "bogue." But when Danny said something, she would crack up. She would shake her head when she laughed—like maybe she was upset at herself for laughing at something so filthy, but still, she would laugh. I met Danny while doing a play in Detroit. How an English dude ended up in the Motor City is another story, but we seemed to keep getting cast together and decided to move out to LA at the same time.

Keiren and I went to school together, and he wound up heading out to Los Angeles shortly after Danny and me made the move. We were all single heading out from the Midwest to pursue our dreams. I was fortunate enough to get some fairly steady work early on. My friends didn't quite catch on with acting gigs, but they did live in LA for awhile and tried to make the most of it. Danny worked at a temp agency, so that he could be available for auditions and potential acting jobs. Keiren was a waiter, or rather, a server, at a beach cities restaurant. He tried to date coworkers there, but they just seemed to want to do cocaine and be friends.

Keiren wasn't into coke, so they really didn't have much time for him. Danny didn't need any help dating. He was constantly with someone. But Keiren did, so...he tried dating apps.

The dating apps were really tough, according to my friend. Just like everyone's head shots have been touched up, a lot of profiles have been "enhanced." Keiren met up with a woman who was also an actor, but she embellished a lot about herself and her career. Keiren was frustrated by the whole date. He could tell that the woman only had gigs as an extra, but she told Keiren she wasn't really into dating an actor and was really only being polite. What she wanted, she told him, was to date a producer; someone who could help her career and take her places (and maybe that's why she embellished her profile). Keiren was really put off by this. Where was the romance and the infatuation? Where was the courtship and the discovery? Why did it all have to relate to the entertainment industry? "We should be falling in love with one another because of who we are, Max. Not for what we do," he would tell me.

And this was someone on the dating app that agreed to a date. Most of the women saw that he was an out of work actor and "swiped left" or whatever it is people do when they're not interested. He started editing his profile in hopes that women would show interest. He lied about his credits and where he went to school, but of course, now he was doing the exact same thing he hated. Nothing genuine. Zero authenticity. He felt guilty about it.

He told me one time when a woman agreed to go out on a date, he confessed to her that he made some stuff up, just so he could meet someone, and they could get to like the "real" him in person. The woman got up and walked out. Then returned only to slap him and left again.

He finally felt that LA had changed him. Keiren lost hope in LA and moved back to the Detroit area. Danny got married while living in Los Angeles but wound up moving back to England and started working at a big insurance company as a filing clerk. Keiren's much happier not living in Hollywood. He's married as well and has a couple of kids. Danny seems happy too (but he always seemed happy) and has come back to visit me a handful of times in LA. Danny loved the LA scene, he just didn't work like he wanted. Keiren says it feels a lot better just being himself and not pretending to be someone else.

I totally get that. And that brings up the other stressful element in LA...work. It's true, I had some success early on in Hollywood. I booked a pilot that didn't get picked up. But then I caught on with a show in its second season as a recurring character, and they kept bringing me back. That show lasted seven seasons. I played a cop. It was called *Men in the Blue*, and it was on Fox. I had a good time on the show and got to work with some really solid directors. The cast was cool for the most part... but even though the show went seven seasons, we never seemed to gel. Or maybe I was just in my head about it because I was always considered a recurring character and not a regular...I felt like a bit of an outsider. I mean, I was treated like an outsider...I was one of those actors called super early to shoot a scene and then I waited all day in my trailer to shoot my other scene at the end of the day. It wasn't unusual to be called at 6 a.m., head to hair and make up at 6:30 and then wait until 9 a.m. to shoot my first scene. Go to lunch at 1pm, and then shoot my other scene at 5:30 p.m. and then head home after we wrapped for the day. Sometimes this was based on location and set ups, but often it was to stack scenes one after another for the leads, so that they could come in, get their work done without waiting, and then leave for the day.

And my character was kind of like Gunther on *Friends*. I would enter towards the end of the scene and make a smart-ass comment and that was that. I never felt like I had anything of substance to play. My character never fell in love or lost a loved one. I'd usually just do something like walk into the precinct with a box of donuts and say, "Someone take these from me…Please!" And all the regulars would shake their heads and return to typing up their police reports.

Still, I made enough money to qualify for insurance. And me and Sophie had a baby boy, so looking back, I can't complain.

Still, I dreamed that that gig would lead to something bigger. And when I say "dreamed" I mean I "expected," and that led to some real anxiety. In hindsight, I guess I should have just rolled with the punches and shouldn't have worried about the next gig, but honestly, that would have been impossible having a young mouth to feed and protect.

I don't know that I worried before I had children. After that, that's all I did. Before kids, I thought if I didn't "make it," big deal; I would find something else to do. But after the kids were born, I kept thinking *If I don't make it, they'll suffer.* And that was agonizing.

You always hope that one gig will lead to another. You see actors really shine in a role—they become trending; they become "it" for the moment—and then, you see them in something else after that, and you hope for that kind of momentum in your own career. But that didn't happen to me.

I did get a couple small roles in some films. In a Jon Lovitz movie, I played a bouncer, who throws him out of a bar. He was really cool and was really kind to me. He made me feel comfortable on set. I thought the scene was a lot of fun, even though my only line was "Get back to your wife, Pauly." Jon bitched and complained the whole way out of the bar. He was funny. I thought I did a pretty good job reacting to him, but after a couple of takes the director pulled me aside and said, "Hey, we already have a funny guy in this scene; we don't need two. Mmm-Kay?"

By the way, I hate "Mmm-Kay." Only dicks say "Mmm-Kay." And this director was a first-class dick. The only people who say "Mmm-Kay" are the ones who project their prowess and expertise but are usually just insecure bitches who are secretly afraid of being found out to be nothing more than a fraud.

I was at first startled, and then I got pissed. I thought the scene was going great. I could see the crew trying not to laugh during our scene. At first, I thought they were just laughing at Jon. Like I said, he was terrific. But then I realized they must have been laughing at my reactions, my facial expressions, because they were also laughing when Jon wasn't talking. I really wanted to ask the director "When is too much funny a bad thing?" Especially in a comedy. But I kept my mouth shut, nodded politely, and toned down my reactions. See, I didn't want this gig to hurt my chances for the next one. Little did I know, that in most cases, the current gig doesn't lead to the next one, nor does it ruin the next one... especially working as a day player like I was.

Turned out the film could have used a lot more funny. I saw it one night on one of the cable movie networks, and it wasn't very good. Jon was good. But the movie stunk. And my scene was cut, so...oh well.

I had a bigger role in another film. I played a construction foreman who falls in love with a transgender woman. It was a great, complicated role. My character was married and homophobic, and here he was falling for someone he used to hate. But one of the producers, the money guy, got into some serious trouble with his finances. Like, he was embezzling from some big political group, a very conservative pact that tried to influence and change the courts in its favor. The producer, Aaron Chittick, was a real higher-up in that pact, and everyone thought that he was the most conservative of the bunch; primarily because he would go on Fox News a lot and troll liberals. He would always get on twitter and post some crazy memes about the virtues of toxic masculinity, the need for women to be submissive, and the sins of homosexuality. He got into some trouble when he was accused of sexually assaulting a guy on someone's campaign. Apparently, Aaron kept rubbing his crotch on the campaign volunteer, who used to play middle linebacker at some D1 school. Aaron took a leave of absence and wasn't invited back to the pact. So, he decided to head into the film industry and produced our little film *Nowhere Home*.

The film never saw the light of day. You can't even find it on IMDB.

I did get another cop show after a couple of guest spots, and this time it was as a regular. I was so excited. It was the highlight of my career to be able to call a set a home, to show up early Monday morning for a table read, and to have the network and studio reps there to hear the script read aloud and give their notes. Oh, and catering and craft services...the food! You could pretty much get anything you desired. I'd show up and a PA would ask what kind of omelette I wanted, and after awhile, they didn't even have to ask…it would just be sitting inside my trailer waiting for me. It was amazing. It seemed like a corner of the sound stage was devoted to food. There were daily thematic displays with decorations. French cuisine one day, Mexican another. Sushi brought in from Katsuya in Hollywood, or Chicago deep dish and New York thin crust pizzas overnighted on Fridays. They spared no expense, which is kind of funny in retrospect, because a good portion of the talent were constantly watching their weight. Not me. They had to let out my uniform pants after a month.

But…*The Unit* only lasted a year and a half because the two stars were all ego. It was supposed to be about two detectives who fall in love and solve crimes together, but these two hated each other. I heard that happened on the set of *An Officer and a Gentleman,* and Debra Winger said something like "hate can look a lot like love" or something like that. I don't know if it's true, but on our set, hate looked like hate. When it first premiered, it drew a pretty good rating, but little did the audience know that the two leads would have screaming matches on set. Then they would give everyone the silent treatment. They then started competing to see who would arrive later than the other to piss the other one off. One time, we didn't start rehearsal until two hours after our call time. After that, they each took to being super nice to the rest of us, hoping to gain allegiances and get the other one fired. It was a mess. We managed to get through the first season and got picked up for season two. I really think the two leads were sabotaging their way off the show. But it was a big enough hit that the network bosses tried to get them to work things out. Plus, the execs waved the contracts in the actors' faces, forcing them to realize that they were obligated to work with one another. But early on in season two, it just became too much. We went on hiatus after the seventh episode, and my agent got the call to tell me "Don't bother coming back, we're done."

Apparently, the evening of the last day of the seventh episode, Lia, that's the female lead, had her boyfriend come to set to keep tabs. During the scene with Brendan, the male lead, Lia kept stepping on the end of Brendan's lines. What I was told by Brad, one of the supporting actors who was also in the scene, (I was done filming for the day and had headed home) was that Brendan didn't break character, but instead started adding some name calling in with his lines. Like "But, bitch, that's not how we solve cases around here." And then Lia took that as a challenge, smiled, stayed in the scene, and kept cutting deeper and deeper into Brendan's lines. This continued, to the point, where Brendan was only getting out three of four words at a time until finally Brendan said, "Listen, cunt—" and Lia punched him. She didn't slap him. She punched him. Brendan almost swung back, I'm told, but restrained himself. He backed away and the director implored a "cut, please." But Brendan said, "Nah, keep rolling," and walked over to Lia's boyfriend and sucker punched him. This was a big mistake because Lia's boyfriend was a professional fighter, and he quickly recovered and got in about five solid punches to Brendan's face before the crew broke everything up. Brad, my buddy on set, told me that Brendan's face blew up sort of like Rocky's after his fight with Apollo Creed, but worse, and his nose was broken in a couple of places. In fact, Brendan tried to swing back after the crew relaxed thinking the fight had finally stopped. But Brendan couldn't see, and swung into the air and fell down. He wound up tripping over a camera operator and tore a knee ligament. Rumor has it, there's footage of it somewhere, because the cameras did, apparently, keep rolling.

I held on to a lot of resentment after that. Why can't people realize when they have a good thing going? We were a hit show relatively speaking...enough of a hit to return for another season. What if it had turned into a detective-style *Moonlighting*, or a romantic *Hill Street Blues*, and grew an even bigger following the more seasons it aired? There were ten regulars and countless guest stars on that show for crying out loud. And the two leads blew it. What really pissed me off was that I thought *They'll never work again.* But if you look up those actors, you'll see that they never really stopped working. I guess if the camera likes you, and audiences like you, execs will hire you. The best times on that show—I mean absolutely amazing times—were when there were these ancillary scenes with the supporting cast, when the two leads weren't even there. Oh God, we had so much fun. I didn't want those days to end. The set was loose, cast and crew were laughing. We'd always shoot a last take "just for fun" and improvise. But never when one of the two leads was there. They brought along this cloud of toxicity whether they were together or by themselves. It was awful. So, no, I didn't think they'd keep on working after the show was cancelled.

They did keep working, but for me, it was tough sledding after that. We had Brianna shortly after Graeme. Two kids growing up, and I found myself averaging two gigs a year that only worked for a week or two at most. A couple of years saw the average go up, but there was actually one year I didn't work at all (while the kids were teenagers). I didn't complain because it meant I got to spend a lot of time with them throughout high school. I even got to coach Graeme in football during his middle school days.

The opportunities that I did get were mostly kid shows. I'd get a guest starring role here and there, and sometimes I had a bit of an arc stretching over several episodes. The biggest run I had was on a show called *Gotcha Last!* It was about two kid brothers who were always up to no good and played practical jokes on their family and neighbors. I was one of the neighbors. I had gallons of paint poured all over me. I was, of course, slimed, I was pushed off a roof, pushed into a number of pools, and even pushed off a low flying helicopter. That last one was both terrifying and exhilarating. I actually jumped out from a helicopter fuselage they had hoisted on the sound stage and onto a huge foam pad. I had a stunt double there ready to do it, but the director said, "You're up for it aren't ya?" I don't think he was supposed to say that, but I did feel the pressure and said, "Yeah…sure…of course."

I tore my meniscus one time but hid it, so that I wouldn't get fired. I was hoping that they would keep using Mr. Simons (that was my character) in more episodes. I had read that there is a part of the meniscus, where the nerve endings are, that will heal itself if there's a tear. If you tear it in the middle, then a doctor has to go in and clip off the loose tear like a hang nail. Well, evidently, I tore it in the middle, because it never felt right after that. I still need to get that thing repaired.

Filming that show was a lot of fun. I began to look forward to the stunts, and the crew was really great. Kids' shows always have a lower budget, especially off-network. And so, there were days where we were responsible for our own lunch. It was a far cry from the network cop show, but we made the best of it. We had potluck Wednesdays, and everyone brought in a dish to pass. It really bonded us and made us more of a family.

However, the show's creator was a pervert, and he got busted during the Me Too movement. I always wondered why he had a new young, female assistant whenever I guested on the show. Each assistant had a story to tell the press…all of them. The show had already been cancelled. Most kids' shows only get a couple of seasons anyway, because the young cast ages so quickly during those years. But the network was quick to wipe the show clean from it's slate. They won't even show the reruns anymore.

Then there's the third stressor: money. I know everyone worries about that no matter where they live. But there's no "Keeping up with the Joneses" quite like in Los Angeles. It seems, more often than not, when I'm out on one of my walks, (I like to get fresh air and listen to music) I would see dudes driving Porches, and women driving Range Rovers. And the rest seem to be in Mercedes and Beemers. It's crazy. I come back to Michigan, and my brain needs a moment to adjust to seeing Fords and Chevys.

When I was working somewhat regularly and had a parking spot next to a sound stage, you would see a Bentley, a couple of high-end hybrids, of course there was a really nice Mercedes, and then you would see my old Ford Expedition. It really stood out. I tried washing it to keep it looking as nice as I could, but the sunroof leaked, and it would saturate the carpet inside. And, as you would expect, the inside started smelling like wet socks. It was a 2003, and the body was falling apart. But the engine was fine, and we couldn't really afford a new car, especially after we bought a house.

And that was another thing. After we bought our house, so many people in the neighborhood started renovating their homes. In no time at all, our home felt out of date. There was just a lot of pressure to keep up, and it stressed me out. It stressed Sophie out. Yet another reason for our troubles.

9

She Just Thought I Was Being Needy

I found myself walking the town streets once again. The sidewalks were more populous this time. Behind whom I assumed was a grandpa were two seven or eight-year-olds walking with their hooded sweatshirts on backwards, and the hoods were pulled up over their faces. Their giggles were so loud as they competed to see who could walk the furthest down the sidewalk without pulling their hood down to see. After a bit more nervous and apprehensive chuckling, they both pulled down their hoods and immediately stopped. The slightly taller girl, who's big strawberry blonde curls were now revealed, was a few steps in front of whom I assumed was her brother. They both let out a huge laugh, the sister exuded a fist pump, and the brother quickly raised his hood to challenge her to a rematch. The grandpa, to his credit, let them play. He was enjoying their company immensely. I'm sure some parents or guardians might put a stop to what these kids were doing. They might run into someone or trip, but that's what being a kid is all about.

I recalled Nate and I making up games when we were younger. Even though Nate was seven years older, he still had a great imagination. Even in his teens when he started dating, (You couldn't blame him if he was out most nights with his girlfriend at the time) he still managed to find time to spend with me. Since we didn't have money, we had to be inventive. And boy, were we inventive. Nate would fashion medieval weapons out of sticks and socks. We were able to get a massive amount of foam from a flea market, and Nate cut up an old broom handle, shoved it into a cut out piece of foam, threw a sock over it, and fashioned a couple of swords. From a dowel, a rope, and a stuffed sock he made a flail. We made all sorts of weapons—spears, battle axes, bolas, maces, you name it, and then friends in the neighborhood would swing by and we'd challenge one another to duals. Soon, Nate created all these rules and gave points for initiative, evasive moves, and parries. He assigned different values for various hits—scrapes, wounds…and of course kill shots were an instant win.

When it snowed, or when it rained so hard the yard got muddy, the neighborhood kids would swing by and play slo-mo football. That was, of course, another Nate invention. No running was allowed. You had to move in an exaggerated slo-mo pace. You were immediately disqualified from the rest of the game if you sped up to avoid being tackled. Because… the whole point was to get a great tackle on someone and drive them into the mud or into a snow drift. It was a blast.

The best invention, though, in my opinion was roofball. Oh, yeah. The greatest unknown game ever created. I wrote a screenplay about it… about two best friends who wound up having a falling out but continued to be the best roofball tandem in the nation. It's a great story. My agent didn't think so.

"Nobody knows what the hell roofball is." My agent told me.

I told him, "That's what makes it so great. This game means everything to these people. The stakes are so high, and the rest of the world could give a shit. They ruin a terrific friendship over some game that struggles to find an audience on some new ESPN alternative sports network that airs right after the National Hide and Seek Regional Finals." He didn't get it.

Roofball is pretty simple and probably closest to the sport of volleyball. You find an A-frame roof—for us it was our shed which stored all the wood for the winter. The server throws up the ball onto the roof. If it goes over the apex of the roof, the opponent gets a point and then serves. When you serve you can spin it, so that it gives the ball some action. You can throw a high arcing lob. You can try to make your opponent run and serve it across the length of the roof. You can try to aim it so precisely that when the ball comes down, it barely nicks the roof. (Nate was particularly good at those, and it drove me crazy.) Our "court" as it were, was really cool, because our shed was attached to the house in a perpendicular fashion, so that when you served, you could really put some velocity on the ball and have it ricochet off the side of the house and roll back across the shed.

Like a lot of "court" sports, there were boundaries. If the ball ran over the side of the roof, that was considered out of bounds. If the ball took a huge bounce, much like volleyball, and it flew back behind you, there was a boundary marker (for us it was our covered well pit, which was about seven yards from the shed.)

When the ball was served, the opponent was allowed to hit the ball into the air and then hit it one more time to get it back on the roof. You didn't HAVE to hit it twice, but you were allowed to. First to fifteen, win by two. Nate and I spent countless hours playing that game, especially when he got back from the service.

Nate and I could make a game out of almost anything.

Back in town, the curly, strawberry blonde with the hoodie on backwards wound up crashing to the sidewalk. She must've tripped over hers or her brother's feet. I was lost in my daydream and only heard a woman gasp, kind of a scream gasp—high pitched and short. The young girl immediately got up off the concrete while pulling down her hoodie so that she could see what happened.

"Are you okay, sweetie?" The concerned bystander asked.

"Oh, she's fine," her grandpa said dismissively. "She's tougher than her younger brother."

"Hey!" The brother protested, as the girl brushed off some remnants of muddy snow from her knees.

The same bystander started to move towards the girl. "Sir, maybe they shouldn't be playing like that. Someone could—"

"And, maybe, you should mind your own business," the grandpa replied.

Before the bystander could get to the girl, the grandpa called out, "Hoodies up!" And both kids raced to pull up their hoodies, rushing to compete again.

"What's the score."

"Ellie, five. Me, four."

"Very good. Get ready and...go!"

And the two kiddoes cautiously stepped forward, blinded by their backwards hoodies.

I crossed the street and finally noticed vast strands of lights crisscrossing one another, illuminating the solstice like darkness that overwhelms Midwest afternoons. Seeing the white Christmas lights dangling from the little shops made me miss my family. And seeing the strands of big hanging Italian lights in various courtyards got me choked up. We put those Italian lights in our backyard a few years ago, and so my mind went racing back there.

We were able to purchase a modest house in the valley when Graeme and Bree were hitting middle school. Up until that point we were renters, and the last house we rented was basically sold from under us. That's when Sophie put her foot down and insisted that we finally become homeowners. I was always hesitant. First, I never understood why the value of most homes in LA started at a million bucks. That to me is insane. Second, if we found a home for a million dollars, that meant we were going to have to put $200,000 on a down payment. We were going to drain our savings, which didn't come close to paying for the entire down payment, give it to the bank, and never be able to do anything with that money. I just never understood any of it.

But Sophie won, and we bought a home. It really wasn't much. In fact, it looked like any other ranch style home in Southern California with its exterior stucco walls and its Mediterranean tiled roof. The house was small, not even 1,500 square feet, but it was nice and cozy for the four of us. What I really liked was our backyard. And I think Sophie liked it too. I remember, after I hung the Italian lights, and she flicked the switch, a big, bright smile filled her face, and her eyes contained so much joy. Sophie's eyes held so much life in them. When she would talk to me, I would get lost in them (like they were these magical orbs) and I was captured by their spell.

Sophie worked. It seems that's all she did. She worked as a reality show producer on startups you'd find on HGTV and the like. She worked nonstop as a mother. And she worked holding together her original family and sorting through seemingly endless health crises that her mother and father were going through.

Sophie would get up at 4:30 in the morning. Friends of ours always thought she was crazy, but Sophie said that she had to have some "me" time. So, from 4:30-7:30am, Sophie would work out or do yoga, then she would journal and sort through her thoughts while she had her cup of coffee, then she would make herself some avocado toast, shower, and then get ready for work. For a while there, she set aside some of that time to make the kids their lunches and help them get ready for school, but as they got older, they no longer needed her to do that. I thought that would give us some added time together, but Sophie managed to fill that block with more of her things. I think she really came to value her time alone in the mornings.

She always had a heck of a drive to work. It's LA, so who doesn't? I've had two and a half hour commutes at different locations around Southern California, but my work was always inconsistent, and Sophie was constantly working.

I think, as I walked down the streets in Greenville now, that really affected me. I don't know if it was shame or boredom or pride, but I always had so much time on my hands, and Sophie was always busy. When we would argue, I talked about us "folding into one another" and she just thought I was being needy. "You'll get another gig." She felt as though I was pressuring her. And the truth is…I was. I was feeling more and more insecure, and I think she was gaining more and more confidence.

I longed to plug in those Italian lights all over again and see her smile. Her smile was brighter than the lights themselves. And I felt like I had a part, a stake, in her happiness in that moment. She smiled because of something I did. But now, that seemed so long ago. She would laugh with the kids, that is, when they actually came out of their rooms during their high school years and gave us the time of day. They were also busy with sports and clubs after school, so we saw them less and less frequently. I think that hurt as well. You dump so much of your energy into your children, and then, like Velcro, they rip themselves away from you. It's necessary for their journey and growth into adulthood…but it really hurts.

Walking down the sidewalk now in town, the music got louder and louder, and I found myself approaching the city park. The townsfolk had gathered at the pavilion, and there, of course, was local legend Mickey Shea talking with all the charm and charisma he could muster over the small band that played behind him. Mickey welcomed the locals and wished them a happy holiday. Mickey had a top forty easy listening hit back in the 80s. I think it went up to number eight even, but again, it was the easy listening chart, and I don't know if a lot of people were tracking that. Still, he was probably the biggest celebrity to come out of this little town, and he was definitely one to milk it. In fact, one of the city limit signs reads "Welcome to Greenville—Home of Singing Legend, Mickey Shea." Rumor has it he paid for it.

"Sing your song!" Some old lady with a walker yelled from the crowd.

"Yeah, don't!" A younger voice called out, and I hoped Mickey didn't hear that, because it was unnecessary and mean.

Whether he did or didn't hear it was immaterial because that unmistakable intro to the one hit he ever had begun to play, and soon after, Mickey began to croon.

"Oh, I never thought, no I never thought I'd see your face again.
You were my best friend.
In the morning…and the night.
Looking around, I finally found what I was looking for.
You were so much more.
Standing in that pale moonlight.
I know now better than I ever did before…
And I know that I love you so much more!
(There was always that big crescendo into the chorus.)
I see you, you see me, we're right here!
I know that I've always wanted you near!
When you were gone, I had to face what I'm really made of.
And I know that I'm so much better with my truest love."

And then he sang the other few verses and the chorus for what felt like a half a dozen times. He just kept repeating the chorus, like he didn't want the song to end. The song finished up, and I couldn't help but notice that there was more polite applause than uproarious cheers. Back in the day, the town seemed genuinely proud of their local hero. But now, Mickey was old, and this crowd, at least, skewed younger. I had watched the crowd during the song, and many were looking at one another, smiling. Years before, this would have been a sign that they were helpless romantics, falling in love with one another all over again. But now, it seemed like they were making fun of Mickey, smirking at him. Some were outright laughing at him. At least that's what it felt like. Yeah sure, the song was hokey. But he did put himself out there…however many years ago. At least he gave it a shot, and for all intents and purposes, made it.

"Thank you very much. I never get tired of that song. That song has stuck by me through thick and thin. In fact, I've been married to that song longer than all three of my marriages put together."

There was a small smattering of chuckles.

"Now, I'd like to sing a brand-new original that I recently wrote."

I swear I actually heard a few moans. And then, as the band started playing the music, several couples and groups began to depart. I hope Mickey didn't notice. But the expression on his face made me think that he did. The park was emptying out. I guess they had better things to do. I felt sorry for the old man. I stayed and listened to his new song along with just a handful of people. When Mickey finished the song, his head sank. He said nothing. No "good night." No…anything. He simply walked off the stage and disappeared into the darkness of the park.

10

Check, Please

I've always had a bit of an issue with athlete's feet. I think that's what it is. It can get really itchy between the piggy that had roast beef and the piggy that had none. And it's on both feet. I've tried all sorts of things to get rid of it, but they don't seem to work. I think, maybe, I just don't give it enough time to heal. I absolutely love when it itches. Or, rather, I should say, I love itching in between my toes, not necessarily the itch itself. I'll scratch, and scratch, and scratch, and wow, it feels so good. But I always take it too far, and then the pain sets in as well as the swelling and infection.

I think it's probably the same as drinking. That initial drink is amazing, and I love the buzz. That hit sends me into such good spirits. I'm always elated. But then that glass of wine eventually becomes the bottle. I think I'm trying to recapture that germinal feeling of the first glass. But it's never the same. So, after that first drink, I'm basically just hurting myself. I mean, I've read that it slows your metabolism…and Lord knows I can't afford that. It also affects your sleep. And, I would sometimes get irritable and often a little clumsy with my speech.

I'm grateful I never got into any legal trouble with my drinking, but I think it affected my marriage. I think I would get snarky and a little bitchy. I thought I was being facetious and funny, but Sophie didn't see it that way. She never told me that. But eventually when she walked in the room and saw that I had a cocktail or a glass of wine, she would go straight to the bedroom and work there or watch TV, and she would just stay there for the rest of the night until she fell asleep. And I'm even talking about when I had a drink in the late afternoon while watching a game or something.

So, I haven't been drinking. I'm sleeping a lot better and having some really crazy dreams. And I'm dropping some weight. Plus, it's way more fun "people watching" when you're sober, and everyone else is drunk. There's not a show on television at the moment that can compare.

So, I walked Chad, fed him when I got back to my brother's house, and then went to The Red Lion, once again, to have some dinner. The server there was really friendly, and she was cute. I imagined making small talk about our day:

She was ready to call it a night but had really only started her shift, and I would tell her that I wouldn't be a bother and that she wouldn't even know I was there. And she would respond by telling me I was the highlight of her workweek...

But, of course, I couldn't speak, so I waved my sign. She gave me a pitying frown and asked, "What happened?" And I gave her a shrug and a smile hoping to convey that I couldn't explain, because I had no voice. After a brief moment, she let out an embarrassed little laugh and said, "Oh right, you can't talk," and she started to walk away. But she immediately spun around and said, "You know, you really ought to get one of those dry erase boards. Just a little one you can keep with you. Then you can talk to folks." I nodded *good idea* and gave it some thought.

"I'll be right back with a menu, hon." And she walked away for a moment. That was fun. Even a little exciting. I hadn't felt energy like that with a woman in some time, and it was just for a moment...how pathetic. But still it boosted my spirits. And then it hit me...*I hope she isn't twenty years younger than me.* I mean, it's not like there would ever be anything more than a little small talk, but I began to feel a little creepy at the thought that she might be in her early twenties.

She came back with a menu and a glass of water and said, "My name's Julie. I'll give you a minute." I smiled and watched her as she walked away. I'll be honest, she had a nice butt. Girls didn't dress like that when I was her age. And yes, that thought did not escape me. I immediately realized that I knew in my heart that she was a lot younger than me, and flirting with her, would indeed, make me a giant pervert. Still, I was right, girls didn't dress like that when I was her age. It must have been her leggings. Back then, girls wore baggy jeans or corduroy or something stupid and unflattering. And when leggings became popular in Michigan (this is just before I moved to LA), women would wear a super long shirt untucked to cover their butts. That was another shocker in LA…women let their butts show in their yoga pants.

Like a camera racking its focus in a movie, my attention went from her backside to the background of the pub, and I thought I noticed an old classmate, sitting at the bar alone. *Actually, was it two old classmates?* (I told you Greenville was a rural hub that attracted folks from around the area.)

Was it him? Wow, he's a lot heavier, but aren't we all. No, it can't be. The object of my focus gave a brief look around, and I saw his face. *Wow, that is him.* It was Mitch McCoy. I wasn't sure if it was Mitch at first, in part because of the weight gain, but also because he wore a uniform, and I thought that maybe he was in law enforcement. *But why would he be drinking at a bar in his uniform.* I soon realized that he looked more like a security officer, and maybe he was having a drink after his shift. Of course, I never bothered to notice at first, sprawled across his back, the words "A1 Security," so…there ya go. He was approached by another former classmate, Crystal Irons—which I always thought sounded like a bad stripper name. (Not bad as in "sinful"…but bad as in "lazy") Crystal once called in a bomb threat towards the end of our senior year because she was so over school. I don't know if they ever found out that it was her. We all knew…because she bragged about it while giving Bobby Stewart a handjob, and Bobby was the most popular guy in our class. So…word spread quickly. Bobby also told us that Crystal's labia was enormous. Even back as a teenager, I thought that was too personal. Still, our immature clique started calling her "Mudflaps."

I kept looking at Mitch. Mitch McCoy was Mr. Everything in high school. He was a grade ahead of me, and when I was a junior, Mitch was the all-state quarterback who led our high school to a rare conference championship and the best record in the school's history. Mitch was a hell of good-looking guy with a strong jaw and one of those dimples on his chin…a cleft chin, I think it's called. Mitch had piercing blue eyes, and he had the confidence to look right at you when anyone talked to him, which made the person talking to him uncomfortable. He controlled the room, that's for sure.

Mitch was also the point guard on the basketball team and the shortstop on the baseball team. He had everything going for him. He was offered a few scholarships for football. I mean, he really was that dynamic. Our offense was boring and pretty predictable. We'd mostly run power right and power left when I was on JV the year before, because we didn't have a quarterback who could throw the ball. But when I was on varsity my junior year, we had Mitch, and Coach Sebring opened up the playbook. We suddenly became an option team, and defenses simply could not stop Mitch. Plus, he had a rocket for an arm. He could throw the ball sixty yards, and luckily, we had a speedster at wide receiver, Steve Bennett. So, defenses really had to pick their poison. They had to keep a safety over the top to help cover Steve, which meant one less defender to come up and stop the run. We were explosive.

All the local colleges wanted Mitch: Hope, Grand Valley, Ferris State, even Central Michigan, which was a big deal because it was D1, and our school didn't get those kinds of looks back then. But then some Big Ten schools came calling, and the town went crazy. Everywhere you went you could hear people murmuring the name "Mitch." Indiana and Purdue were the first to come up to our school. Then Illinois and Wisconsin. But when an assistant coach from Michigan stopped by…wow. We all went absolutely nuts.

I never knew if Michigan ultimately ever offered Mitch a scholarship or if Mitch just decided to stay closer to home, but Mitch chose to go to Ferris State in Big Rapids. Back then Ferris wasn't very good. They were nowhere near the program they are today. It puzzled a lot of us, because it was also a D2 school, which is cool and all…I mean, you still get to go to college and get a degree, but if Mitch was really as good as we all thought, why not go to Michigan or any of the other big schools and take your shot at being "big time?"

I even asked him at his high school graduation party why he picked Ferris. "Bennett's going there. I figure we can be a great combo and put that school on the map." I think the answer I was looking for was somewhere in there. In high school, Mitch was a big fish in a very small pond. In fact, he was a whale in a puddle. Maybe he needed to keep being the big fish. Would he be just an average fish somewhere else…and would that be unbearable?

As he walked away from that conversation so many years ago, he turned back to me and said, "Trust me. You haven't heard the last of Mitch McCoy." I remember smiling at him, wishing I had that kind of swagger.

And so there he was sitting at the bar with Crystal. She was rubbing his back, as he sat there watching some bowl game; I couldn't tell which teams were playing from where I was sitting, but I could see him finish a pint and ask for another. Crystal slammed her half-finished cocktail and signaled for another as well.

I had run into Mitch a couple of times before since our days in high school. One time I got into a little bit of trouble thinking I could make some money gambling on NBA games. I hadn't realized how flakey NBA players can be during the long, regular season. I mean, some of those guys phone it in. It can really make betting unpredictable. Anyway, I was back home for winter break; this was in college, and I ran into Mitch at the grocery store. We asked how one another was doing, and I guess he could read on my face that I was stressed.

Looking back, it wasn't a large sum of money at all. In fact, it was small. I had bet on a slate of twelve games one night at $10 a game…and I lost ten. I was down $80 to a friend's bookie. The thing is, I didn't have $80. I was on financial aid, and I had the bright idea that since I liked sports and followed them, I could pick some games and make some quick money so that I could get Christmas presents for my family.

As soon as I lost, my mind began to spin, thinking this bookie was going to break my legs or cut off a finger when he found out I couldn't pay. My college buddy, who was friends with the bookie, suggested I just bet on the next slate of games. "Nobody's luck could be that bad." I had mentioned all of this to Mitch that evening at the grocery store, and he immediately gave me four twenties. "Here. It'll ease your mind."

"No. No way. I can't take this."

"Please, I'm doing just fine."

"I can't, Mitch. But—"

"Max. Please…Please."

"Yeah? Wow, thanks, Mitch."

"It's no problem at all."

"I really appreciate it. And I'll pay you back just as soon as my loans come through next semester."

"It's not a loan. It's a gift."

I didn't know what to say. I just shook my head. The only thing that came to mind was…

"So, how's Ferris?"

"So good."

See, I had heard the opposite, so this took me by surprise.

"It's going really, really well, Max."

I had actually heard that Mitch got kicked off the team and then dropped out of school, but I didn't want to get into all of that. Besides, my mom was finishing up paying the cashier, so I just thanked him again and joined my mom as she grabbed her bags and put away her cart.

"I'll be seeing you around, Max." He shouted in my direction as I left, and I gave him a grateful wave.

"I owe you big time, Mitch."

"You don't owe me nothin'."

I had run into Mitch another time, after that. It was after I had moved out to California and came back to visit my brother and his family. Mitch and I would've been in our late twenties at that time; like I said, he was a year older than me. And oddly enough I ran into him outside the Red Lion. He was coming out, and my brother and I were about to grab some lunch inside. I remember Mitch wearing his old high school jersey, which I thought was odd for someone our age to be wearing, and my brother thought it was downright pathetic.

Mitch was awfully excited when he left the bar, as I remember, and he was already drunk around noon on a Saturday. As I recall, he wouldn't let me just say "hi." In fact, he kind of cornered me and got between me and Nate. I remember because my brother just decided to head in and leave me alone with Mitch. Mitch went on and on about this new business he had going. It was some window business, and from the moment he started pitching me on it, it felt like some sort of scheme. But he was certain it was going to make him a lot of money, and he wanted me to invest.

I, instead, really wanted to ask Mitch what all went down in college. He went in as one of the best quarterbacks in the state and now he was approaching thirty, selling some pyramid scheme bullshit wearing his old high school jersey. *What happened?* Did you have a great college career and set the local D2 world on fire, and then set out into the real world? I never heard any buzz from folks about Mitch in school. Never heard about any fun games or comebacks or playing football at all to be honest. So…what happened? An uneasy feeling shot up my spine, thinking for some reason that if I did ask him, I would embarrass him, and I didn't want to do that. I guess if he had set the football world on fire, he'd let me know…"You haven't heard the last of Mitch McCoy." I liked Mitch. I didn't want to risk making him feel bad. So instead I told him that I didn't have any money, especially with two kids and being an actor and all.

"Man, when you gonna give that up?" He asked playfully...I think.

"I know, I know. It's a rough road."

"Nah, I'm happy for you. You pursued your dream. That's what it's all about." And he softened his posture and opened a path for me to get into the pub. "Hey, give it some thought," he told me.

"What's that?"

"This window business. I'm telling you, every house around these parts is gonna have 'em."

"Okay." I had no plans of giving it anymore thought. "I'll think about it, Mitch."

"Right on. I'll see you around, Max." And he sort of stumbled away.

Looking at Mitch and Crystal sitting on their stools at the bar, I noticed Mitch's left hand sitting in between Crystal's thighs and her right hand gently rubbing his back, then sort of sink into the top of the back of his uniformed pants. I would have never predicted them to be a couple. Or maybe it was more like when Pink Floyd sang about two lost souls, and they were simply enjoying one another's company.

Crystal kept rubbing Mitch's back, her hand sliding up and down and side to side, sometimes over the untucked uniformed shirt, and sometimes her hand crept under it. Mitch kept staring at the game on the screen, occasionally taking a swig of his beer. Crystal began to use her other hand to rub Mitch's chest. Maybe it was because she couldn't get Mitch's attention, but she stopped after a minute or so. And as soon as she pulled away, Mitch's head turned and his face sunk deep into her neck, and he pulled her close to him. He was there, tucked into Crystal's neck, for more than a moment, as his hands moved down and squeezed her left ass cheek. She let out a near silent squeal as his face seemed to bury deeper into the crevice between her shoulder and her jaw. His face seemed to move down towards her breasts, and that's when she pushed his head away with a playful laugh. She was still in his arms, and he stared at her... Then he released her and turned his attention back to the game.

I thought about the last time Sophie and I had sex. I couldn't remember when it was. I remember what it was, because we had gotten into a routine where we did the same thing every time. And the number of times we had sex became fewer and fewer. When we were first intimate, we couldn't have enough sex. And, man, we were adventurous. Back in those days, we were both up for trying different things. One night, when the kids were with friends, Sophie came home with a silly couple's game… kind of a truth or dare type of thing. We would read cards from a deck and revealed secrets and things we had done in past relationships. There was no jealousy; if anything, it was a huge turn on. I had no idea that Sophie entered a wet T-shirt contest on a college spring break in Florida. Or that she dated a 6' 5" defensive end from Penn State, who signed as an undrafted free agent with the Giants. Or that she had sex at the LA Zoo! And the "dares?"…They made us laugh and giggle. One card read "Grab something from the refrigerator and act out the scene from 9 ½ Weeks." I left the living room and headed to the kitchen. I came back with a container of squeezable mayonnaise and flipped the top open.

"Don't you fuckin' dare!" She screamed and howled with laughter.

I doubled over, laughing so hard, that I tripped and dropped the mayo and it squirted across the floor.

"I knew you couldn't last!" She shouted. And I laughed even harder. I even peed a little.

Then as the relationship became more steady, the number of times a week went down to around two. Once we had kids, that number went to once a week…typically, not always. I remember one of our fights was about the math. Sophie asked what I was complaining about. "Once a week is still four times a month!"

"No, you have a period every month. So, that's three times." That was my comeback.

"I'm tired. I'm tired, Max. And I've got a lot on my mind."

I wonder if it's typical between men and women that women need to be in a certain frame of mind to enjoy intimacy, while the majority of men use intimacy as a stress reliever. That may be a gross stereotype, but it was true of myself and Sophie.

Like draining a rain barrel, "all the time," turned into "a lot," which became "often," down to "a trickle," and once a week became every other week, which became once a month, which became…

Random…and rare.

To…nothing.

Crystal went back to rubbing Mitch's back. And though she had pushed him away with his seemingly too much public display of affection, she did sneak her hand around the front of his pants, and underneath the bar…began to rub his crotch.

Check, please.

I flashed a credit card to Julie as she walked by with food for another table, and she smiled and nodded. Julie swung back by after a moment and took my credit card.

I was definitely ready to call it a night.

That night I reached out to Sophie. I texted her and asked *how are you*

I guess I had gotten in the habit of not adding punctuation. Our kids had so many rules when it came to texting. They basically age shamed us. (Is that a thing?) We were so out of touch, according to Graeme and Bree. If they asked for something, and I replied *okay*, they would respond, *why so aggressive*. Apparently, typing "okay" is combative. I guess it means you're put off from whatever it is they're asking for. And God forbid you type "k," or you'll get a *what's wrong?* "K" is hostile according to my children because that means you feel put out and you're completely over them. You have to type "kk," and that evidently means you're happy to get or do whatever it is they want. The same is true with punctuation. Periods are belligerent. Question marks are too formal. *what is this a job interview, dad*

So, my text to Sophie asked how are you…and she didn't respond. I waited for bit.

I stroked Chad's fur and scrolled the menu on my brother's cable. Maybe it was the way I texted her. Sophie always hated how the kids texted, and she never played along with their "rules." So, I texted again…

I mean, How are you?

And I waited.

And waited.

I saw one of Sophie's shows coming up on the Food Network as I continued to scroll through the guide. *Cooking Off the Chainz* with 2 Chainz. Evidently, he's terrific in the kitchen. I started to get jealous of 2 Chainz for being talented at multiple things. Then I got to missing Sophie, so I turned off the TV.

I just sat there, starting to think that our marriage was, in fact, over. I couldn't move. Or rather, I didn't want to move. I just stared off into space, looking at my brother's fireplace, which didn't have a fire going. I couldn't even be captivated by flames. Then…I fell asleep.

VVVP. VVVP.

I awoke to my cell buzzing in my hand. I was still sitting on the couch, but Chad had left for something less boring than spending time with me. From my slumber, I looked at the phone. It was a reply from Sophie.

Sorry. Took my parents out to dinner and forgot my phone.

It's plausible. I mean, maybe she did and maybe she didn't. And that right there made me sad. Yes, it's plausible that she forgot her phone. She did it a number of times throughout our marriage. But that was usually when she was heading off to work, and she worked so hard throughout the day that she didn't have time to check her phone anyway, let alone look at social media. But I was sad that our marriage had sunk to a place where I was questioning whether she actually forgot her phone, or she had her phone with her and simply didn't want to get in a texting conversation with me.

I looked at the time on my phone…10:48pm

I noticed she didn't answer my question *How are you?* So, I simply texted

kk hope it was fun gnight

11

I Don't Want to Say It

I drove the familiar roads back to town looking for a place to have dinner. There was static coming through the speakers, and so I hit "seek" and noticed numbers rapidly changing as the system raced through the radio dial trying to find a station with a clear signal. It finally landed on NPR and a voice said, "This is All Songs Considered." A tune came on the radio that I didn't recognize. It was an indie type of folk group. The harmonica and banjo started things off, and I immediately liked it. I listened to the lyrics while periodically glancing at the infotainment system to see the name of the song and the group scroll along…but it never did. The call letters of the radio station were the only things that scrolled across the monitor.

"I keep waiting for your calls
Staring blankly at the walls
Was this our last chance or do we have another
And my head hurts from drinking
And my head hurts from thinking
But it's my heart that will never recover
And if this is it, know that I loved you
And please know, I held no one else above you"

A familiar anxiety shot through my spine, and all I could see is Sophie walking away. Not walking away from the relationship, but more like leaving the house for the day. I had seen that visual so many times in the past. She left the house while I stayed home, waiting on a call from my agent or waiting…for God knows what. I just kept seeing her walk… in super slow motion…out the front door as the music played. She then looked back at me. The motion of her head turning threw her beautiful hair softly across her face, and she gently moved the stray strands back behind her ear. Her face had no smile. It held no anger. In my daydream there was nothing. I realized I started to veer towards the shoulder of the road, and that brought me out of my trance…in time to hear the last lines of the song.

"…For a while we had it all. Wasn't it incredible?

I admit I used you as a crutch

I feared I loved you too much

It's my fault, darling, I put you on a pedestal

Know that I'll always cheat, steal, and lie for you

And know this, my love, I'll be first in line to die for you."

Needless to say, I had to turn that shit off. Great song. Bad timing.

In town, I spotted a Big Boy up ahead and decided to go there. Growing up, Big Boy was a real treat. We went out to eat when my mom got her income tax refund. My dad usually took any extra money she had, and he would go off and spend it on a trip for him and a "friend" or he would throw a party. But my mom was pretty sly about hiding a little here and there. And every time she got her refund, we managed a trip to Big Boy. I could have had the classic Big Boy burger or the Patty Melt or the Slim Jim…maybe get a side of their battered onion rings…but I always opted for the salad bar. And, I wouldn't put any lettuce on my plate when I made my salad. I would load my plate with eggs, cheese, turkey slices, bacon, tomatoes, olives…you name it. Anything but lettuce. I felt that, at an early age, lettuce was a racket. That was the big cheap item that filled up your plate and your tummy, thus preventing more trips to the "All You Can Eat" salad bar.

I was led towards the back by a short, elderly woman with a duck waddle. She seemed to be favoring one of her hips. I grimaced for her as I walked behind. There weren't a whole lot of people who patronized the place. I noticed random townies occupying a table by themselves, eating alone. However, there was this one older couple I noticed sitting in a booth, seated next to one another on the same side. They sat so close to each other, there was no noticeable gap between them. They looked at one another fondly, even playfully. Then, as I passed by, they both reached for their mug and took a sip. Both nearly did a spit take, laughing at how they just acted in the exact same manner. And then they let out another laugh at their simultaneous spit take. At least that was my assumption. It was a really sweet moment, and I was glad I got to witness it.

I was seated in the back room of the restaurant, which struck me as odd, since there seemed to be plenty of room out front. It was really quiet, and I was the only one there, apart from two women. And wouldn't you know it, those two women were Janice and Michelle. They sat across from one another in a pleather-seated booth and leaned into the table almost every time they spoke. It seemed intimate and private, and it was hard to hear what they were saying. I chuckled to myself when I thought about that last part. That's exactly what they were trying to do... Talk without anyone hearing what they were saying, and I'm sitting here becoming addicted to the gossip in this town.

Since they were barely whispering, picking up anything they had to say was going to be impossible. So, I just sort of visually "took" them in peripherally. Janice and Michelle were a good ten years younger than me, I guessed. I had seen Janice before...obviously, but I don't think I really looked at her. She was fit and seemed to me that that was really important to her.

I imagined her Instagram photos were pictures of her workouts, while Michelle posted pictures of her kids. Janice seemed to be the kind that would talk about world hunger and somehow manage to get a shot of her robust cleavage in frame, while Michelle would post about world hunger and have a link to a charity.

I saw Janice look around before she said anything else. I avoided eye contact with her when I felt her gaze. That seemed to happen to me a lot. I would look around, and see someone, and I would start to stare. Sure enough, our eyes would meet, and I invariably looked away as fast as I possibly could, which, then, I would get all in my head thinking *They must think I'm a real weirdo*. Well, this time, I think I looked away before Janice's eyes and my eyes met.

"What is it?" I finally heard Michelle ask.

Janice glanced towards me once again, then gestured by twitching her head towards my direction. I don't think she wanted to talk about anything while I was in the vicinity.

"Him? I think he's deaf. Or something." Michelle tried to relieve any worry.

"Isn't he an actor?" Janice asked.

"Not really. I mean, I haven't seen him in anything in a really long time."

Ouch.

"If he is, he gave it up. Maybe it's because he lost his hearing. That's what my nephew told me. He waited on him the other day at Jack's."

Janice paused. Was she working up some sort of courage? Was she getting her thoughts together? I was going to covertly listen like hell to everything they said after Michelle's actor slight. Who am I kidding; I was going to listen regardless of what Michelle had said.

"I don't know how to tell you this, Michelle."

"You can tell me anything, you know that."

It was quiet.

Michelle broke the tension. "Janice…I know…Gary told me."

"Told you what?"

"Told me about you…and…Kirk's…brother." That seem to take Michelle a long time to get out.

"See…" Janice whispered. "See, that's just it."

"What's it?"

Janice shook her head, trying to get the right words out of her mouth, it seemed.

"Gary…"

But that was all she could manage.

"What?"

Nothing.

"What, Janice?"

"It's a lie, Michelle."

"What is?"

Janice shook her head again.

"Nothing. Never mind."

"No. Tell me."

But Janice didn't say anything.

"Don't do that, Janice."

Still silent.

"Hey, we're too close for that."

Janice looked at Michelle.

"You're my best friend, right?"

Janice nodded, which seemed to give her courage.

"It's a lie."

"What is?" Michelle treaded slowly.

"Sleeping with Ray. What Gary told you."

Michelle half smiled and half winced, perhaps trying to understand.

"I didn't sleep with Ray, Michelle." Janice stared point blank at her friend.

"But—"

"I wouldn't sleep with my husband's brother."

"Um—" Michelle seemed confused.

"I mean, do you think I could do anything like that?"

Michelle gave that universal eye raise *Well*, which in this case, I think meant I *suppose not.*

"Do you, Michelle?"

Michelle looked conflicted. I'm not sure. But she certainly hesitated.

"Oh my god!" Janice seemed alarmed, which sparked Michelle into action.

"No, no. Of course not."

"Michelle!"

"Of course not, Janice."

"God."

"No! I don't."

"What?"

"I don't believe it…I don't believe you could do such a thing." Michelle was trying to convince Janice.

"Thank you."

Silence once again. I felt really uncomfortable watching Michelle try to convince Janice that she did, in fact, believe her, when, from my vantage point, it seemed Michelle could imagine Janice sleeping with Kirk's brother…that her reputation did lend itself to being attacked.

"I just wonder…I mean…why would Gary say that?"

And more silence as both women fidgeted in their seats.

"Well…" Once again, Janice stopped herself.

"What?"

"Oh Michelle, shit."

"Janice. What?" Michelle now asked pointedly.

"I—I—don't even know how to say it."

"Then just say it."

I was really wishing Janice would just come out and say whatever it was she was holding back as well.

"Gary told you that…" Janice let out a deep sigh. "To cover for himself."

"What?"

"Oh God, Michelle."

Michelle stared straight at Janice, waiting for her to speak.

"I don't want to say it." Janice murmured.

"Well, we're way beyond that now."

"Forget it. Just forget I said anything."

"How?"

"I don't want to hurt you."

"Janice?! What is it?"

Janice's body swayed back and forth as she avoided what was inevitably coming.

"Oh for God's sake, Janice!"

"Gary has been having an affair with a student!"

It came out so quickly; it was alarming. I almost gasped, which would have ruined my cover as a deaf, out of work actor.

Michelle was in shock as well. Her head moved back and forth as she registered what was said. Before Michelle could head down a road of denial, Janice jumped in…"I saw Gary talking to a girl…a senior…Don't ask me who, there's no way I can say that. It'll just destroy this girl, and she's just a girl."

Michelle's eyes were wide. She was now frozen, staring at the table.

"I approached the girl and pressed her. And, well, she confided in me. She told me…Oh God, Michelle…" The words rapidly poured out of Janice's mouth.

The two sat there for a moment, but then Janice continued.

"She showed me a picture. A selfie…you know, um, of her, um, naked…"

I could see Janice's foot tapping as she tried to say what she was about to say.

"…That apparently Gary had asked for."

"No," Michelle whispered to herself.

"I'm sorry."

"No."

"Michelle."

"I—he—no…"

"I can show you the picture. I mean, I told the girl to send it to me, because, you know...you know...I have to report it."

Michelle looked at Janice in disgust.

"Sorry. I just thought you might need to see it...to believe it. I'm sorry."

Michelle began to rub her head. The waiter entered the room to check on us, and as he made his way towards Janice and Michelle, Janice waved him off. So, the waiter made a turn towards my table, and I quickly held up my water glass and pointed to it.

"More water. Coming right up." And he left.

"Michelle...Gary found out that I knew. The girl must've told him. And so, he...I don't know...cornered me...after school. He came into my classroom...and...basically...threatened me."

I thought Michelle might pass out. I really did. Janice waited for a response, but none came, so Janice just sat there, seemingly studying her friend.

"I'm really sorry."

"Let me see it."

"Sorry?"

"The photo. Let me see it."

"Um...uh, yeah. Sure."

Janice rummaged through her phone, until she finally landed on what must have been the picture. She turned the phone to Michelle, who started to cry.

"I'm really sorry." What seemed to be a sympathetic smile swept across her face. It stayed there, which started to then feel patronizing, like *Ah, poor thing.*

Michelle wiped her eyes with her napkin, but from what I could tell, it didn't do any good. More tears followed, and she wiped again; her eyeliner streaked across her cheeks. She then made her way out of the booth while grabbing for her coat.

"Michelle?"

Michelle hustled out of the room, and Janice, who seemingly forgot about my presence yelled after her and filled the room with, "I haven't reported anything yet!"

Michelle was gone, but I figured she heard what Janice shouted.

The back room was dead quiet. It was very awkward. Janice started to gather her purse and coat, as the waiter returned with a pitcher of water.

As he filled up my empty glass he asked, "Have you decided on what you might like?"

I gave him a smile. I completely forgot about eating. I quickly flipped through the menu trying to locate the salad bar. My finger stopped on the "Famous All You Can Eat Salad…Please No Sharing."

I pointed to those words as Janice quickly swept by us, leaving the restaurant.

12

We Change, Folks Change

The next day, as I walked the downtown streets with a cup of hot tea, a boutique caught my eye. I didn't catch the name, but I liked the window displays of candles, coffee cups, and crew neck sweatshirts with various references to the state and area—One had an oven mitt with the words "The Mitten" above it. Another had an outline of all the Great Lakes with the words "Salt Free." And another had an outline of the lower peninsula but had an added index and baby finger drawn pointing up to make the ASL sign for LOVE. So, I went in.

I had been so caught up in my current situation with Sophie that I forgot to get Christmas presents out to the kids. Anything I bought now would arrive much too late. Still, the trinkets and such were cute and worthy of a looksy. Inside was a cluttered mess of knickknacks with a main room and little, tiny, adjacent walk ins. The main room had more candles. I love candles especially earthy scents. I like sandalwood and balsam and smoked cedar and tobacco, myrrh and frankincense. The candles in this shop had some of that, but I quickly noticed that they were all holiday themed—"Christmas Tree"—which I assumed was coated in pine, "Peppermint Mocha," "Winter Fire," and what I assumed were holdovers from Thanksgiving—"Pumpkin Pie" and "Turkey Dinner," which sounded like it smelled terrible, so of course, I couldn't resist. Wouldn't you know it, it smelled like apples and vanilla. I was disappointed.

"Hello there! Whatcha lookin' for?"

I only heard the voice and half-turned my neck, hoping that the slightest of handwaves would do the trick. I really didn't feel like trying to explain why I couldn't answer questions or participate in a discussion.

"You like candles, huh?"

Oh, boy. I'm gonna have to expl—

"Me too. I could fill a whole store with candles if you let me. But I know the folks that are a shoppin' want more than that, ya know? Anyway, we got all sorts of things…"

She continued to talk, and I thought it rude to keep my back turned to her, so I gave her a smile. I couldn't get a real angle on her age. She had shoulder length grey hair and sort of a squarish figure. I'd say she wasn't much more than five feet tall. She had a white crewneck sweatshirt over a white turtleneck, and the sweatshirt read "SHHHH. I'm on Santa's Naughty List." And it had a woman with her roundish, shortish build in a string bikini, posing in a Marilyn Monroe sort of way with her tushy sticking out, slightly bent over, with her right, index finger up to her lips. I smiled at the sweatshirt, and she must've noticed, because she quickly transitioned from whatever she was talking about to…

"Oh, you like the sweatshirt, huh? Yeah, I modeled for it. Yep. Can you believe it? I was dating an artist who—clever guy, cute too. Shame it didn't work out. Anyway, he's gotta T-shirt shop. Ya know, a press type of thing, where he designs and makes T-shirts outta his garage.

Cute guy. God was he fun. Anyway, he had this idea, and asked if I'd pose, and I says 'Sure, why not?' I think that surprised him, but I like my body, ya know? I mean, it's the only one I got, so, yeah, sure, it's been through a bit. Lotta history, ya know, but what the hell."

My smile grew, and then I noticed books that had been cut into letters. Old, hard cover books that had been placed on a band saw and moved and fashioned in such a way as to make capital Ps and Ts, Rs and such.

"Oh, you like those?" And I smiled again. "Yeah, a guy outside of town makes those in his spare time. He finds old books at garage sales and yard sales and what not. Nothing famous, mind you. Probably end up in a landfill, if he didn't rescue 'em. But they make great gifts.

I'm Mary Ellen, by the way. The guy made me a whole set, ya know, to spell out my name. I got 'em at the house. Pretty neat. He was fun too. Super sexy in a back-woodsy sort of way. So, real sexy, ya know? Almost married but nah. Anywho, feel free to look around. We got all sorts of things."

And so, I did. And she continued talking with just the slightest of pauses.

"We. Listen to me. It's just me. Never married. Never saw the point, really. It's a construct, right."

That wasn't a question, because she didn't wait for an answer.

"I think people get married because it's expected. Then look what happens. Heck, I don't see a whole lot of divorces around these parts neither, believe it or not. I just see—what's the word? Resignation, ya know—or not even despair, but rather, what, an acceptance that this is it. What the hell kind of life is that."

Again, not a question. She continued on, and I poked my head in a small room that had a kitchen look. There were shelves of coffee cups with sayings ranging from inspirational like "Be a small light in a world of darkness" to downright dirty—"I'm not a gynecologist, but I'll have a look." *I don't think you can take that mug to the office.*

The coffee cups ran from floor to ceiling on one wall. There was an old wooden stove that I assumed did not function with new copper-style pots and pans, and an old antique table in the center of the room with placemats and serving bowls, plates, and glasses. It was a tight fit, as I shimmied around the table, trying to clear my ass without knocking anything over.

"They tell you to build a life together with this one person, and yet people don't seem to like that person…I mean after a while. Sure, it's probably fun at first. I mean, I have fun at first with all the guys I see. But then it gets, what, familiar, yeah? Yeah. But you're some sort of failure if it doesn't work out. I got news for ya, buddy…It's not working out. So why stay married? And you know what? People change. Of course they change. You ever get on Facebook and connect with someone you went to high school with? Well, of course, you have. Duh."

I had made my way around the small room and entered the main room again just in time for Mary Ellen to smack her forehead with the palm of her hand.

"What's wrong with you, Mary Ellen?" She asked herself but didn't answer. "Anyway, I get friend requests like that, and I add 'em, don't know why in God's name I do. Because do you know what? Huh? They wind up asking if you still like red licorice or going to horror movies or whatever memory it is they have of you when you were, like, twenty years younger. I got one the other day asking if I still dyed my hair. Does it look like I dye it? I mean, how would they know? My profile pic is a picture of my chickens. I have thirteen. Although we lost Henry last week. Weasels. God, I hate weasels. Absolutely what's the point with those guys, huh? I mean, I really have no idea how those li'l bastards contribute to this crazy, circle of life, like, at all. Jesus. Anyway..."

I had made my way to another small room and this one was bathroom themed, complete with a toilet and sink. There were shelves of liquid soaps and bowls of bar soaps and small tables with lotions.

"Toilet works! If you need to use it. Honest to Pete. And those bar soaps are handmade by a friend of mine. She's a riot. A real hoot. You'd love her. Anyway, where was I? Oh, my hair. Yeah, no, I don't dye it. And to tell ya the truth, I think I only dyed it a couple of times. Went blond. You know, had a bit of fun. Big whoop. But then I started to grey, and I thought the heck with it, I'll just let it go. Kinda liked it. My sister asked, 'Aren't you worried people will think you're old?' The hell with them, right? I greyed prematurely. I don't know...I find it sexy. You?"

There was a pause after "You," and I worried for a moment that she was looking for an answer. But then...

"I don't know, I guess my point is. We change. Folks change. Like, of course, we change. How could we not? I don't like the same things I did in my twenties. Hell, my body's changed. I used to love tomatoes... all of the sudden, can't eat 'em. Garlic. Nope. Developed an allergy. So, you change in that way. But you know, you start to experience things. You go off and you visit places, or you meet someone, and you're affected, yeah? You're affected...and...you change. You change in that way too. Experience changes you. How can it not? So, what do you do with that when you're married? I've been with a lot of men. I mean, my fair share. Oh God...I don't mean—well, you know what I mean, yeah? I've been with some guys. And it starts out great, or not so great, but whatever. But let's say it starts out great. Some were great. Others? Not so much. But—God, Mary Ellen, get to the point. My point is, let's say it starts out great. Well, something happened—you find out more about the person. That's the other thing, right? When you meet someone and you fall in love, you want it to work. Sure, you get to know them a li'l bit, but I don't think folks really wanna know everything for fear that what they find out won't—what—be to their liking? Because you want it to work out, ya know? So, you don't wanna know too much. Or they don't tell you everything, 'cause they think you'll end it and leave 'em. So, they reveal it later. Whatever. I don't know. But what I do know is is that people change.

And sure, you know what, the guys I've been with have changed. Or heck, I've changed. I don't know. My point is is that I'm glad I didn't marry them. Had some fun. And that's that, ya know? On to the next. Finding everything alright?"

I came out of the bathroom room and gave her a smile. I imagine she needed to go on a rant. I'm not sure why. Maybe this was her only socialization. Maybe she needed to get some stuff off her chest. I was happy to listen. She was darling, and I say that without any sort of a patronizing tone. I guess in my heart, I thought she was a lot older than myself, and that's why I say 'darling,' but if high school was only, what, twenty years ago for her, then she's only in her late thirties and younger than me. I guess the grey hair threw me. "Prematurely grey" would be such an LA thing to say. Except the folks saying that out there would be in their fifties hoping you thought they were in their late thirties or early forties. But I believed Mary Ellen. No sense in not believing her. As she kept talking about whatever she was talking about, I started to wonder *How in the world am I going to leave here without it seeming rude? I mean, all I can do is smile and wave.*

"...You're at a crossroads. I totally get that. You have a decision to make. Do you and your spouse (Oh, she was still on about relationships and change) have a meeting of the minds, and compromise or do you say, 'Hey, good game. Attaway. I'll see ya later?' I don't know. Most people stop talking anyway, so that's gotta make it even harder. Like you're supposed to know what the other person is thinking. I hate that. I have no idea what you're thinking right now. Probably, 'God, I wish this woman would shut the hell up...'"

I put both hands up to my chest, palms out, and waved to let her know that I was, in fact, not thinking that. And I really wasn't. I was enjoying myself. Just wasn't sure how to make my exit.

"Anyhoogle, I don't think you can go into a relationship though thinking it'll all fall apart. Otherwise, we'll all just throw our hands up in the air and not even try. Right? Am I right?"

As I started to nod, a woman entered the store, but it barely altered Mary Ellen's focus.

"Oh, hello, let me know if I can help with anything." And the woman gave a slight smile.

As Mary Ellen went back into what she was talking about, I noticed this was the same woman from Jack's Café. The beautiful woman with the cheekbones that seemed to scoff when the host asked if we were together. Huh.

"I have a…oh a whatchamacallit…a…QUADRANGLE," Mary Ellen shouted when she found the word she was looking for. Like that monk with the peas…In France, right?"

I wasn't sure where she was going with this now.

"Oh, Mary Ellen, you dolt." She chastised herself but kept going. "The monk who studied genetics or something. Oh…who cares, right? Anyhow, I have a quadrangle that's done me good. You separate it into these four squares when heading into a relationship. It'll be good…and it turns out good. It'll be good…but it turns out bad."

Her voice rose and dropped when she alternated between the positive and negative outcomes in a sing-songy way.

"Then, of course, the other two are it'll be bad…and it turns out good. And, it'll be bad…and it turns out bad. That last one. That one…" She then whispered out the side of her mouth, "Sucks. But you knew it would be bad, and you were right…so there you go."

The beautiful woman was now at the counter—the register—ready to check out. I suppose she knew exactly what she wanted and found it. She sat a small, beautifully painted bowl on the counter along with a card. (I hadn't noticed the card room. That must be upstairs, hence the stairs, that I had just now noticed.) The whole time Mary Ellen was talking, my focus was split from looking and listening to Mary Ellen, and sometimes side-eyeing the beautiful woman to see if she remembered me. She never looked at me.

Mary Ellen continued, even while ringing up Ms. Cheekbones. "But, you can't let that last square of 'You think it's gonna be bad and sure enough it's bad' ruin the other squares. Follow? And even that square where you thought it would be good and it turns out bad…even that square started out with excitement. So, that leaves you with good, good and bad, good. And both of those are happy endings. So, heck…why not go for it? At least that's always been my mantra. And so…I keep dating. Heck, at least it's a new adventure, right? Now don't get me wrong…I've had some—I've made some mistakes…big ones. But the way I live is this…'Forgiveness turns regret into experience.'" Those last set of words were inflected like some famous quote, and she gave some space to let those words sink in.

"Know who said that?" She had been busy ringing up the attractive woman, but in just this momentary instant she stopped and looked right at me after asking her question. I managed a shrug...and a smile.

"Me." And she gave me a wink.

Mary Ellen managed to wrap the bowl, bag the card, handle the credit card transaction, and give the sold items to the beautiful woman without missing a beat in her story. I used the brief moment of silence to smile and wave goodbye before the attractive woman could leave, which would have left me in the shop by myself with Mary Ellen once again.

"Oh, okay, bye, hon. Thanks for the chat."

As I stepped outside, I chuckled to myself at the word "chat." I still had my hot tea, which was now cold tea, and saw a trash can up the block. There stood another whimsical looking storefront—this a small book and card shop called A Novel Idea.

As I roamed the isles, I figured I would email Graeme and Brianna a gift certificate, so that the kids at least had something from me for Christmas, and then I would mail out cards to celebrate the new year. Everything I read, though, was far too hokey.

"Finding yourself is never easy..."

"What is a son?"

"You're not only beautiful, daughter. You're smart and funny too."

Oh God...I kept wishing there was a section in the store where the cards simply told it like it was...

"So, your parents are separated, huh?" And you turn the card, and it reads, "That sounds weird and sucky." Or...

"If things don't work out with your folks...You'll at least get two Christmases!" Or... "Parents are separated?..Don't blame me it was your mom's idea!" I managed to chuckle to myself and thought the next chapter of my life could be to write out funny greeting cards that people could relate too. I turned and saw a whole aisle devoted to birthdays. Sophie, the kids, and I had a long-standing tradition in our family. On someone's birthday, after they blew out the candles, we would go around the room and say one thing we were grateful for or something we loved about the person we were celebrating. "You make me laugh everyday," Sophie told me on my birthday early in our marriage, "God, do I need that." That line became a mini-tradition inside the tradition on my birthday for several years following. "I know I say this every year, but..." or "I'll add something else also, but...You make me laugh everyday."

And then one birthday...probably around five years ago...it

stopped. She started saying "You're so devoted to the kids. I love that about you." In her defense, I used to describe her and her talents and her savvy and her feistiness, her commitment, and how clever she was, and get very personal with all the things I loved about her…but those trailed off as well. I would say shit like "You're very dedicated to your job." Or "You're a wonderful mother."

Damn…did we just get tired and hurt and let it all slip away? And the poor kids…They must've seen and felt the change in how we talked to one another. Kids know. We may have thought we were being sly, but the kids knew. No wonder they saw this coming before I did. I picked out the best of the worst cards this shop had to offer. At the check-out the tall, jet black-haired woman started to ring me up.

"Just want to make you aware that today I'm allowed to select my favorite item in the store and offer a deal to everyone who buys something. Here…" and she gestured to a stack of paper napkins adorned with decorated Christmas trees. "We have a package of two dozen disposable napkins with Christmas trees designed by children in Botswana. Adorable, huh?"

I nodded and smiled.

"Would you like me to add this to your purchase?"

Before I could manage a gesture that would convey, "No thanks. I'm good," she continued rather quickly. "Yours for only five dollars… today."

I guess my head shake wasn't big enough because she exclaimed rather loudly, "Terrific!"

And so, I walked out of A Novel Idea with a few cards and two dozen disposable napkins that I didn't need.

"I mean, what the actual fuck, Gary!" That's what I heard as I was rounding the corner of the card shop and headed to the back parking lot towards my brother's car. As I stepped towards the parking lot, I first saw Michelle from the restaurant, and of course, there was Gary, her husband.

Michelle was standing outside a large SUV looking over the hood of the car, and Gary emerged from the driver's side.

"Once again, Michelle, you're not listening to me!"

"I'm done listening, Gary."

"I am trying to expla—"

"I'M. NOT. LISTENING!"

She was basically screaming, and I wondered if anyone else was hearing this.

"But it's not true! It's not true, Michelle."

"I'm so sick of your lies."

"I'm not lying."

"Gary, you were caught—"

"Oh, because Janice told you that?"

"Not just Janice, Gar—"

"Because Janice is a bi—"

"Not just Janice!"

"I didn't sleep with—"

"I can't believe I stayed for as long as I did."

They were basically just talking over one another. That is until now. Now, there was a moment of silence, as Gary processed what Michelle just said.

"What does that mean?"

She slowed down her speech as she repeated the exact same thing.

"I can't believe I stayed for as long as I did."

"Yeah, I heard you, Michelle!"

"I mean, look at you."

"What?"

"You fat fuck. You fat fuckin' piece of shit."

"Me?"

"Who do you think I'm talking to, dumbass?!"

The language was cranking up a bit.

"No, I know who you're talking—"

"I defended you to my friends—"

"I know who you're talking to, Mich—"

"I mean—"

"But why are you calling *me* fat?"

This stopped Michelle.

"You...of all people," Gary continued.

"Don't..."

"Oh, really? Don't?"

"Don't, Gary."

"It's not so much your body, Michelle, but—"

"But what?"

"It's you. Your attitude."

"My attitude?"

"It's shitty."

"Go to hell, Gary."

"Nothing I do is ever good enough…"

"Oh, Gary."

"Never—"

"My attitude?"

"All I've ever tried to do—"

"Gary, you are an emotional infant."

"…Is make you happy."

"You are a moody fuck."

"I'm an Infant?"

"I walk on eggshells waiting to see what kind—"

"Bullshit!"

"—Of mood you're going to be in."

They were letting it all out now. It felt like years of pent-up resentment was pouring out of them.

"That's rich, Michelle."

"It's so true, Gary. You just never grew up."

"Oh, Michelle."

"You're stunted emotionally. Like you're perpetually twelve years old."

"Fuck you."

"See."

"No! No! You don't get to say 'see'."

"See."

"Fuck. You!"

"You're a child, Gary."

"And you're a fucking cunt who refuses to ever be happy."

"It's over, Gary."

"I've worked my ass off for you!"

"You're such a dick."

"Just so you could keep up with your bitch ass friends."

Michelle stopped responding.

"Fuck, Janice! Fuck Heather! Fuck, Myra! Fuck 'em all."

"You'd love to fuck 'em all." She couldn't resist, I guess.

"I didn't cheat on you!!!" Gary was screaming, throwing his arms in the air, and turning in circles as though he was trying to let the whole town know.

"I don't believe you."

"Janice is the one who's been cheating."

"She told me you would spin it like that."

"She's been fucking Ray."

"More lies, Gary."

"I'm not—"

"I can't take anymore lies!!" She bent over howling saying this.

"As God is my witness, Michelle!"

"How dare you?!"

"What?!"

"You lying fuck!"

"What is wrong with you?!"

"The photo, asshole!"

"What photo?"

"The one with the naked girl?"

"What?!"

"A *girl*, Gary!"

"The fuck you on about?"

"Janice showed me the photo of the student, you dumb fucking pervert!"

"Oh my God, Michelle!"

"Don't!"

"That's RAY!!"

"Stop!"

"But it's not true, Michelle!"

"I saw the photo!"

"And I'm telling you—"

"I don't believe you!!"

"You've never believed in me!"

"In you? I never believed IN you? I've worked my ass off for this family."

"You're out all the time getting drunk with your girlfriends!"

"Fuck off."

"You gave up on me a long time ago!"

"No shit."

"What?" Gary just started shaking his head, trying to process what was just said. "Why?" He asked.

"'Cause you gave up on you…on us."

"Bullshit."

"I was never good enough for you!"

"Bullshit."

"Well, obviously, you fuckin' sick ass fuck!"

"STOP!" Gary screamed. "IT'S NOT FUCKING TRUE!"

Michelle could only shake her head. Gary started to move towards her, and her body tensed up. Her disgust was so evident, it stopped Gary in his tracks. The screaming had stopped, and in the silence, I heard cars driving in the distance and the calls of a few winter birds.

"You've never been good enough for me?" Gary asked rhetorically. "What a joke, Michelle. It's me. I've never been good enough for you!"

It was quiet again. I took a quick look around to see if anyone else was watching this, but it looked like I was the only one.

"Well, Gary, let me be the grown up in the room and tell you, that at least I can admit it…You're right…You're not good enough for me. Not anymore."

"You're a weak, brainwashed woman."

"And you suffocated me during sex."

It seemed she knew how to hurt him because it was immediately silent. Gary's head sank, and he stood there for a moment.

"I faked every orgasm I ever had with you." Michelle didn't yell but said it so determinedly that even I heard it from a bit of a distance. It was another plunge of the dagger into what remained of their marriage. Gary just stood there. Then he reached in his pocket, fumbling for something. Michelle studied him. He then managed to pull out the car keys and tossed them to her.

"Here…keep it." And Gary stuffed his hands into his jacket to seemingly keep them warm and started to walk away. He then turned back…"You realize what you're accusing me of. I mean, fuck. Michelle, you? I—I can see Janice…she's fucking lying. She's warped—fucking desperate!" Michelle shook her head, as Gary went on…"She is a desperate, sick piece—not the point. It is. It is the point. But more—but fuckin' more importantly—"

"Gary."

"You. Michelle. That you could think I would do…THAT? FUCKING THAT? Sleep…have sex with…fuck." His voice went from a hard-to-hear, monotoned whisper to a quick scream, and back again.

Michelle kept shaking her head. I think she was done…or she

didn't want to hear what Gary was truly saying.

He started to cry. "You fuckin' believe that shit?"

It was so quiet as they just stood there.

"My Michelle?" I think that's what he said. I could barely hear it.

He then turned again and walked away. I kept waiting for Michelle to yell out "wait" or for Gary to turn around, but he had already done that, and those kinds of moments of reconciliation seem to only be in movies. It was just a painstakingly slow exit on Gary's part, and Michelle finally broke down crying, as Gary disappeared out of sight.

13

Ghosts and Demons

It was Christmas morning. I woke up to Chad licking my face, and as I was trying to get my bearings, it dawned on me that I had forgotten to take him out for his evening wiz. I sat up on the bed, and Chad, as old as he was, was dancing around the room, anxious to get outside. I let him out and watched him sniff and find a familiar patch of snowy grass, and I swear he must have peed for a minute and a half. *I'm so sorry, Chad. I'm such a bad dog uncle.*

I made a pot of coffee and looked out the living room window. My brother had built a wrap around porch, and it was really quite a scene to see that in the foreground of a wintry wilderness landscape. My brother had ten acres out back, and it was a mix of fields and forest. I looked out sipping my hot coffee. It was Christmas morning, and I missed my family. I missed the kids. I missed Graeme and Bree being the first to wake up and jumping on top of Sophie and me. Heck, I missed when they had gotten older and were in their teen years, and seemingly over everything and so judgmental, and it was me and Sophie going into their rooms and jumping on them to wake them up to open presents. I missed it all.

We would open stockings first, which was a departure from when I was a kid. For some reason it was a big tradition in my original family to open stockings last. I don't know why. In hindsight, it was pretty anticlimactic. We didn't have money growing up, and Nate's and my stockings always had the same things in them: An apple in the toes to fill up space, some walnuts, Brazil nuts, chestnuts, and the like filling in the foot area, an orange taking up the heel, some wrapped chocolate pieces in the ankle and calves, and then something special like a *Star Wars* figure or a pack of trading cards or a small bottle of Jovan Musk for Men near the top.

But it was tradition, and those are hard to let go of. So, I tried to sell Sophie on waiting until after we opened presents to open our stockings. But again, Sophie always pointed out, and I admit, correctly, that stockings were the appetizer to the presents, which were the main course. I think for me, the stockings represented that Christmas morning wasn't, how do I say...over. Stockings were something additional to look forward to. It didn't matter that my mom filled them mostly with cheap fruit and nuts. It was something else, something more. When you grow up, and your friends go out to eat, but you don't...when they head to McDonald's and your mom makes you a homemade patty and puts it on bread...when you wear last year's worn-out sneakers to your first day of school...you look forward to something else, something more. And on top of that, a black cloud would slowly move in when the holidays were over, because our dad would go back to operating out of anger and manipulation.

But the adult me relented, and we started with the stockings. However, (I guess this was my little compromise) I liked to make the stockings special. I put an anniversary diamond band in Sophie's stocking one year. Another year I got her a bracelet with the kids' birthstones. I would get Graeme the newest and latest game for his Xbox. One year we got a young Bree a couple of American Girl dolls, and I stuffed her stocking with a complete wardrobe. I did this all on my own. Again, I wanted the stockings to be special. Of course, loading Bree's stocking with American Girl clothing ruined the surprise of getting a couple of $100 dolls. Sophie, needless to say, shook her head when she saw Bree open her stocking. Sophie shook her head a lot at me. How did things get so bad? Sophie and I had our ups and downs, but we always seemed to pull through. I never would have guessed it would have come to this. I mean, I guess I just didn't want to face the fact that we were at rock bottom, but here I was, completely alone, on Christmas, of all days, while my children ran to friends for comfort and my wife ran to her parents. I stood, eyes fixed on Nate's backyard, but my head was lost in the memories of my family. I wondered how their Christmas mornings were going. Fear and anxiety swept over me as I imagined them all together at my in-laws... that somehow this was all a big lie, and I was simply left out. There was a rush of worry that was so irrational. I was able to dismiss it. *You're just lonely.* So, I went back to wondering what they were up to this Christmas morning—separated and in different time zones, I know, but what did they do on our once special day? I could only imagine.

I thought about Graeme. I saw him with his host family in Dublin; the son and Graeme were best buds. He probably opened a gift or two but then landed at a nearby, tiny, corner pub with wainscoting and a tin ceiling, sipping Guinness and doing shots of different Irish whiskeys. I imagined him happy, and that forced a smile across my face...a small smile. I texted.

Merry Christmas, my son. I love you more than life itself.

Bree, I thought, was already on the slopes, having a ball on her board. Maybe she was already done and was soaking in a Jacuzzi, laughing with her friends. She and I both loved hot tubs. Our vacation planning revolved around which hotels advertised their whirlpools. I mean, we would do our research and see which resorts, not only had a hot tub, but were proud of their hot tub. And then, we would book it immediately, whatever the cost. Much to Sophie's chagrin.

Merry Christmas, Bear. Thanks for the playlist. You are my dream that came true.

And then there was Sophie. I hoped she had a nice Christmas morning. She was with her parents, whom she loved. But I imagine it was not without its challenges, not only with their failing health but maybe more importantly, all the ghosts from the past. We all have ghosts, and sometimes its hard being back with your parents no matter how much you love them. Sophie always felt a strong pull to see her parents, and I think it was more than obligatory. I think she enjoyed their company. Still, after a day or two, Sophie would start getting agitated, and she would get impatient with me. It took me a couple of trips to realize that she felt trapped—she was frustrated with her parents but felt that she couldn't say anything. Maybe, like most of us, she weighed the pros and cons of challenging her parents on these trips or staying silent and enduring what they had to say.

I always got along with Sophie's parents. They seemed to enjoy my company, and I enjoyed theirs. We made one another laugh, and of course, they were always interested in my career. Sophie's relationship with them ebbed and flowed. She and her mom were tight, but Sophie adopted her poor body image from her mother, who was always quick with a "You sure you want to eat that?" to both Sophie and her dad.

Margie even did it to me a couple of times, and my response was always the same…"Oh, I'm sure. Positive." And I was easily the biggest one of the group. Sophie also had her challenges with her dad. Sophie was, to put it mildly, a liberal. And her dad seemed to be a founding member of the Grand Ole Party. So, the two would butt heads at least once every visit. Me, I got a charge out of it…but I don't have a political affiliation.

Merry Christmas. I miss you.

I erased that last part. Felt like I was pressuring her. I gave it some thought.

Merry Christmas.

I couldn't just send that. Sure, I didn't want to force anything, but I certainly didn't want her to think I had given up.

Merry Christmas. I love you. Always.

And I sent it, before I could overthink it anymore.

I sat down for a while waiting for a response, hoping for a response…from any of them.

And I sat there.

I reached out to my brother and texted

Merry Christmas, Nate. Hope you got to Florida in one piece. Enjoy the in-laws!

And to my mom I wrote

Merry Christmas, Mom! Hope you are enjoying your time with Aunt Rosemary. Tell her HI from her favorite nephew. I love you, mom.

I started thinking about other people as well. Maybe Gary and Michelle made up for the sake of their children…but after the fight I witnessed, the things he was accused of, and the things that were said, I had my doubts. But hey, relationships are weird and crazier things have happened. Maybe it was all a big misunderstanding. Maybe Gary and Michelle were sitting around the tree waiting to see their kids' reaction when they opened their presents. Then, hopefully, they looked at one another and managed a smile…a forgiving smile…to one another. And from there, they could build, rebuild, on that one moment.

I thought about Mitch. What was he doing this morning? I could only guess. I really didn't know Mitch anymore. Maybe he was with Crystal, but I didn't know…that felt more like lonely people hooking up, rather than a real, committed relationship. Maybe he went hunting. He was always a gifted hunter. So, my mind went further into that thought. Mitch went hunting super early and sat in his safe space—his hunting blind. This, I thought, was where he found peace. He would re-energize out there. And then...along came a big ole buck. And Mitch lined him up in his sites and took it down. I saw Mitch tracking the buck and then dragging it back home. Then there was Andy, the sheriff's deputy, and his family. I assumed Andy had a family. He never mentioned them, but that's kind of what people do in the Midwest. They meet someone, and maybe that doesn't work out, but it doesn't take long to meet someone else and just kind of decide that you're going to settle down and start having kids. Maybe that's why divorce rates are so high. Maybe, like Mary Ellen suggested, folks settled for the second or third serious relationship and figure time was passing them by. Mind you, a lot of my friends out west don't have children. They've decided that they don't want them. But back here in the Midwest there seems to be this unspoken pressure by the older generations, an ancestral code, to start baby making before it's too late.

So, I pictured Andy divorced. No idea if it's true, but I figured who the hell would want to be married to that guy. Still, I imagined that he was on friendly terms with the ex, and she invited him over to her place and watched their kids open presents.

I looked at my phone. Nothing. I waited.

I looked at my phone. Again, nothing. And I sat there...hoping for a response to the texts I had sent out.

But nothing happened. I took another sip of joe still wondering how I ended up alone on the one day I absolutely treasured being with family. Then, in a very cinematic way, a rack focus pulled the trees outside of my brother's house into a sharp, crisp picture. I was no longer wondering and daydreaming. I only saw those trees. And one tree in particular which had remnants of an old fort that my nephews had built a couple of years ago. And then...I saw my old fort...in the back of my parents home. It was a cool structure, fairly high up on a wide, old oak positioned on the other side of a decent-sized creek. To get to the fort you had to cross a swinging bridge my brother had built before he enlisted and left me—left home.

I shook my head and looked at the last few gulps of coffee that remained in a cup that read "My Wife is Hotter than my Coffee." I smiled. Sophie and I used to get each other stuff like that. I wished in that moment that there was something stronger in my cup, and I wanted to find a bar... that early in the morning. But, more importantly, I couldn't shake the image of that old fort. And a stronger urge overtook a desire to drink, and so, I grabbed my brother's keys and made a decision: Instead of finding a bar, I was going to drive up to my parent's old house. I was going to go see some old ghosts…maybe they had some answers that would help my marriage.

Downtown was empty given that it was Christmas Day. I made a right on M57, a rural state road and headed out of Greenville. I drove past empty cornfields with pockets of snow scattered about listening to Bree's Moody Winter Vibes playlist she had made for me. These were terrific songs that hit just the right tone for how I was feeling at the time. Before I knew it, I was heading up US-131 and was a good deal away from town. For a moment, I didn't really know where I was. I mean, we're never really lost anymore with a map right there on our cell phones, and I had traveled this stretch in the past; but I had gotten so lost in the music, I didn't realize that I had been driving for close to an hour.

I had forgotten how brown it was when the snow didn't cover the earth. I drove past acres of harvested grows laid baren from the plummeting temperatures. There were fields with pockets of old, beige stalks of corn, which somehow were ignored by farmers in the autumn for reasons way beyond my brain power, although I kept wondering why they were left behind as I raced past them. What a dreadful pallet Mother Nature used to paint this time of year…a gunmetal grey sky above a drab oatmeal or, what, mushroom, maybe? Yeah, the ground was the color of mushrooms. Maybe it was my mood that day; I truly love the winter. The colors I observed that Christmas morning seemed in constant use in Andrew Wyeth's paintings, and they told quite a story—fenced in horses or a dog snuggled by the pillows on a bed—but that day, I just wished, prayed even, that it would snow, and a sheet of white linen would cover the drab, puke nutmeg that surrounded me.

After a while longer, my throat started to tighten. It was hard to swallow. It wasn't impossible, but I was concerned. What had come over me? And just as soon as I asked myself that, I started thinking about my parents. The closer I got to the old farmhouse where I was raised, the more anxious I became. I guess the ghosts were trying to talk to me after all.

Parents have a picture of us, and more often than not, you can't change that picture. My parents loved me with conditions. They loved me transactionally. If I fulfilled my role, then they demonstrated their love. And while it was more true of my dad, my mom had her moments, and when I didn't fulfill her expectations, there was no bigger guilt trip to go on…trust me.

I now sat at the end of the driveway of our old home on County Line Road. The house had been long abandoned. My mom sold it after the divorce and moved into town, and I guess whoever bought it let it go. That's when I saw the ghosts. "Ghosts" was an expression of Danny's. While we always had a festive time together, he found it hard heading back to England after one of his LA trips. Hell, he found it hard on the rare occasion I visited him in England.

"I can see your ghost sitting in my conservatory."

"Ghost?"

"I was pulling some barbeque off the grill from out back and I walked through the conservatory to the kitchen, and I saw you smiling at me…right where you were when you were here."

"Ahh. I get it. Yeah, I get those pictures in my mind too."

And there I was at the end of the driveway of the old farmhouse seeing ghosts. The first one I saw was an eleven-year-old me throwing a football to myself in the front yard with the huge snowflakes smacking my face as I dove for an errant pass. I played quarterback, I played running back. I played by myself, so I was everybody. I could spend hours out there in the snow.

Then I saw my dad screaming at my mother through the big, front kitchen window. The dishes weren't washed correctly, or God forbid, put away. That was a big rule for my dad. It wasn't enough that the dishes were washed; they had to be dried and put back where they belong, and the counter had to be clear. He hated clutter. Mind you, he never did the dishes. That was beneath him. But he expected my mom to do them after she got home from work and made dinner. I saw my dad raise his hand and scream "You never learn!" and then the back of his hand came down hard on my mom's face. I looked down from where I was standing at the edge of the driveway, and I saw the thirteen year old me wide-eyed and trembling. I've always harbored a bucket of shame for not running into the house and heroically defending my mom. I then looked back into the kitchen window and saw my dad throw my mom across the kitchen, slamming into the stove. My head turned to that thirteen-year-old boy again…to me…paralyzed with fear. How difficult it must have been for my mom to never live up to my dad's expectations of her. I winced thinking of that memory, much the same way I winced when I was a kid.

I saw my brother leaving on a wet, humid summer afternoon, heading to the army. Dad thought he was crazy, so it was Mom who was sitting in the old Datsun, waiting to take Nate into town. But then memories jumped to when he first visited on leave. I ran up to him and he had a gift waiting for me. I pushed it aside and hugged him, and I remember Nate saying "Be careful. You don't wanna drop it." I opened the gift, and it was a brand new Sega Genesis with both Sonic the Hedgehog and Mortal Kombat. I was blown away. The gaming system was brand new back then. We had an Atari system that no longer worked, but we never bothered throwing it away.

I saw my mom on her knees next to the silver maple in the front yard. There was a fairly decent sized flower garden next to her with rocks lining the outside edge. The flowers, tiger lilies, were in full bloom. My mother was grabbing at the shirt tail of my dad's untucked button up. He was walking away from her. He was leaving her...leaving the marriage. He was telling her that he was moving downstate where he could finally pursue his dreams. I never knew what dream it was that particular time. The dreams were always inconsistent. What was consistent was my dad blaming my mom for always holding him back. I stayed with those ghosts for a good while. I always found it hard to wrap my head around why my mom, who suffered so many different abuses from my dad, would beg him not to go. If I'm honest, I had blamed her for not leaving him sooner. But then I started thinking how I chased after my dad's love and attention as well.

I saw my dad in the driveway. Some friend of his that I never really knew had pulled up in a big pickup truck, and my dad was presenting him with a new compound bow. The guy—damn, I can't remember his name—was ecstatic. That was days before a Christmas when Nate was getting ready to be discharged from his military service but couldn't make it back for the holidays. I remember it was then, because that Christmas morning the gifts I opened were all hand made. My dad, who thought he was skilled at almost everything, sewed me what I guess you would consider sweatpants and a sweatshirt...except they were clearly homemade and ill fitting. I must've been around fifteen years old at the time, and I remember feeling embarrassed to wear them to school when we got back from our break.

"Just don't have the money this year," my dad said as I unwrapped the presents. "So, I saw the cheap stuff they sell in those catalogues and decided to make 'em even better."

As he said those words, I wondered how he had the money to give his new friend a compound bow but didn't have the funds for his own son. Nate told me later that Dad had pressured him into sending some money home, and Nate obliged. I guess my dad used that money on his buddy.

And yet, I would continue to chase my father's affection until he died seven years later.

I saw my mom running out of the house after me. I was borrowing her car to go on my first date since getting my driver's license. She gave me a hug and told me to be careful. I smiled at the gesture. But then she grabbed hold of my cheeks with both her hands and said, "Don't ever get married, Max. Promise me." I laughed. Surely, she was joking. "I won't let you go until you promise me." And wow, I remember her really grabbing my face. Still laughing I told her, "Don't worry mom. It's just a date."

"Promise?"

"I'm gonna be late."

"Then you better promise."

"Okay, Mom. I promise." And she slowly let go of my cheeks.

I always thought that was a joke. For the longest time. But, when Sophie and I got married, my mom found a moment to whisper in my ear, "You made a promise to me." And she walked away and didn't talk to me the rest of the day. I still thought at that time, that it was her weird sense of humor...but there was never a "Just kidding" or "Ha, pulled your leg."

My dad's narcissism forced me to immediately recognize how he loved. With narcissists, love is always transactional because everyone is meant to serve *their* purpose, and when you no longer serve the purpose of a narcissist, then they want nothing to do with you. But it's not that easy, because when your parent is a narcissist, they secretly focus on the opinions of others, while vocally talking down to those very same people. But deep down...they desperately worry about their image. So, they kind of have to stick it out and raise their kids—it's sort of in the job description. Some don't. I get that, and the other parent is left to raise the children by themselves. But my dad was so worried how other folks perceived him that he was determined to stay until I was eighteen, then he would leave. At least then he could tell his friends that he was there until his boys were adults and out of the house...that he did his job as a dad.

Truth be told, my dad had that plan as soon as Nate was eighteen, but then I came along seven years later and ruined things for him. This is why, I imagine, he told me, just before he died, that "My biggest regret in life was not leaving before you were born." I was kind of hoping for an "I love you," or some words of advice or wisdom, but...

I was eleven when Nate left home. I didn't think my dad's behavior could get any worse, but in Nate's absence, it did. My mom's did as well. I looked up to the second story of the house and saw my old bedroom. I spent so much time there entertaining myself—playing with Star Wars figures or army men. My dad didn't leave my mom and me at that time, but he wasn't present at all. He was never around. He had abandoned us without the mess of doing it legally. I felt unwanted. My mom grew resentful.

My mom's passive-aggressive behavior took me a little longer to understand. Her transactional love presented itself as the good ole silent treatment. When I didn't do what she wanted she would withdraw and avoid. I would always have to go to her and say "Mom, I'm really sorry. Please don't be mad," even if I had no idea what I did wrong. And...I had to do that at least a few times. This set forth a bad habit of me constantly looking for ways to make my mom happy, but also, (and I realized this staring up at that window—the window that I looked out of so many times growing up) I adopted this type of behavior that would play out through my adult years—I desperately didn't want to jeopardize what little time I had with my father, so I would never challenge him for fear he'd outright leave. And I didn't risk telling my mom my truth, because I always thought she'd go into one of her "Whoa is me" deep funks, and those were unbearable. So, the behavior I adopted was...that...I learned to swallow shit and keep quiet. I guess...

I guess...

I guess I was terrified of not being loved. Yes, my mom's relationship with my dad frustrated me, especially after Nate left. I kept wondering why she didn't leave him. He didn't work. He left a lot. He had affairs. He abused her. It took me years to understand that she was terrified of him, but more terrified of being alone; and she either chose to ignore the situation until it temporarily corrected itself, as it had so many times before, or she just tried to make the best of a really bad deal. But I can't really blame her. I kept hoping my dad's behavior would change. I longed to hang out with him. I don't know if I had some sort of weird Stockholm Syndrome or if it's just normal for a son to want his dad in his life.

I was desperate to be loved.

I did this in my marriage...quite often...and set us down a destructive path—one I hope we can still navigate away from.

Demons are different than ghosts. Ghosts I've always thought as pleasant...visitors, memories, or reminders. Demons I've always thought are...real.

I kept staring up at that bedroom window. My throat was still tight.

I told my brother once about a recurring dream I had in which I was a kid afraid to go into the back room off of the living room.

"Because of the demon." My brother added. My eyes widened. "He took up the whole room with his shoulders hitting the ceiling forcing it to scrunch down leaving his face right at the door when you finally opened it."

"Yeah. That's it. Yeah."

"Yeah...I had that dream too," Nate added.

"I always closed the door as soon as I opened it," I confessed.

"Me too."

And then...I stayed," I told him. "About six months ago. I had the dream, and I stayed."

"Yeah. I finally looked at it as well. He had yellow eyes. I thought they'd be red. So I got caught up in his yellow eyes. Not gold, but a sick... mucousy yellow."

"Yeah." I couldn't believe what Nate was describing.

"And it had two sets of wings. Like a normal set and a super set over them."

"They made the room even smaller. The demon, like, barely fit."

"Did you stay?" Nate asked.

"Yeah. You?"

"I punched it." Nate smiled. "Then I stabbed it. I didn't have a knife at first, but once I started to attack it, I had weapons. But all medieval, ya know? Like a dagger and a silly broad sword...And so...I just kept stabbing it."

We sat there for a moment. Then he asked, "You?"

I paused. I didn't know what to say. Nate did what I imagined Nate would do. He always had courage. He was always so damn brave. I didn't really want to share what I did. So, I sat there, and Nate sat patiently waiting for me to answer.

"I stared at its face. I mean, it was like Alien or Predator or something with my face inches from his. There was slobber and dripping shit. And I…"

I went quiet again.

"What?" Nate asked.

"I…I reached out my arms." Nate gave me a quizzical look, as I continued. "Like for a hug."

Nate gave me a look. But it wasn't judgmental. He wanted to know more. So, I continued as I stared out into space.

"The face…of the demon. I thought for sure as it was hovering right there in front of me, that it was dad, somehow. Ya know? That under all these layers of blisters and hanging skin, I'd see Dad. But it wasn't Dad."

"Who was it?" Nate asked.

I shrugged. "I don't know." And I shrugged again. "But, it took on or embodied, I don't know, um…fear. Fear. It was a demon. And I always thought when I would wake up after—in the dream, I always fucking closed the door, about to piss myself—I'd wake up, and I always thought that must be dad. But it wasn't. It was more universal. It was fear…. So I tried to hug it."

I was looking at nothing, out into some ether, but I could feel Nate looking at me, and I could see tears rolling down his face.

I kept staring into an abyss and finally whispered, "I wish I had attacked it like you. Goddammit. I wish I was brave."

Nate grabbed hold of me. He rocked me back and forth and just held me. I thought he was pitying me…feeling sorry for me. I didn't attack it. I tried to hug it.

He pulled back and looked into my eyes…"You're the bravest guy I know, Max."

Ghosts and demons.

Ghosts are the memories—the ones that spread an instant smile across your face or perhaps make you ponder and long for those days gone by. Demons are the horrors. Nothing lives on like the horrors of the past. One minute you're fine and then they're there…uninvited. They can be fleeting and vague as if in a dream, or so brutal it fills your soul with a silent scream.

Ghosts and Demons.

Demons and Ghosts.

14

The Pagans Are Out in Full Force

I don't know if it was helpful or not going up to the farmhouse, but I had decided that I had seen enough. I turned the car around and headed back. I wasn't in a hurry to get back to my brother's, so I thought I'd take the backroads south. I was once again lost in Bree's playlist, not knowing a single artist but loving each and every song.

"Strawberries" by Caamp

"Julia" by Mt. Joy

"Young Bodies" by Westward the Tide

"Smooth" by Jack Stauber

"The Feels" by Labrinth

"Love Brought Weight" by Old Sea Brigade

"Pat Earrings" by CASISDEAD

Bree had something magical about her spirit. She had a real sense of style without even trying, and while she could be so cutting with her sarcasm, she had an empathy about her when you least expected it.

A sign reminded me that I was on M-66, and I headed through a small town called Remus, which was also dead on this Christmas day. When you fly into Detroit, you're actually flying into Romulus. Michigan has a Romulus and a Remus. It also has a Paradise in the upper peninsula and a Hell in the southern lower peninsula. As those thoughts went through my mind, I was now outside of Remus and back on what felt like a very rural road. As quiet and empty as it had been on this Christmas day, up in the nearby distance was some activity. Cars filled up the parking lot just ahead on the right, and as I got closer, I made out the sign of the place on an attached billboard: The Fat Cat. I really didn't care what kind of ambiance or motif it had. It was open, and an overwhelming desire to have a drink consumed me. (Thinking about those days growing up has that effect on me.) I found a spot to park and headed inside; a few flurries that had started to fall tickled my face.

Wow, the place was packed. *The pagans are out in full force*, I thought. I went from a quiet, emo music-playing car ride to a ruckus, lively pub scene. All attention was given to a bearded, heavy-set, flannel-clad gentleman on a little stage...just him and his guitar. The crowd was laughing and cheering as the inebriated singer hit the chorus of an "adapted" cover.

"Can you take me higher?

Some place where they play Golden Tee

Can you spell fire?

Yes, sir...F. I. R. E."

At first, I couldn't tell if he was too drunk to get the words right, and that this was what held everyone's attention. But then he hit the bridge:

"Well let's go there...

Let's make our escape.

C'mon let's go there..."

And then the entire crowd, and I mean the ENTIRE crowd joined in.

"We'll get so fuckin' baked!"

And as he went back into the chorus, I realized this was all intentional, and everyone here, on this Christmas Day, was having the time of their lives. I could get into this.

"Can you take me higher?

Some place where they play Golden Tee

Can you spell fire?

Yes, sir...F. I. R. E."

As he jammed an instrumental portion on his guitar, I made my way to the hostess and her stand. She had to sort of scream to be heard.

"Hey there! Glad you're joining us. We're pretty packed today!"

I pointed to my throat and silently over-articulated the words, "I can NOT speak." "No problem." And she scoped out the joint for a chair. I was a little shocked and pleasantly surprised that I didn't have to go into some long, detailed mime work about losing my voice.

"Lookey there! There's one spot at the end of the bar. Will that work?"

I gave her a thumbs up, and she walked me over.

"My son is deaf! So, I read lips!"

Without thinking, I mouthed the words "Wow. Cool."

"Yeah, it is cool. Here ya go." And she sat me down in what seemed like the only remaining seat. "My husband's the bartender, so he'll take good care of you."

"Thank you," I mouthed.

She signed to me by holding out her hand with all five fingers spread, then tapping her chest with her thumb and said, "You're welcome."

This is a cool ass place.

The dude onstage wrapped up the jammin' instrumental portion of the Creed cover and finished the song off by singing his chorus one more time…again with the entire crowd joining in. After he had finished, the crowd erupted in joy and laughter. The first few notes to the next song got everyone excited once again, but I admit, I couldn't quite recognize it.

"When the days are cold
And you're feeling bold
And you lose that shirt of lacey gold.
You're mostly tanned as hail,"
I think he means hell, but maybe he's trying to rhyme.
"But those boobs are pale…"
Yep.
"Babe, you got me horny as hail."
There's that word again. Damn, what song is this?
"I wanna hide MY truth
And get inside you
Unzip this beast inside
There's nowhere for it to hide
Come on baby let's breed
We still are made of greed
It's time for me to come
It's time for me to come."

As he jumped into the chorus it was feeling more and more familiar. And, of course, the crowd jumped right in.

When you feel my heat, look into my eyes
It's where my penis hides. It's where my penis hides
So let's get close, to your dark inside. It's where my penis hides

It's where my penis hides"

Oh. My. God. Wow, that's hilarious, I thought. The singer looked like Zac Brown singing dirty Weird Al-style parody, and the crowd knew every word as he belted his song. This must be a weekly show or something, and this dude had a cult following. The bartender stopped by and asked if I wanted a drink.

I mouthed the words "May I get a red wine?"

"Cab okay?"

I nodded.

"You got it."

And so, there I sat. The crowd was rambunctious, obviously feeling good . Small groups swayed back and forth with arms around one another's shoulders, while a couple of random guys high-fived and then downed their full pints of ale. There was an uncoordinated clump of folks dancing in front of the stage, occasionally bumping into one another. When they did drunkenly and mildly collide, they smiled and toasted one another. One particular gentleman on the outskirts of the dance party kept knocking into a couple sitting at a high-top who were crudely making out. They didn't take any notice. The guy onstage continued to belt out the Imagine Dragons song in a way only he could. A nice big glass of wine was set in front of me. I closed my eyes and saw the faces of Sophie, Graeme, and Bree, and then I took a hearty gulp.

Damn, been awhile. That tasted great.

The night moved along, and the drinks kept coming. Every now and then a random stranger would set a shot in front of me. I knew it was a bad idea, but I guess I was caught up in the euphoria of the evening. I remember drinking what tasted like a creamsicle, and I remember definitely tasting Jäegermeister, because I hate that god-awful poison. I know there was Fireball at one point, and then there was a small group that decided that I needed shots of cheap tequila. It was a frat-looking guy, complete with ironed khakis and a white, heavy cotton Ralph Lauren button up, who approached me first.

"Hey, Harvey, right?" To which, I shook my head "no."

"Harvey, Trevor Reese. Over on Pine Lake? You replaced my pipes." I shook my head "no" again.

"Tina!" And Trevor pulled a nearby woman into the conversation. "Look, it's Harvey."

Tina laughed in an exaggerated, inebriated way. "You dumb ass!

That's not Harvey."

This drew what I assumed to be Tina's girlfriends and another dude into a small, half-circle that encompassed me at the bar. "Trevor thinks this guy is Harvey!" And the rest of the group laughed with Tina.

"I swear I know you," Trevor defended himself.

In his defense, I get this when people recognize me but can't remember from where. Folks have thought I was a contractor, a plumber, all sorts of tradesmen.

"Where do I know you from?" Trevor asked, and everyone waited for me to reply. As I started to squirm wondering how the hell I was going to answer, the bartender saved my ass.

"He can't talk."

"Oh." And immediately it seemed that everyone felt sorry for me. Trevor's friend piped in, "Well, then he for sure the hell isn't Harvey." And everyone obnoxiously cracked up again.

They started to vacate my bubble, but then one of the girlfriends turned back to me.

"Wait. You're an actor." And everyone returned to their exact same spots and surrounded me again. I gave a polite smile as they tried to figure out what they might have seen me in.

"Do you host a game show?" I shook my head.

"No, no. He was the sidekick on that talk show." And I shook my head again.

The bartender passed by and jumped in. "You ever see *Men in the Blue*?"

This time the group shook their heads.

The bartender then offered up "*The Unit*?"

"Is that a porno?" Trevor joked, and his buddy cracked up and slapped Trevor on the back.

"No, dummy, it's a cop show," Heather's girlfriend clapped back. "That's it! Yeah."

I gave the bartender a grateful smile. "I'm a fan. You grew up just north of here, yeah?" The bartender asked, and I nodded. "Right on," he said with a smile and dashed to refill someone's drink.

"This calls for shots!" Trevor announced.

"Thumb suck!" Tina yelled, and everyone delightfully groaned... if that's a thing. Before I knew it, Tina grabbed my hand and squirted lime on my thumb. She then dashed salt on it a few times. I looked around to see everyone in the circle getting this treatment. I was then handed a shot of tequila, and the "thumb suck" began. I had never seen this before, and to be honest, I was a little taken aback. Tina then grabbed my thumb and put it in her mouth. When I witnessed the others do it, they were pretty quick about the whole thumb in mouth thing, but Tina kept it in her mouth and moved my thumb back and forth. My face must have told the story as I looked at the others, because Trevor chimed in "Oh, don't worry. I'm happy she's getting some action." And Trevor's buddy once again cracked up and patted Trevor on his back.

Tina set my thumb free after she sucked on it, to the point that, upon release, it made a loud popping sound. She then threw back her shot, squealed, and then…very determinedly…looked straight into my eyes and said, "Your turn!" I looked to my right and saw one of Tina's girlfriends smiling at me. She presented her thumb, and I, like I so often did before, didn't know what to do. I mean, I didn't want to put her thumb in my mouth…and yet, there was this thought that overwhelmed me that I didn't want her to feel bad. I absolutely didn't want this woman's thumb in my mouth…and yet, I placed it there and licked the salt off of it. Even upon pulling out her thumb from my lips, I gave her a smile. She smiled back flirtatiously as Tina moved the shot of tequila towards my face. I instinctively drank the shot, and the small circle cheered. Tina's girlfriend began rubbing my back, and a waterfall of guilt ran down my neck through my spine. I wondered, right at that moment, what Sophie was doing.

"Another round!" Trevor's buddy yelled, and the group screamed.

The songs were hilarious from what I remember. The singer twisted that love song that was in Footloose, which was sung by the lead singer of Loverboy and one of the Wilsons from Heart. In the chorus he belted out "I can see forever in your thighs." He kept it dirty with Creedence CIearwater Revival…"I wanna know, have you ever seen Lorraine…going down on a sunny day." And in that one Buffalo Springfield song, he used some sort of sound machine, and instead of singing the word "stop," he would hit the machine with his foot and a loud, fart noise would ring out. "You better *FART* Hey what's that sound? Everybody look, what's going down?" It was juvenile and the more I drank…the more I laughed.

Since I hadn't drank like that in a long time, I started feeling nauseated. I was also really uncomfortable with Tina's girlfriend looking for reasons to get closer to me. I mean, every time someone said something she thought was remotely funny, she would begin rubbing my back and would let her hand linger…way longer than your average "That was funny, right?" touch or pat. So, I made my escape by looking for the bathroom. It was packed, and I worked my way outside. The snow had really kicked into gear, and large flakes were sticking to the ground and parking lot. I made my way to my brother's Jeep, took a whiz, and then managed to get inside the vehicle.

I then remembered my promise to never drink and drive.

So, I put the seat back and quickly fell asleep.

I awoke to a knocking on my window. I had no idea where I was. My eyes didn't want to open, and I instinctively kept blinking them to help me focus. There was a giant face just outside the driver's side door. In my slumber, I tried to hit the window button to lower the glass, but of course, the engine wasn't on, so that didn't work. I pressed the ignition button and cracked the window. It was so dark.

"Hey man, you're going to freeze to death out here."

I'm not sure if I nodded. I probably just stared, still trying to figure out what the hell was happening.

"Go on and head home, buddy. We're closed now anyway."

Who the hell is this guy? Where the hell am I? I gave him a thumbs up, and he walked away. As I tried to sit up, it all hit me. I was still drunk, which meant I had gone out drinking. I hadn't done that in awhile, but I obviously did it where it snows quite a bit. The front windshield was covered. I fumbled for the windshield wipers switch and turned it on. The wiper blades struggled to throw the snow off the windshield but managed to clear two arching openings to see through. *Wow, that's a bunch of snow.*

Oh right, I had gone out drinking in Michigan on Christmas. I guessed it was a little after 2 a.m. since the helpful guy knocking on my window said that they were closed. Thank God he came by; it was absolutely freezing in the Jeep. I cranked the heater up, remembered my promise, and went back to sleep.

It was the sun that woke me up the next time. I was no longer drunk, but I did have a monster headache. It was as if there was some sort of MMA bout going on inside my head—The kind where one dude knocks the other one out, jumps on top of him, and manages to get in half a dozen more violent blows to the face before the referee gets between the two fighters and puts an end to the bout. And, oh, how I craved water. My mouth was so dry. I looked around, shivering. I thought I had left the car running, and so I wondered why it was off. These newer cars don't seem to stay on when idled for too long. You get a warning after a bit that the engine will shut down if no further action is taken. I fired up the engine once again, and cold air blew out through the vents. Snow had once again covered all the windows, and so I rummaged through my brother's car looking for his scraper. I struggled to get out of the Jeep. Is there some invisible somebody that keeps smacking me in the back of the head? Desperate for some form of hydration, I cupped a ball of snow from the hood of the vehicle and started biting into the frozen concoction like a sno-cone. I swore I would never touch another drop of alcohol.

Once I had the windows cleared, the car had warmed up. I scoped out the parking lot. To my California eyes, it looked like we got around four or five inches of snow, and I wondered if I was going to make it out of there. But I did…and pulled out of the Fat Cat and started to make my way back to my brother's home and some desperately needed ibuprofen.

But…that didn't happen. Long story short—I had a hell of a time driving on the road leading back to town. The plows were not out yet, and it was tough sledding…literally…I was sliding everywhere and ended up in a ditch along the side of the road when I tried to avoid a couple of deer darting in front of my brother's car. My brother had told me that the deer population had gotten so out of control, that there were accidents everyday. "You shouldn't try to avoid them," he told me. "Just hit them and take the front-end damage. Otherwise, you could really be in a mess."

I debated walking the rest of the way; maybe the frigid air would help my head. Instead, I threw on the hazard lights and hoped someone would see my flashers as they drove by.

And someone did. And of all the people to see them…it was Andy in his patrol car. Actually, he was in a large, police issued SUV.

"Max? What the hell? Whad'ya doin' out here in this weather?"

I did not have the patience or the energy to go through the mime work needed to explain to Andy that I still couldn't speak. Plus, he didn't seem to understand what I was trying to "say" the first time. But he just stood there, standing, wearing a corduroy hat with flaps with aviator shades, looking all kinds of goofy; and evidently waiting for an answer.

I marched through the snow and made my way up to him, all the while, pointing at my throat. I kept mouthing the words, "I still can't talk" and tried my best to silently enunciate to the point that it hurt my jaw.

"Holy shit, what happened to your voice?"

And he waited.

"Wait. Are you injured? Did you lose your voice from this accident?"

I shook my head.

"Ah, shit, it don't matter. Let's get you outta here. I'll call for a tow truck, and you can ride with me. I got all sorts of shit to tell you."

15

What a Strange Conversation
This Has Been

Here's what Andy told me...

The police received a call yesterday around 10 a.m. regarding an altercation at the home of the Careys...that's Kirk and Janice. When Andy and another officer arrived, Kirk had some blood on his face but told the officers that it wasn't his. Janice was holding her left arm and then told them that the blood was Gary's. According to Kirk and Janice, they noticed an old, beat-up car, sitting on the side of the road next to their driveway. They said they saw it after they had opened presents with the kids and Kirk was heading back to the hotel he was staying at.

"Apparently Kirk and Janice had recently separated," Andy added as we drove along. It struck me that Pat and Sue's gossip session held some truth, and Kirk and Janice were no longer together. Andy then told me this...

Gary stepped out of the rusted, old car and walked around to the opened truck.

"I shouted out 'nice wheels!' I'd never seen that car before. I mean, it wasn't Gary's." Kirk told Andy.

Gary pulled out a bat from the trunk and then approached Kirk and Janice, talking about how Janice had ruined his marriage with Michelle, and that Janice had ruined his life. This was all according to Kirk.

"I didn't know what the hell he was going on about," Kirk told Andy.

"Gary looked insane." Janice jumped in. "He just kept muttering 'you fucked everything up.'"

Kirk stepped to stop Gary from coming any closer and said "Just calm down. What are you talking about?"

"'Ask that bitch ass whore wife of yours'…Those were his exact words."

Janice told Andy that she had no idea what that meant, but that it fired Kirk up because he told Gary, "Now you watch your mouth."

"Or what, Kirk? Huh, tough guy? Or what?"

"Or I'm gonna beat your ass!"

"That's fresh when I'm the one holding the bat."

And that's when Gary whipped the bat around like he was going to take a swing at Kirk. "And that's when I stepped in the way." Janice told Andy. "Like a dummy…and the bat grazed me on the arm."

"It was more than a graze, Jan," quipped Kirk. "He assaulted you." (Andy was acting out the characters to me, changing his voice trying to imitate Kirk and Janice. He would periodically give me an eye raise and a nod like, *You like my impressions? I can do this acting thing too.*)

"I mean, I tried to get out of the way…so I guess, I mean, it wasn't the full impact if that makes sense." Janice added.

Andy asked if it was broken and neither Janice nor Kirk thought it was. They had iced it, and Janice thought she'd be okay. But that's when Kirk started pummeling Gary.

"I guess I just lost it. Seeing Gary hit my wife. I just charged him."

"He was defending me."

"Am I in trouble?"

"Maybe you should stop talking, honey."

Andy told me that he assured them that they were fine and to just tell him the facts of what had happened.

"Well," Kirk added. "I tackled him, and then I guess I just started wailing on his face."

"I tried to pull him off."

"And I stopped hitting him when I could no longer see, because the blood kept splattering in my face."

"I asked him 'About how many times do you think you hit him?'" Andy told me. (What I found funny is that Andy lowered his voice when impersonating himself, like he was some tough guy around them.)

"I have no idea…I wasn't counting." Kirk told Andy.

"It wasn't that many, honest. I'd say five, maybe seven shots," Janice chimed in.

Andy asked them what happened after that.

"Well, Gary just sort of laid there on the ground. Wasn't moaning or anything. I mean, he was moving, real slow, so we knew that he was awake, you know, like...not dead. But he just sort of rolled in place, holding his face." Kirk told Andy.

"And then?" Andy asked.

Janice added "We went inside to call you."

"But when we went inside and called you, I, of course, wanted to look at Janice's arm—"

"And I wanted to clean up Kirk's knuckles, you know?"

"We've been..."

"Separated," Janice finished.

"And I guess I wanted to take that moment to also figure shit out. Like, why are we not together, ya know? I don't know. I just kept looking at Janice, like, we can work out some misunderstanding, right?"

And Andy added a facial expression of a puppy's face saying "Ahhh," telling me that Janice had looked like that after hearing what Kirk said.

Kirk finished with, "Then I looked out the window, and...you know...um...Gary was gone."

"Gone?" Andy questioned.

"His car too."

"He must've drove off."

"You're telling me," Andy asked, "That you beat a guy senseless to the point where he couldn't much move...then went inside, then...when you looked after him, he was gone?"

"Exactly." And "We were inside longer than we thought." Kirk and Janice said together.

"And where is Gary now?"

"How the hell should we know?"

Andy half-jokingly told me that he had known Kirk for a long time now and wanted to ask him where they were keeping Gary's body.

"Kirk's always struck me as having that kind of arrogance about him...like he could get away with anything, ya know?" Andy could spot that kind of arrogance in others but didn't seem to have any of that awareness about himself.

Andy continued with his story. He told me that he had a suspicion that things went too far, but he said that he had to go on the evidence and not jump to conclusions. "It just didn't feel right, Max, you know?"

"Yeah...I'm gonna need you to come down to the station and fill out a report." Andy told the couple.

"I thought I wasn't in any kind of trouble."

"You're not...yet."

"What does that mean?"

"We just want to get your side of the—"

"It's not Kirk's side...it's the truth."

"Got it. We just want to get Kirk's truth, officially, and take it from there, okay?"

So, Andy told me that they all met down at the station. On the way there, Andy said that he tried calling Gary using a number that Kirk gave him, but there was no answer.

"I wish I would have thought to do that at their place, Max." Andy said. "Some people are dumb enough to just leave the phone on the body. Might've heard the 'bzzz' from the phone from some fifty gallon drum near the garage, ya know?" Andy said with a laugh.

I wondered if there was anything to what Andy suspected or if he was creating a scenario to add more drama to the situation. I thought what had already happened certainly didn't call for any more gas on the fire. I wanted to ask questions, and, of course, physically I couldn't. I was curious why he was unloading all this information on me. It seemed a little unprofessional.

"So...you can't talk, huh?"

I half smiled and nodded.

"Well, good. You'll keep this between us. They better hope Gary turns up at an urgent care or motel or something. What the hell was he doing there on Christmas anyway?"

It actually made some sense to me, given what I had witnessed the past few days—Janice and Michelle at Big Boy...Gary and Michelle yelling in the parking lot—but I was forced to keep that to myself. Soon enough, Andy pulled into the driveway of my brother's house and let me out.

"I'll keep you updated," Andy said with a grin. "Oh..."

He stopped me as I was closing the passenger door.

"We still have to do that ride-along."

I nodded and started to shut the door, but he interrupted.

"I know, I know. You've must've done a bunch of those out in LA but I want you to see how a real pro does it." And he gave me a wink. *Why does everyone wink at me?* Not knowing what to do, I winked back and finished shutting the door.

I had let Chad out and fed him. I had already taken the Ibuprofen; that was actually the first thing I did. There were only two pills left in a giant bottle, and I was grateful to get the last of it. Still, I made a mental note to restock my brother's NSAID addiction. I was now waiting for it to kick in. I was on my third big glass of water, and my belly felt full to the point that I started feeling nauseated. It was all due to my water intake... and, of course, the worst hangover I had had since college.

I sat on the couch in now what was seemingly more "my" spot than my brother's, and I pulled out my phone. I had a bunch of text notifications. Wow. I hadn't been on my phone since I arrived at the Fat Cat yesterday. That must be some sort of modern-day record for me. I didn't think to check it listening to the music and enjoying the ambiance of the bar scene. I didn't think to check it when I stumbled out of the bar, drunk and tired. I didn't think to check it, as I was passed out, of course. And I didn't think to check it as I sat there listening to Andy. But now...

There was a text notification from Graeme. Another from Bree, one from my brother...and another from Sophie. I can't believe I didn't check my phone.

> *Hi dad merry Christmas not the same without you wish you were here you'd absolutely love Dublin. Love you G*
> *Hey pops merry Xmas what doin? Wish I was there with you doesn't feel right ya know? Tell uncle nate and aunt mara hi and the boys. Kk love you Bear*
> *Yo pops where you at? I'm bored. I know you said you lost your voice but text me back k? Kk Bear*
> *Pops what up?*
> *Everything cool, pops?*
> *I'm getting a lil worried.*
> *Merry Christmas, lil bro. Is Chad still alive? Kidding. Love you.*
> *Hey Max. Not sure what to say. So I'll jus say Merry Christmas. Hope you're enjoying your time with Nate and Mara. Mom and Dad say hi.*

My first text was to Bree. She sent so many; I wanted to alleviate any worry she had.

Bree. Sorry. Didn't have my phone. Well, that's a lie. I had it but didn't look at it. I went to a bar, that you would have loved, and got drunk. I know, I know. But I'm fine. Back at your aunt and uncle's. Love you very much.

Then to Graeme...

Wish I was there too, pal. I love Dublin. But I would love it even more sharing the experience with you. Maybe another time. Love you, my son.

I had been to Dublin. I went during a hiatus of a show I was recurring on. I can't remember which one. I met up with Danny after he had moved back to England. We had a great time in Temple Bar. We saw a good bit of Ireland that trip after a quick tour of Scotland. I remember it had been a chunk of time since we had seen women milling about. Even in Edinburgh, (What a gorgeous town especially in the rain!) there didn't seem to be the foot traffic of people when we were there. And then we hit the countryside and traveled up to Inverness and didn't see much of anyone. I remember from a distance seeing a woman working on the side of the road on her farm.

"Wow, look at her," giving Danny, who was driving, a playful slap on the arm.

As we got closer, she was quite into her work with mud and dirt covering most of her. She was throwing out some sort of slop from her pigs.

"Mate, I think you got your Scoggles on." Danny laughed heartily.

"Scoggles?"

"You know, like beer goggles but we're in Scotland."

And that became the bit on the trip. So, when we were in Temple Bar and Danny was horny and was just being flirty, he bought a round of drinks for a group of Swedish women in their sixties. I, of course, told him he was wearing "Swoggles." It wasn't lost on us that we weren't much to look at, so we kept trying to think what those women would be wearing if they were looking at us.

It was always a great time with Danny. And today was Boxing Day. So, I sent him a text as well.

Happy Boxing Day, brother. Really miss hanging out.

Sophie loved Boxing Day as well. I'm not sure why. Maybe it's because those years when Danny and his wife, Jessica, lived in LA they always came over on that day. Sophie and Jessica were tight. It was hard when Danny moved back. I imagine it was just as hard on Sophie when Jessica moved back with him.

I wasn't sure what to text back to Sophie. I didn't want to push anything, and I didn't want to ignore her message. I just stared at her little note on my phone.

Hey Max. Not sure what to say. So I'll jus say Merry Christmas. Hope you're enjoying your time with Nate and Mara. Mom and Dad say hi.

First, I analyzed her text. Not sure what to say. Well, we are separated after all. "So I'll jus say Merry Christmas." She forgot the "t" in "just." Did that mean she was in a hurry? No "I love you" or "I miss you." What did that mean? And the rest of her text just felt trite to me. Like she was just being nice. Or maybe she just wanted to be left alone…you know, "separated."

I started to type…"Hey Soph"—but I erased it. I must have read her message ten times. Then

I decided to "love" the message, and a heart popped up next to her text.

I asked myself once again *What happened?* Every time I had asked that before, I kept heading to the same answers *She just stopped loving me, I guess. I guess she changed. Everyone changes. She's grown tired of me.*

But this time was different. Maybe my ego softened. Maybe it was the trip up north. I don't know. But I couldn't help but think of my role in all of this. Waves of memories kept rushing in, and they didn't stop.

I remember coming home with gifts when I had one of my recurring roles. I would dance around the house. I would play with the kids. I came home with a Wii gaming system one Friday after getting released early from filming, and we played bowling and tennis and laughed. I remember Sophie and me getting buzzed on wine that day. Oh man, we went through a bottle and then opened another bottle and went through that. Graeme and Bree, who were a lot younger then, of course, kept jumping around the room when it wasn't their turn. It was an impromptu moment of joy. I know there were so many other days like that…they just felt so long ago, and it was getting harder to recall them.

I remember thinking at one point that maybe that was my role… to be, I don't know, the clown. To brighten everyone's day. Sophie was disciplined. She could have fun, don't get me wrong, but like I said before, she had her day planned down to the minute with working out, actual work, all of it; and she wasn't one to veer off course. She needed that routine to keep it all together. She was also practical. It was a gift, even though there were times I resented it. But without her discipline, our family would have fallen apart. Had we been at the store together and I would have tried to put the Wii in the cart, she would have talked me out of it. So, I did things like this sometimes to create that spark I thought we could use in our family.

But after awhile, I think I resented "having" to be the clown.

"No one is asking you to be a clown, Max." I remember Sophie telling me in one of our arguments later in our marriage. "You decided to do that," I remember she added.

"Well, if I'm not, then what will happen?"

"I don't know what you mean."

"If I'm not the clown, then things get so serious around here."

"Don't be the clown then and see what happens."

"Fine, I won't."

"Good…what a strange conversation this has been."

If I'm honest I was trying to tell her that she didn't know how to have fun and cut loose anymore. But I didn't want to hurt her either, so most of the time, looking back, I just wound up uttering passive-aggressive, hard to translate bullshit. But she wasn't always like that. She could party. And she was so much fun when she cut loose. In the beginning of our marriage, she reminded me of Meg Ryan in *Top Gun*, you know, before Goose died. "Take me to bed or lose me forever!" And no one will ever have a better laugh than Sophie. Her big, glowing, big brown eyes would squint shut and her shoulders would convulse. I felt like the king of the world every time I made her laugh. (I actually have a video on my phone that's about ten years old of her laughing at one of my jokes. One of those laughs where she just couldn't stop and that made her laugh all the more. I can't look at that video anymore because I just start to weep. But I can't delete it either.)

She just sort of stopped laughing.

Maybe being a mother changed her. I already mentioned how frightened I was when we had kids. I remember when Sophie and Graeme were released from the hospital, and I loaded Graeme into his car seat. I actually said to the nurse who was helping Sophie out of her wheelchair and into the car, "This is a bad idea. I mean, I kill house plants." The nurse laughed it off, and I said "No, I'm dead serious." I was terrified. Isn't it something that I never thought how scared Sophie must have been? She always…I mean always, seemed to have her shit together.

And so, I'd have these bouts of self-pity, and I would just, kind of, mope about. Eventually she would pull me out of it. She would relent and apologize, and I would soften and then start to goof around again. Is that co-dependency? I'm not sure what to call it. But as the memories kept rushing at me, I know that we played mind games with one another. I mean, she didn't have to apologize. It was me who got all moody. And it happened when I wasn't working. If I was getting gigs, then I was fine, or even more, I was fun. But if I didn't, I was hopeless.

What a terrible roller coaster I made my family ride.

And, I admit, I would get clingy when I wasn't despondent. I would crave Sophie's attention, and of course, she kept herself busy. I'm one of those people who likes physical contact. I like to touch and be touched. When there was a window in Sophie's schedule, I wanted to be close to her…which she interpreted as "always wanting sex." This was another bone of contention. Yeah, sex was nice. But I don't know that I immediately thought of sex. I immediately thought to be physically close to Sophie, and if it led to more…cool. But when she would scoff, or shake her head, or exhibit some other negative view of intimacy with me…I would react with…sarcasm and quips. I remember calling her a puritan, which then turned into "pilgrim" for some reason. So, those times when I would try to cozy up to her and she would let out an exasperated sigh, I would say something like "Oh, sorry, pilgrim. Didn't know you were doing something important." This would come at a time when she was unwinding and watching some old, syndicated sitcom. So, she would come back with…not so sarcastically…"You're such an asshole."

And then one day, not too long ago, the hamster wheel I described above, where I would get down and Sophie would apologize and pull me out of it, then I would be fun and want her to be fun, and when she wasn't I got depressed again, and she would apologize and pull me out of it…it stopped spinning. That day, when I got all quiet, out of work, and mopey, Sophie made a decision that she was no longer going to play along. And instead of apologizing, she told me she wanted a trial separation.

I wondered in that moment of going down memory lane, what on earth was in those ibuprofens I took…and I wished, in that moment, we were all together.

I was brought out of my daydream when I heard the sound of the tow truck dropping off my brother's Jeep. I had two choices. I thought about heading into town, but I also thought about crawling into bed. I decided to do both…but first, the nap. Just as I was about to doze off, my phone vibrated…It was a text from Danny.

Mate! Happy Boxing Day! You need to head over when you can. I need my friend.

I smiled as I lay there, thinking of the time Danny surprised me for my fortieth birthday party. He was just there at the house when I got home from an audition. What a feeling that was to see my dearest friend, who I had missed so much, standing there to greet me at the door. As I started to doze off, I thought *How cool would that be if I could return the favor and just show up at his door?*

I set my phone down and closed my eyes. *Vvvp.*

Okay, I'm starting to actually worry. Is Chad okay?

Oops. Forgot to text Nate. I typed a quick note.

Chad's fine. Seems happier. Ran your Jeep into a ditch, but it's fine too. Happy Boxing Day!

I took a nice long nap, and when I woke, I decided it was still early enough in the late afternoon to go get a meal in town.

16

What Are You Doing Here?

I sat inside the Red Lion waiting for a server to come by. It was quite busy in there, (I imagine because they were closed Christmas Day) so I decided to entertain myself by reading the menu. The menu gave the Cheesecake Factory a run for its money. I mean, it was a small book. How did I not notice this before? They had some interesting choices that all seemed to revolve around cheese. Deep Fried Cheese Sampler, Deep Fried Bacon Cheese Curds, Smoked Trout Dip and Brie, and I kid you not… Cheese Kabobs—Ten small squares of artisanal cheeses stacked on top of one another. I glanced up and took in the room.

There was a couple sitting across from one another at a small rectangular table. The woman looked like Mama Cass with a perm…her dress was, well, big and unshapen. Her partner was bearded and burly and had on what I can best describe as a "dress" flannel and what I assumed were his nicest jeans. I got the sense they dressed up for their date, and I smiled to myself in appreciation of their effort. They had been sharing a large platter of spaghetti and meatballs, which sat at the center of the table.

After the flannelled man swallowed and wiped his mouth with his sleeve, he pulled a large noodle from the massive plate and offered the woman one end. She giggled and placed the end in her mouth. He must have said something like "close your eyes," (I couldn't hear them with all the ambient restaurant noise) because she closed her eyes and smiled. While he placed the other end in his mouth, he fumbled for something in his jeans pocket. His thick hand had a challenge ahead of it because those jeans looked "snug." They both started to slowly slurp up the long noodle, and their faces merged closer to one another. His hand continued to struggle until it managed to pull out a small box…seemingly just in time. As the two lovebirds finished their noodle and predictably kissed, the man had the small box waiting just under their chins. The woman opened her eyes, looked down, and immediately teared up.

A voice stole me away from this wonderfully romantic scene, and it was the same younger woman from before.

"How's that voice?"

I shrugged and smiled, and she said, "Hold that thought," and scurried away.

Not much else I can do with it, I thought. And I waited for her to return.

She came rushing back with a small, dry erase board and handed it to me with one of those Expo blue markers.

"Here ya go."

I gave her a look, and I really hoped it conveyed my gratitude. I mean, who does something like that? She was kind enough to think of me…and then!..She actually followed through and bought me a board and marker. She didn't have a guarantee that she'd run into me again, and yet she still bought them. I thought that was really sweet.

I took the board and wrote "That's the nicest thing anyone's ever done for me! Thank you, Julie!" It took her too long to read it, because I wrote in cursive, and my cursive is absolute garbage. Her lips moved as she read it to herself (which was really cute), and I worried the message had lost its impact. But she stopped, looked up at me and gave me a big hug.

"You remembered my name."

Why aren't you ten years older?

I felt bad as soon as I thought it, but I was pissed Sophie was only answering my texts and not reaching out to me on her own.

"Can I get you a drink?"

I wrote "Just a water please."

"And a shot."

I smiled, waved my hands in protest, and shook my head.

"C'mon, I'll do one with you."

Well…I couldn't say no to that. Hell, I couldn't say anything. I wrote on the board…"Thank you!"

"Leg Spreader?" She asked.

The look on my face must've conveyed my utter confusion.

She laughed through saying, "It's one of our signature drinks. Coconut Rum, blue curacao, pineapple juice and midori."

I grimaced. That sounded like a lot of sugar and after my adventure yesterday, I needed something simpler.

She leaned into me and whispered out the side of her mouth, "Not gonna lie. It's pretty good." She pulled away from me and said with a brightness, "But I'll get us a Duck Fart."

What the hell kind of place is this?

I smiled. She smiled. I smiled again, and then felt stupid.

As she left, I scanned the bar but didn't see anyone I recognized, until Mitch made his way from what I guessed was a bathroom break. He made it back to the bar stool he had called home from the time before. I watched him signal for another round and noticed that he was watching someone. Mitch was watching Crystal, who was sitting at the end of the bar on the opposite side. She was laughing with a cowboy looking dude, who was ordering drinks from another bartender. I couldn't make out what they were saying, but whatever it was Crystal enjoyed it. Then he would tip his cowboy hat, and she seemed to dig that as well.

The bartender sat a couple of pints and some cocktails in front of the cowboy. The cowboy picked up two shots and handed one to Crystal. They raised the shot glasses and then downed them. The cowboy winced and shook it off, which made Crystal laugh even more. The cowboy managed to gather the remaining drinks and made his way to a group that awaited him at a nearby table.

More and more customers entered the restaurant, and it was becoming quite packed. Julie, the cute server, who had been kind enough to give me the dry erase board, made her way back to my table, but I think she forgot about doing shots together…which made me feel relieved.

"Anything look interesting to you?" She had a terrific smile. I smiled back, and even though I could tell she had been in a rush, running from table to table, to the kitchen and back, she stood there and waited. And I sat there, lost in that question. Oh, my order! I used the board and started to write down what I wanted, but she stopped me.

"And what's your name?"

Duh! I erased what I was writing with my sleeve, and wrote "Max." "Max Sheffield?"

And I nodded.

"I know. I'm just playin'. You were in that Nickelodeon show…"

And I nodded again as she continued, "You were the neighbor. And you would get slimed. Oh, and that one time you fell into that pool of pudding?!"

And I nodded some more, thinking *You must be even younger than I thought.*

"So, what would you like to order?"

But in my mind, I thought, *the hell with it*, and wrote "Just how old are you?"

She laughed loudly and told me, "I'm twenty-eight."

Oh…Well, at least it's not a twenty year difference.

"I have younger siblings I was forced to babysit. How old did you think I was?"

I shrugged and wrote down my order. As I finished writing, Julie leaned in "You were really great on that show…really cute."

And she left to get back to work. Wow, a boost of adrenaline or dopamine or both shot through my body. She made me feel so damn good in that moment. And…I'm terrible with signals, but even I could finally tell that she was flirting with me.

I wound up having a nice meal. As Julie periodically made her way to my table and then would hustle off again, I couldn't help but think about Sophie. If Sophie and I couldn't fix our marriage, how awkward would it be to start dating again? Sophie and I had been married for so long, we could finish one another's sentences. We knew what would upset the other, what would make the other laugh. *Thorough*…That's the word. But maybe *Thorough* can mean…I don't know…*Complacent* and taking one another for granted. I guess we got too comfortable. And "too comfortable" turned into "uncomfortable," and we simply decided to live with being uncomfortable…until Sophie decided not to any longer.

Throughout my time at dinner, I also kept tabs on both Mitch and Crystal. At first, I wondered if Crystal and Mitch were actually an item, and Crystal was playing with him. But Crystal didn't seem to acknowledge Mitch at all. She wasn't checking in to gauge his reaction, and I began to think that maybe I was falsely assuming Crystal to be up to something nefarious…although this was the same Crystal who called in that bomb threat to get out of final exams our senior year of high school.

As for Mitch, he just periodically watched Crystal. He didn't socialize with anyone or flirt. When he was drinking his beer and shooting whiskey, he would grab a look at the game on the screen behind the bar…and then look over to get an update on Crystal's activity.

Watching them, I decided that Crystal and Mitch didn't come here together tonight. They just both happened to be here. And even though Mitch was in his usual spot drinking, Crystal was going to have her fun.

Crystal gathered her purse and threw on her coat and scarf and headed towards the door, which was near where Mitch was seated. As she walked past Mitch, he grabbed her wrist, which stopped her and swung her back around to him.

"What?" Crystal asked.

Mitch gave her a drunk smile and tried to pull her into him. She was having none of that and pulled away. But Mitch wouldn't let go, and Crystal got frustrated.

"Let me go, Mitch."

It was really lively in the restaurant, and nobody seemed to take notice of the two.

"Let go, or I will make a scene," Crystal said slowly.

"Who is he?"

"Who?"

"The cowboy."

Hey, that's my nickname for him as well.

"Why do you care?"

"I don't."

"Cool. So let go."

I noticed Mitch still had a hold of Crystal's wrist.

"So, who is he?"

"Why are we doing this?"

Doin' what?" He asked with a grin.

"Last week you had your ex-wife in here—"

"We never married."

"Okay, great. Who gives a fuck?"

"Obviously you do."

"No, Mitch, I don't. That's my—"

"You do."

"The fuck I do."

Why'd you ask?"

"I didn't ask, Mitch. I brought it up because you were asking about—"

"Uh-huh. Sure." His smile kept broadening.

"Goddammit! These games of yours."

"I'm not playing—"

"You're something else, Mitchell. You really are."

"Well, you're the one who—"

"LET GO OF MY FUCKING ARM!"

Crystal had had enough, and the restaurant immediately went silent. Wow, she had some pipes. Mitch, perhaps too drunk to be embarrassed, released his grip, and she pulled away from him. As folks slowly started back in on their own conversations…

"WE DON'T HAVE A RELATIONSHIP. GOT IT?" She was still screaming, making certain she kept her audience. "WE JUST…HOOK UP. LIKE THE TWO LONELY FUCKS THAT WE ARE."

Now, Mitch seemed self-conscious, and he swiveled on his stool towards the counter of the bar.

The cowboy approached with a weird sort of swagger, "We got a problem here?" In tow were, what I assumed to be, two friends of the cowboy. The cowboy couldn't have been taller than 5'7", and it occurred to me right away that his buddies, skinny and short with trendy trucker hats and their snap up plaid shirts with the top three snaps undone to show off what chest hair they had, always did this sort of thing—group together as a team in case something went down.

Mitch stood up. Mitch always had that prototypical size for a quarterback. He was 6'3" and the years only added weight to his playing frame. So, I would guess he was pushing 230-240 pounds. He towered over the little cowboy, and his two buddies suddenly didn't seem too keen on a physical altercation. However, the cowboy didn't see the expression on his friends' faces as I did, and so he stepped right up to Mitch's face— or rather, chest.

"If there's a problem, big guy, we can settle this outside."

"I don't fight anymore." The tiny cowboy strained to look up to Mitch's eyes. I could see Crystal shake her head. "You're welcome," Mitch added.

"Welcome for what?" asked the cowboy.

"You're welcome I don't fight anymore." His eyes met the cowboy's friends…"You too."

I had no doubt Mitch would throw all three of them across the bar.

"Well...I don't recall saying 'thank you,' asshole." The cowboy doubled down on his bluster.

A cascade of emotions seemed to rush through Mitch as he let out a hearty laugh and then looked down shaking his head. He then slowly tilted his head back up and with mouth agape, shot a murderous look at the cowboy before the biggest smile appeared across his face. He then raised his right hand, and the cowboy physically flinched ever so slightly...I'm sure he was hoping that the rest of us watching hadn't noticed, but of course we did...I definitely saw the blench. Mitch then gently patted the cowboy on the shoulder and then pinched his cheek. Mitch then waited and I wondered in that moment if he was hoping the condescending pinch would provoke the smaller man and his friends. But the cowboy remained frozen.

The cowboy, habitually addicted to shit talk I suppose, muttered "You...may have...been big time years ago...But you're jack shit now... tough guy."

And Mitch stood there, in a stand off for the briefest moments, until finally, he inhaled the deepest breath and let it out slowly through his mouth. Even through the tension I laughed a bit on the inside when it seemed the cowboy's face contorted in reaction to Mitch's breath from his exhale.

"I'm leaving," interrupted Crystal. "The dick measuring is way too much for me."

"Don't leave on my account." Mitch then tossed back his whiskey, sat down, and watched the game.

Crystal stood there for a moment, looking at Mitch's back. She then looked around the restaurant to see everyone staring at her. And then? Her eyes landed on me.

"Fuckin' Max Sheffield?!" Everyone, including Mitch, seemed to turn and find me. "Shouldn't you be off trying to get all famous and shit?" I wanted to say, "Hey Mudflaps" but couldn't, so I managed a modest wave to the room and smiled. I have no idea why she singled me out, but she finished with a "Huh" and left.

Slowly, everyone went back to their conversations, but I kept watching Mitch. I wondered how many guys have challenged him over the years. Countless, I thought—aging men, prideful and impertinent, trying to desperately cling to that last bit of youthful vigor. If you can take down the biggest name in the entire area, then perhaps, you were really "somebody" after all. My thoughts were quickly interrupted with a quiet, lower resonating voice, "Max?" During the time I studied Mitch, I thought to myself I know that voice. So strange, voices from the past... especially ones you cared so much about. And this one, so smoky and sultry...I slowly turned my head towards the voice. Was it really her?

"Hi Max."

Yep...it was Emma, my girlfriend from my senior year of high school and during the first part of college. Holy...well, holy shit, she looked the same. Her face was older, but it was her. There were crow's feet at the end of her eyes, and a few wrinkles on her forehead. She reached out her hand, and her forearms had a few age spots. But her smile...it was the same.

I held on for dear life trying to stay in the moment. My brain started to catapult back to the past to our time together. It was over three years. That's a long relationship especially when you're young.

I smiled back. More of a "can you believe this/no I can't" sort of smile. A tall, professional looking man with gray hair donning the sides of what was still an incredible head of hair approached and leaned into Emma.

"I'll warm up the car." He buttoned up a charcoal grey trench coat, popped the collar, and threw a plaid cashmere scarf around his neck. Then he left.

"What are you doing here?"

I wanted to ask her the same thing. I had heard she moved to New York with dreams of being a fashion designer and married a guy who worked on Wall Street. I, instead, reached for my new dry erase board and started writing.

"Oh sorry, I didn't know you were busy." She said rather defensively.

And I held up the board that read: I LOST MY VOICE. MY NEPHEW. LONG STORY.

"Oh..wow. Um, okay." She seemed confused by it all, and who could blame her? "You can't talk at all?" I tried but pain appeared before any words, so I shook my head and quickly wrote: I WISH I COULD. I smiled and gave a shrug.

It had been so long since I had seen Emma. We had split when we were, what, twenty? We were inseparable when we were together for the first couple of years. But I think I suffocated her. In fact, I know I did. Our breakup was ugly. She had wanted to split during the relationship. She wanted to experience life as I was talking about marriage. Ha! Marriage at nineteen. That must've freaked her out. She had come up with "I want us to be boyfriend and girlfriend but see other people." I was so afraid of losing her that I went along with it. (I remember telling Graeme and Bree the story a couple of years ago and made sure to tell them that her idea never works. Too much jealousy.)

I freaked out. I didn't want to date anyone else. I just wanted to be with Emma. And I was hurt that she wanted more. So, I didn't...I didn't date anyone. But she did. Summer after our freshman year of college, she got a job as a lifeguard and started seeing a guy who she worked with. It didn't help that he looked like an Olympic diver. It did help that he was a wet towel when it came to any sort of personality. However, my desperation at wanting her back hurt my best assets...my personality and sense of humor. She was so annoyed with me. In her defense, I would desperately show up at the beachfront on the lake they both worked at to see if she needed a ride home, or I would "coincidentally" appear at a party where I knew the lifeguard crew would attend. I was pathetic and lonely and, quite frankly, a bit stalkerish.

As it turned out, he wound up sleeping with Emma's best friend. He actually got her friend pregnant, which caused a big controversy around our small town. Emma called me and told me she wanted to be exclusive again. Looking back, I so wish I had said "No, thanks." It would have done us both so much good. I mean, she wanted to spread her wings or have new experiences that didn't include me, and I should have just realized that and let her go when she originally wanted to break up. But I didn't. And when she wanted me back...I went running to her. I was also super horny as well. Nineteen! When you're young, you can do it all the time. And when we got back together, for the rest of the summer, that's all we did.

But the following summer, as I got more involved with theatre and had really developed a passion for the craft, she told me to decide between her and acting. I had an opportunity to do some summer stock in Illinois and she wanted me to stay. That was a deal breaker for me. I always thought we would grow old together—dating douchebag lifeguards aside—and support one another in our careers. But when I was delivered an ultimatum, I chose theatre.

We went our separate ways, and with the advent of social media, I found her years later and DMed her. I was with Sophie, and I wasn't looking for anything other than to say, "I hope you're well." And to apologize. I didn't like that there was this energy out there…something negative standing in the way of two people who once loved one another. Hell, we were so young. I know that she felt rejected when I broke up with her. She even accused me of only breaking up with her to get back at her for taking breaks from me, so that she could explore what I would only call back then "other options."

It also didn't help that after our breakup I had quickly started to date again, this time a fellow major in the theatre department. Staci was her name. And out of the blue, she asked me out, and I said "yes." And as luck, bad luck that is, would have it, Emma needed to get some stuff out of my apartment—some clothes, some of her favorite CDs. I had forgotten that one night when Staci stayed over, I had been chewing gum, and when we fell asleep, the gum fell out of my mouth during the night and got tangled up in Staci's hair. In the morning after trying to pull it out to no avail, I cut the gum out and a small chunk of her hair with it. Well, when Emma came over to get her things, she saw the chunk of hair on my nightstand and went, how do I say, ape shit crazy. She accused me of being some sort of serial pervert who obsesses on keepsakes. "What fuckin' weirdo shit did you have of mine, you fuckin' psycho?! Do you have some hidden toenails somewhere? My god, you're such a strange fucking human being." It would have been easy to dismiss what she was saying because she was completely wrong about the circumstances, but it hurt nonetheless, because I felt like she was using the gummed-up hair as a way to express all the things she hated about me while we were together.

"You obsessive Freak! I can't believe I spent three years with you! What a fucking waste of my life. Do you know how many people begged me to dump you? Huh? Do you?" She may have wanted an answer, but there was no way I was going to say anything. She was just trying to hurt me. I mean, after all, I hurt her. When you find someone else's hair in your ex-boyfriend's apartment, I think that spells the end. I guess, maybe, she thought that since we got back together when she broke up with me… then we'd probably work things out after I broke up with her. But then I went and slept with Staci, and that sort of sealed the deal.

"All of my sorority sisters. I mean, all of them. 'You're dating a theatre nerd!' I mean, c'mon, Max, you play fucking Dungeons and

Dragons…"

That was unnecessary. But this was her moment, and nothing was going to stop her.

She continued with a crazy-mocking voice, "How many hit pointth do you have? Are you a magic uther or thome big, tough warrior? Oh, my glatheth!" She spoke with a lisp and motioned her finger towards her face, pushing an imaginary pair of glasses up her nose closer to her eyes. Then, she went back to her Emma voice.

"And my brothers…"

They like me.

"They hate you! My parents? Oh my God, my parents. They think you're such a fucking loser." She started imitating her dad. "Emmer, isn't he getting a theatre degree? How the hell are you supposed to make ends meet with that?"

I could actually see her dad saying that. He worked middle management at GM and went into the office faithfully for over twenty years. They lived in a nice home in Farmington Hills and also had a summer home up on Crystal Lake near Frankfort.

"What a waste! A fucking waste. Oh!" She screamed as though a new idea had just hit her. "I can't believe I let you fuck me."

Well you did.

"I mean look at you!"

Eh, it's true. I had actually always thought the same thing. I mean, to me, Emma was a knockout. She was a wild flower with her fantastical thoughts and her adventurous spirit. She was willing to do a deep dive about religion and politics and happenings around the world. Hell, she could've been a doctor, but she was so creative, she stopped taking her chemistry classes and focused on apparel and design. She did what she wanted, and that was really what attracted me to her, because secretly I always thought I had to toe a certain line to be acceptable. She would fashion two bandanas into a top, tie them in such a way that they covered what needed to be covered, and then headed off to class. And that body of hers? Jeepers. Any time I saw her naked I just shook my head, part of me not believing I was in the same room as her. Blame it on my youth, but back then I thought she was a walking Playboy magazine, and she always accused me of obsessing over her breasts. To be fair, I also loved her butt. Ah, hormones.

I don't know what it was in that moment. I think it's that she started to cry after saying "I mean look at you." I've always been uncomfortable when people cry in front of me. I think it's a defense mechanism to start chuckling. But that's what I did. Also, after everything she said, or rather screamed, to now, in this moment, choose to start crying after making fun of my body was a little absurd. Boy, did she not like that. She just started maniacally grabbing for anything she could find that may or may not have been hers...all the while screaming "Fuck you! Fuck you! Fuck you! Fuck you!" In fact, she scrambled out of my apartment, stumbling into the couch and invariably dropping a sock or CD and leaving them...still screaming. I could hear her outside of my apartment and when I walked over to look out my window, she was staggering down the sidewalk trying desperately to hang onto all of her belongings, still screaming "Fuck you!" I saw a dude walking by her, giving her a bit of space. To which she replied, "And fuck you too!"

To think all of this could have been avoided, the break up notwithstanding, if I hadn't been so lazy and thought to throw away the hair with gum in it. I just forgot about it. So, in my DM on MySpace or Classmates or whatever existed back then, I wrote that I was sorry for how I handled the breakup. I was immature and I didn't take her feelings into consideration like I should have.

Well, she answered that DM in the early 2000s to tell me how needy I was during those three years. How I was high-maintenance, and how it was super hard to love me.

None of what she wrote was incorrect or wrong. I was needy, and...I was high-maintenance. I put a lot of pressure on her considering that I had felt so alone and unloved during my teenage years after Nate left for the army. When I met Emma, I dumped everything, every part of my being, into her. I always wanted to be with her. And it wasn't just the sex...especially young lovers' sex, which seems almost daily. I wanted to explore ideas and philosophies. Like I said, she was brilliant, and there was a time when we really fed off of one another. I wanted to tell her about my acting scenes, and I wanted her to show me stuff from her subscriptions to Vogue and Harper's Bazaar that inspired her fashion ideas. I was making up for all those days I'd get home from high school and just be by myself, especially in the winter after football was done, and I didn't have anything after school to occupy my time. I was just alone. And because my mom worked so much and often took the bus home...which would add another hour to her day...sometimes I would make myself something to eat, do a little homework, and go to bed. My dad was gone with the car having an affair or camping with his friends or God-knows-what. And, so, yeah...I was all alone.

Then I met Emma, and...I suffocated her.

And now she stood before me...smiling. Her smile was, I don't know, warm, mature. There was compassion and a wisdom to it.

"Max..."

I looked at her.

"I wish I had never sent that email back to you. That message, you know?"

I smiled and began to write.

She continued, "I was a bit shocked to hear from you. And I initially thought your message was, I don't know, patronizing, and so I guess I let you have it. I'm sorry."

I finished writing and showed her: I'M GLAD YOU DID. I NEEDED TO HEAR THAT.

"It was cruel."

And I wrote IT WAS HONEST.

"Still..." And her voice abruptly stopped, and her eyes welled up a bit. "I had a great time with you, Max. There were, yeah, there were tough times—hell, we were so young. But damn, Max...could you make me laugh. I had taken myself so seriously back then."

She still seemed pretty serious, but I listened.

"Truth is I still do. Everything is so important in my world. My husband, the stock market, my deadlines. Is Penelope going to Columbia or Yale? Did Thomas get into Deerfield? And then I think about those times you would walk around my dorm room with your butt hanging out...God, your ass was SO hairy." She laughed. A couple next to me gave me a look and silently chuckled.

"Do you remember...God, I don't even know why we had those Barbies at the Sig Kap house, but do you remember—"

I was already starting to nod my head, knowing where this was heading.

Laughing through it, Emma said, "You popped the head off that Ken doll, pulled out your wiener and said 'Hey everybody, it's Dickhead'!"

The couple beside me gave me another look. This one seemed a bit more judgmental. Still, they laughed.

"I'm thankful for you, Max. We had fun, yeah?"

I nodded very sincerely, smiling back at her.

"Oh! You know my aunt?" Julie approached from behind Emma, and I couldn't help but shake my head at the coincidence, my smile still plastered on my face. Emma sort of ignored Julie and leaned in very close to my face. She gave me a small kiss on my cheek and whispered, "Thanks for making me laugh." She pulled back but just slightly. "Times are never as bad as we think they are, ya know?" And she gave me another kiss on my cheek and stood up, stepping away from me.

"It was so nice running into you, Max Sheffield."

And I nodded...and smiled some more. Emma walked away, giving Julie a quick embrace. "See you before we head back?" She asked Julie, and Julie responded with a big smile, "I sure hope so."

And then Emma was gone. I watched her exit , and my thoughts were immediately interrupted by Mitch. He was struggling to stand and make his way from his barstool. He rummaged through his pockets and pulled out a set of keys but immediately dropped them. When he bent down to get them, he smacked his forehead on his barstool and dropped his keys again. Believe it or not, when he bent down to get them, he smacked his forehead on his barstool again. If an actor did this in an acting class, the teacher would accuse them of "playing" drunk and would tell them "It's way too big." It seemed like I was watching a sketch.

The bartender who kept serving Mitch asked, "You alright?" And Mitch nodded. The bartender added, "Doesn't do me no good to say anything anyway. You don't never listen to me." And I saw Mitch hold out his fist, and the bartender responded in kind and bumped Mitch's fist with his own.

Mitch stumbled, bumping into the counter of the bar, and prepared to walk out. I quickly looked around to see if anyone was going to stop him. There was an older couple who kept staring at Mitch, but neither made a move to help him or grab his keys. Is this the age we live in? Have we been told to "MYOFB" enough that we just watch when someone needs help?

Is today's society too litigious, so we don't want to risk it...Or are we just lazy? The couple went back to talking to one another...I guess they figured the show was over as Mitch made his way to the door. I scanned the bar, but nobody else seemed to see what was going on. *Surely, someone will take notice and go after him.* But nobody did. Mitch struggled to open the door and then left.

I don't know how long I sat there, it couldn't have been too long, or I never would have caught up to him…But I got up from my table, threw on my coat, slapped down too many twenties for the bill, and rushed out of the restaurant hoping I'd catch up to Mitch before he decided to drive off.

"You leavin'?" It was Julie. I looked at that beautiful smile and gave a wincing nod. "Damn," she said. *Yeah…damn.* I joined my hands together and gave her a "grateful" gesture and rushed out.

17

I Was Really Good, Max

On a visit one time to see Nate and his family, we played a round of golf nearby, and he filled me in on the latest local gossip. That's when he told me he had started coaching with this younger guy who was cocky and arrogant and inappropriate...and a lot of fun to be around. That was Kirk. This was a few years ago mind you, but I had the feeling even then that Nate felt young again around Kirk, and so where Kirk's behavior, for the most part, annoyed and even slightly revolted Mara, Nate found it refreshing and, I would even guess, exhilarating to some degree.

Nate also brought up Mitch. "Did you ever hear why Mitch dropped out of school?" He asked me right in my backswing...which didn't really make much of a difference. Still, I gave him a look, and he smiled.

"I never knew...still don't. But I saw Mitch the other day in town," Nate continued as we hopped in the cart and chased our balls. "His arm was in a cast. He told me that he got into a fight. Some guy was yelling at his wife in Meijer and apparently Mitch asked if everything was okay, and the dude told him to mind his own business. And Mitch ignored the guy and directly asked the wife, who wouldn't dare answer. Mitch took that to mean everything was indeed not okay, and so he jacked the guy in the face and broke his nose. Well, a bunch of guys who thought Mitch started everything came from various isles and took him on. Mitch told me one of the guys, who happened to be friends with the dude he just knocked out, recognized him and said something like 'Well, well, well, if it isn't Mitch the great college drop out.' Other guys started to chime in with 'Oh yeah, I remember you.' And 'No way! This fuckin' guy is THE

Mitch McCoy?' This really incensed Mitch, and he told them to all fuck off and started to walk away, but apparently a couple guys stopped him and cornered him, and I guess the whole thing triggered Mitch, and he asked who wanted to get fucked up first. He told me they all jumped him. He told me he took three of them out, throwing one of them into the glass in the meat section, if you can believe that shit. You never know with Mitch. Sounds exaggerated if you ask me. But evidently enough of them got him down to the ground, and I guess one of them held out his arm and curb stomped it, busting up his elbow."

"Jesus." I don't ever recall an exclamation like that coming from my lips before, but I was astonished. And I never knew Mitch to brag or inflate himself like that. Sure, he was trying to make money and had plans when I would run into him back in the day, but I never heard him make stuff up about himself. I never thought he had the need to…so I was prone to believe the story.

"Anyway, that's some of the drama in big bad Greenville, Maxy. By the way, I'm about to par this hole."

My brother was such a cheater.

"You know what was strange though, Max?"

It's gets weirder? I thought.

"When I took a closer look at his cast, I saw all of these scars on his hands. Weird old cuts, that sort of thing. And his fingers were all bent to hell, which I assumed was from football. I mean, c'mon, look at this guy." And my brother showed me his right middle finger revealing the top of it bent towards the ring finger by at least forty-five degrees. By the way, that was probably the hundredth time my brother showed me that finger. He was also prone to show me the top part of his left ear which was an eye sore from wrestling.

"Mitch must've saw me staring at his hands, because he kind of shouted out proudly 'Go for the knife.'"

"Huh?"

"Exactly. I didn't know if he was giving me a command or what. I mean, I always found him a bit out there whenever we'd run into him, but he repeated it 'Go for the knife…It's a game. I got involved in a bit of a tournament…trying to make some money,' Mitch told me. Evidently, this knucklehead, Max, was in some sort of Russian Roulette except you find a knife with a flat based handle, like a hunting knife, yeah? And you set the knife up on a table standing on that flat base so that the blade is up, top sticking out. And then, like fucking idiots, you see who can grab the knife first. I guess other guys were faster and grabbed the handle and he grabbed the blade, but shit, bro, his hands were covered in these scars."

I don't know what happened to Mitch in college or after college, but he wasn't the same Mitch from high school. Hell, none of us are, of course. That's kind of a stupid thing to say, but he was different. Way different. How could he not be. He was the biggest thing to come out of our area. I think he still has all the big high school records…and not just in football.

Outside the restaurant I caught up to Mitch in time and tapped him on his shoulder, since I couldn't say anything. He whipped around, I imagine a little startled, perhaps thinking the little cowboy and his gang were following him. His momentum from spinning so fast made him fall. I helped him up and grabbed his keys. I went to write on my new board that I would drive him home, but realized quickly, that I had left it in the restaurant. So, I began to mime driving and pointing to myself, and then walked Mitch over to the passenger side. He didn't object. After I helped him up into the seat of his truck, I hustled over to the driver's side, and got behind the wheel.

As we drove through the streets of town which were periodically lit by street lights, I checked in every now and then with Mitch by giving him a look. He was drunk…and looked, well…empty. I saw someone who seemed utterly broken.

"I was really good, Max."

That's what Mitch said about five minutes after we were on the road, and it would be another five minutes before he spoke again.

"I fucked up, Max. It was me. I always said it was the coach. He was a dick, for sure. But it was me. Did you know I tore my hamstring my freshman year?"

I looked over at him and shook my head, but he was staring out through the front windshield.

"Yeah. I tore it up pretty good. I was having a hell of a camp too. I just—I don't know—I just didn't wanna fall behind. I mean, I could've started. My freshman year. I mean, I was on track. I was getting half the reps. And Webber, the senior, got the other half. And then, snap, ya know? I felt a pop during a scramble drill, and I knew. Right away. I knew it was bad, Max. I never told anyone that before. Hell, I've never told anyone any of this."

That surprised me. Was that true? Maybe hyperbole? If it was true, then he's kept all this hidden until now. *He didn't have anyone he trusted enough over the years to talk to?* That thought disturbed me.

"But I knew it was bad. I tried right away to brush it off. Mind over matter, ya know? If I didn't dwell on it or...I don't know...then I could get back out there sooner...'minimize,' that's the word."

And he got quiet again. And, I just kept driving. Graeme messed up his hamstring his senior year of football. He was really bummed because we all thought his season was over. But a friend of mine, a doctor, spun the plasma from Graeme's own blood and injected it right into the injured area. Graeme missed two weeks but was back in time for the playoffs. They lost that game, but I know Graeme was grateful to get back on the field one more time. They didn't have that kind of technology or know-how back when Mitch and I played. And Graeme's hamstring wasn't necessarily torn. Mitch's was by the sound of it. I can't imagine how much pain Mitch tried to stomach in order to play.

"But that fucker wouldn't heal." He shook his head. "I know I came back too soon, but I couldn't get better. It just wouldn't heal. And Webber got the start in our scrimmage. And that shit sophomore—God, he was terrible—started getting my reps."

Silence.

"I got desperate. That's it. That's what it was. I got really fucking desperate. I mean, Max...It's all my dad talked about all summer. I remember we had a family reunion, and I never saw my dad happy. Like... Ever. At that reunion, he was just going around to aunts and uncles, cousins, you name it, and he would just...I don't know, brag about me. Yeah, I mean, he was talking shit about me being the first college football player in that big ass family, but Max...Max, I was going to be the first college grad in the family period. Nobody else had even gone to school. I mean, nobody. Did you know that?"

I shook my head again, but again, he just stared out the window.

"So, I rushed everything...and that's when...you know..."

I didn't know, and he seemed to have a hard time saying it.

"My roommate gave me a muscle relaxer...and...fuck...fuck, Max...that fucker..." He trailed off.

And then...

"I was really fucking good."

I just kept driving. After a while, Mitch opened his glove

compartment, and pulled out a prescription bottle. He presented it to me and shook it. The sound indicated to me that the bottle was getting low. He opened it up and emptied the bottle in his hand. Two small pills tumbled out.

"These things…man. They're motherfuckers," and he popped both into his mouth…and I think he chewed them. He gave a hard swallow and just stared straight ahead.

"They're amazing…Until they're not…I don't know if I even feel them anymore…Did you know I got a girl pregnant around that time?"

I didn't know that, and again, shook my head.

"Yep. I have a twenty-five-year-old daughter somewhere out there…someplace. Came back home. Met someone I didn't like…ha… did that a few times. The fuck? Tried. I dunno…Tried."

We were finally at Mitch's place, and I pulled into his driveway. I got up close to his front porch and put the truck in park.

"Take my truck back. So you can get home. I'll get it in the morning."

I couldn't really protest, and I was actually grateful he said something, because I had no idea how I'd get back to town, and I really wasn't looking forward to crashing at Mitch's for the night.

"My dad died…You knew that, right? He—twelve years ago now. And from that time—" He opened the passenger door…

"That I dropped out of college—"

He climbed out of the truck…

"Til the day he died—"

He was now standing outside his truck, and he finally looked at me…

"How many years is that? Fuck, I can't do the math. My dad, maybe, said a few dozen words to me…maybe." He looked at the ground, shaking his head. "That's like fifteen years, right, Max?..My dad fuckin' ghosted me. That's what they call it now, right?"

He was about to shut the passenger door but looked up first.

"I was really fuckin' good…Max…I was really fuckin' good… Now, I ain't. I ain't been good for a long ass time."

He stared at me. I really wish I could say something. I wanted to. I wanted to tell him that's not true, and that things don't always work out the way we plan, but I couldn't speak. And at the end of the day, those things I wanted to say were just to comfort him. And it wouldn't have comforted him. I guess I wished I would have had the right thing to say…and could have said it…but I didn't. So, I just sat there, uncomfortable.

I decided I would get out and help him up the driveway, but as soon as he heard the door crack open, he cracked the smallest of smiles and said, "Don't get out. I got it." And his smile grew bigger, trying to assure me.

"Thanks a lot for the ride, Max." He smiled and slammed the door. I watched Mitch make his way to his front porch. He stumbled but made his way inside, shutting the front door behind him. I sat there for a moment, taking it all in. Then I backed up and drove back into town.

18

I Used to Wonder What Motivates
This World of Ours

The next day I tested out my voice. I just sort of moaned, and some noise came out. I didn't want to push it, but I was also tired of not being able to speak. I could feel the moan on my throat, and so I muttered a few words as a whisper. I was speaking. That's kind of what I was whispering.

"I am speaking. I am speaking."

I could hear it. I was relieved that it was healing, but I also started to worry the moaning and whispering were directly impacting my larynx and throat area. That's where the pressure is when we talk softly. I started to raise my voice to open up my throat, and there was some relief, but I couldn't hear much more than I did before, so I thought I better not push my luck.

Now, if I'm honest I'm not much of a breakfast guy. Because of that, it felt too soon to meander into town and get a bite to eat. One thing I hadn't done since visiting my brother was go for a walk. In LA, it had basically become a ritual—a way to clear my head and sort out my thoughts. And I enjoyed it on previous visits to see Nate and his family. So, I headed out.

Just like where I grew up, there were several acres between houses. Sure, there was a newer development, here and there, where some heir to a great-grandpa's farm sold off a corner of the inherited four hundred acres, which was then converted into a neighborhood of ten or so new, manufactured homes. But my brother's neighbors were a good eighth of a mile down his rural road. There was an older couple that lived across the street. It was an adorable looking cottage, set in deep from my brother's street—especially in the summer—with a beautiful grove of weeping willows in the back yard, which led to a dock on Bass Lake. *Wait, is the yard and the side of a house facing a body of water considered the front? I never knew which was which.*

I rarely saw the couple. And I hadn't seen them on this trip. I figured they wintered in Florida or Arizona. In the past when I did see them, say, doing yardwork or jumping in their car to go somewhere, I would wave, and they would wave back. But that was the extent of it.

Nate told me that they kept to themselves. He had tried to make conversation with them but given the age difference and infrequency of their presence, nothing ever went too deep.

"I couldn't even tell you what they did for a living. Her name is Evelyn…" And I forget what Nate told me the husband's name was. Samuel, I think.

He said that Mara would drop off homemade chocolate chip cookies…a specialty of hers—she uses way too much butter and mixes in an extra bag of chips, which means they're absolutely terrific. But even that stopped.

"It's not that my gesture wasn't reciprocated, Max." Mara piggybacked on what Nate told me not only to add to the conversation, but also, I think, because she would hate for me to think she was shallow. "I'm not sure why I stopped dropping them off," she added and gave it some thought. "I think I got a little tired of ringing their doorbell and having nobody answer and just leaving a Tupperware bowl full of cookies on their stoop. Heck, I didn't even know if they got 'em or if the racoons did."

It's just one of those things that sometimes happens, I suppose. Relationships no matter how casual or serious can often fade away…like a wilting flower left unwatered.

I became slightly irritated on my walk because the wind kept hitting the spot on my neck just under my Adam's apple. I had forgotten to wear a scarf, and damn, it was cold. I had worn gloves and a hat—I was even using one of my brother's ski masks he used when he went hunting, so that just my eyes were exposed. But the mask barely went down past my chin and my coat only zipped up so far, and by the time I had felt the chill focus in on that one spot, I was too lazy to turn around. And yet, I became preoccupied with…that one spot. To make matters worse, I began noticing how snug the ski mask was. I know I have a pretty large head, but so does Nate. *Wait…am I wearing one of the boys' masks?* No wonder it didn't cover my neck. Now I had two things to obsess about. *Terrific.*

Suddenly I stopped. I stopped dead in my tracks. My head had been looking to my right where I had an unobstructed view of dense hardwoods and a splattering of conifers. They were all barren of leaves and color, of course, save for the wonderful green needles on the evergreens. But in that moment, everything in my periphery was trees. Just trees. Grey massive trunks of oaks and maples, some occasional groupings of white, flappy barked birches, and brown, sappy boles of the pines.

I immediately recalled my favorite poem: "Stopping by Woods On a Snowy Evening" by Robert Frost. I had recited it in a poetry class I took in college. A short four stanza poem that was an instant classic and loved by so many. I think it's the last stanza that really "gets" folks…at least it does for me. It always makes me stop, pause, and reflect:

The woods are lovely, dark and deep,

But I have promises to keep,

And miles to go before I sleep,

And miles to go before I sleep

The wind hit that spot once again and brought me out of my trance. My impatience got the best of me, and I turned back towards my brother's place.

As I approached nearer to home, I noticed my brother's neighbor bent over towards the end of her driveway. At least I think it was her. From the distance and my vantage point, it could have very well been the old man. But, the closer I got, I could tell it was, who I assumed to be, Evelyn. She was struggling to shovel snow. And at the particular moment I walked up to her, she was bent over, her shovel was used as a crutch preventing her from falling, and she was breathing rather hard.

Since I couldn't yell, I waved my hands rather demonstrably in order to get her to look up. She did, and I waved. She gave me the sweetest, faintest wave back. I stepped closer, too close really, but I wanted her to hear me.

"Please, allow me?" I asked. She looked at me inquisitively. I'm not sure if she was reluctant at a strange man standing too close wearing a kid's ski mask or if she didn't understand what I had said.

So, I ripped off the hat and repeated myself, "Please, let me do this," and I finished with some awful miming of shoveling snow.

She smiled (so many wrinkles filled her face when she did that) and handed me her shovel. She then immediately plopped herself down on the nearby snowdrift, basically using it as a stool.

"Thank you." I had never heard her speak before. Her voice held weight. Just those two words seemed to contain a lot of life…and wisdom.

She had shoveled most of her long driveway, so there wasn't too much for me to do. I was impressed with what she had accomplished. While shoveling we managed to formally introduce ourselves, since we had never exchanged names before, and I was surprised that she never asked "What" or asked me to repeat what I had just said. She was able to hear my faint speech…at her age? *Wow…impressive.* I finished up in no time and made sure to clear the extra hard snow at the edge of the road where the plows had already been through.

"Won't you come inside?" She asked. "Let's have some tea."

I nodded and smiled and then said, "okay." And she gave me one of the warmest smiles that I can remember. Actually, I don't recall if she smiled at all. It was her face. Her face smiled at me. She made her way back towards her home and I followed, shovel in hand.

Inside she invited me to have a seat and pulled out an old antique chair, which was part of an intricate set in her kitchen. There were so many beautiful furnishings and exquisite pieces of art. It felt like a small museum, yet somehow it felt empty. Perhaps it was the silence. It was awfully quiet.

We sat there each with a cup of piping hot tea. She had seemingly struggled to make it, limping around the kitchen, and I wished I had arrived sooner and shoveled the whole damn driveway.

"Thank you, Max. Is that short for something?"

"It is." I then lied and told her, "Maxwell."

The truth is my mom and dad made a deal. (Actually, it was my dad's idea, and he convinced, connived, or demanded—take your pick—that my mom go along with it.) He got to name the boys, and my mom got to name the girls. Well, they only had boys and, so my dad got to pick them. And he named Nate "Nate" and me "Max." Not Nathan or Maxwell. Just Nate and Max. We were named after people from my dad's past. Nate, I was told, was an old work buddy at a tool and die shop that my dad worked at before he married my mom. He had worked there a few years before getting laid off. (That would be the longest running job my dad would ever have, as he bounced around from gig to gig before getting bored and quitting or getting fired.) He and Uncle Nate, that's what we called him when we were kids, were pretty inseparable…they were best friends, really…until a mysterious falling out. I don't recall Uncle Nate coming around after my brother left for the military. And me? Well, that's a mystery as well. When I asked my dad who I was named after, he always used to say, "I just like the name." There didn't seem to be a Max in our lives growing up. And when I would ask my mom, she kept quiet and wouldn't answer. Years later, shortly after my father died, she told me that there was a Max from our past. But it was a Maxine. Maxine was a former lover of my dad's that he was with early on in his marriage to my mom. It was an affair that lasted almost ten years. Which, and I've done the math, means the affair ended around the time I was born. I don't know if I was named after her—or rather, I wouldn't put it past my dad to name me after Maxine, but I refuse to believe that I am named after one of his mistresses. It just never sat right with me.

And so, I lied to Evelyn…I always lie about it. Whenever anyone asks what Max is short for, I tell them "Maxwell," "Maximillian," "Maxim." Anything to try to create a reality from…well…the truth. If it even is the truth.

"Maxwell…hmmm." Evelyn gave that some thought, and her words pulled me out of that crazy memory of the possible origin of my name. "I've seen you before. Is that your brother across the street?"

I nodded, and she added, "You two look so much alike."

I chuckled to myself. Neither Nate nor I would take that as a compliment. We often made fun of each other's looks.

"It's hard, Max, to manage the chores around here…especially in the winter. Well, especially after Simon died.

Ah, Simon not Samuel. And then I felt a touch of remorse that I wondered about the name instead of first feeling sympathy. I slurped my tea, not knowing what to say. But after I sat my cup back down on the table, I managed an "I'm sorry."

"Thank you. It's been almost a year. He died on New Year's Day. Not that that is of any significance. January first has never meant all that much to me. Plus, he had been in the hospital for about a month and a half." Without skipping a beat she asked, "Did something happen to your throat?"

Defensively I gestured and quickly whispered, "I'm not sick or anything." I didn't want Evelyn to think that I was contagious. Old people tend to get worried about things like that.

She looked at me patiently waiting for me to tell her what happened, but in my discomfort, I took another sip of tea. I didn't much feel like straining what little voice I had telling her how I lost my ability to speak.

But she just looked at me...and waited. I took another sip of tea and then lifted up the mug as a way to say, "Good tea. Thanks."

She smiled a smile that had experienced a lot of life...and a lot of bullshit.

"I took a log to the throat. My nephew...he...we were cutting up wood and he...didn't see where he was throwing it...the log." And then I gestured with my hands holding a small log and it slamming into my larynx.

Her eyes brightened slightly. "Wow...and you lost your voice from that?"

And I nodded...and drank some more tea. I then stared at my mug as I sat it back down. I sensed she was studying me...staring at me, and so I avoided looking up.

"Are you here with your wife and kids?"

I shook my head and then looked up..."No."

She nodded and finally took her first sip.

"I seem to recall you having a wife and two children. I think I recall the little ones playing out in the yard over there if memory serves me correctly."

I gave a slight nod. It's true, Sophie, Graeme and Brianna made a handful of visits with me to see my brother and his family, though the last visit had been ages ago.

"But they didn't make the trip this time?"

I imagined she could tell by my fallen face what had happened. Not all of the details, of course, not every little occurrence that had led to this moment in time, but judging from her chin momentarily lifting up as if to say "ahh," Evelyn knew the broad strokes of a breakup.

It may have appeared to Evelyn that I was lost in thought about Sophie and the kids, but truthfully, I was thinking about the way Evelyn spoke. She had a cadence to her voice...a deliberate inflection. There was a slower rhythm to it, and it was—in musical terms—legato.

We sat there in silence. Given the way I think about things, I wondered why she spoke like that. *What was she up to?* I thought that about almost everyone I encountered. I've thought that way since I was a child. I can chalk that up to always wondering if my dad was going to pivot in mood swings and attack one of us in the family or…the times trying to interpret my mother's passive-aggressive language. In the quiet…at the table with Evelyn, I couldn't tell if she was playing some sort of mind game like my parents did or if she was just comfortably patient with stillness.

The only sound, for what seemed like ten minutes, was the creaking from my chair as I tried not to squirm, sitting there uncomfortably…but obviously failing. I was not comfortable with stillness. I had finished my tea as the silence began, but I continued to sip from my empty mug so that I had something to do. *What an idiot…*Everytime I took a fake sip…*What an idiot…*but yet, I still reached for my cup and sipped my drink that was no longer there.

Evelyn finally broke the tension I felt. "I have to tend to those stretchers."

I looked up at her, confused, and she added, "Those pieces under the chair that support the legs…you know, the horizontal ones?"

Oh, I expressed but didn't say.

"They're awfully loud under your seat," she said with a smile. She didn't wait nearly as long to ask, "And what is it that you do?"

I immediately replied, "I was an actor."

"Was?"

I looked at her, befuddled. She looked at me and waited. God, she was in no hurry to be understood. Here I am, so quick in life to make sure that I am understood that I overexplain everything, and here's Evelyn… so capable of being misunderstood, that she's just willing to sit there. I looked at her inquisitively because she asked "Was?" and I didn't know why she asked that. Then finally it hit me…*Did I tell her "I WAS an actor?" Oh boy, I didn't realize I said "was." Wait, did I? No. Surely, I said "am." Shit. No. I said "was." Wait.* I had a feeling my face torqued in different directions while I sorted this all out in my head, and so I looked over to Evelyn to see if she noticed, but, just like other times I had looked at her, all she did was give me a reassuring smile, seemingly loaded with wisdom…and patience.

"I am an actor. Am. Just…"

I got quiet.

"Haven't been working much?" She asked.

All I could manage was a series of short nods and a stupid, short smile.

It got quiet again, and now the chair was really creaking. But... neither of us spoke. I wanted to say something but only because I wanted to cut into the hushed lull. Evelyn seemed to be at peace with it. I...was not.

"Grief."

That's all she said at first.

"I used to wonder what motivates this world of ours. Love... power...revenge...money."

"But I think it's grief. Simon and I lost our only child when he was twenty."

I've always been triggered by the thought of one of my children dying before me. It's my worst fear. So now, I was even more uncomfortable. I know I should have probably looked at Evelyn, if only out of kindness or etiquette, but my eyes darted sneakily around the room and then back down to my mug. I never knew this about her. I doubt my brother even knew. But instead of ingesting this information, my eyes surreptitiously started to dash again.

I then wondered if she noticed me trying to find a clock. *It's gotta be lunchtime soon, no?*

"Drunk driver. Robert was on his way home from college. Spring break."

Now, I felt bad for not listening. *Why was I so antsy?* I forced myself to stop looking around...to, instead, focus on what she was saying. It wasn't easy. And just as I made a deliberate effort to listen, it was quiet again.

"I think everything I did after that was in response to that grief. I so loved that boy. Still do," and she took another sip of tea.

I found it hard to swallow. My mouth had filled with saliva, and it was hard to move it down my throat. In fact, it caught in my throat, and I became restless. I tried so hard to not move in the stillness. It was becoming a bit unbearable.

"No family. Not working. That's got to be hard for you, Max. Yet...here we are...enjoying our tea."

I had no idea how to respond—to what she had just said...to the loss of her boy—so I just said, "And thank you for it. It was lovely..."

We then talked over one another with...

"You're welcome." And "…But I must be going."

And I stood up, grabbed my mug—

"Oh, leave that. I'll get it."

And again, I thanked her. Struggling, like a lot of the elderly do when they've been sitting in one spot for a while, Evelyn started to get up from her chair, but I immediately stopped her with "Please—please don't get up. I can show myself out."

"Okay." And she relaxed back into her seat.

"And thank you, again."

"You're welcome, Max. Thank you for the company."

Outside, I hustled down the driveway, and I kept telling myself to slow down. I thought it would look rude if she was now standing at a window watching me. Why was I moving so quickly anyway? Why was I so uncomfortable sitting there with Evelyn? *Slow down, Max.* And I did. I tried to walk like a normal person. I took a quick look back to see if she was indeed staring out at me, watching. But when I did, she was not there…at any of the windows.

19

Please, Sir, Don't Be Mad.
I'm Falling in Love

A shower helped. My nerves had peaked. I had become discombobulated. But the hot water hitting and massaging my neck and body, some music playing from my phone, and a handful of deep breaths seemed to bring me back to some sort of state of calm. I didn't want to figure out what the hell just happened to me. This was not the first time I felt the onset of this kind of angst, and I just wanted to forget it. So, I tried my best to get lost once again in Bree's playlist.

I pulled out of my brother's driveway and turned on the radio. Now, growing up in Northern Michigan, there weren't many genres of music to listen to. There were a couple of oldies stations, three country stations, and then there were a few religious stations that didn't play music but instead had fiery sermons…like the peace sign must be satanic because it's never mentioned in the Bible. And the oldies were more easy listening in nature…like Roger Whitaker as opposed to the Beatles. So, imagine my surprise when I turned on the radio and Mazzy Star's "Fade into You" was playing. Was this on one of the oldies stations, and now considered some sort of classic rock? I didn't care. I loved this song. One of my all-time faves. The lead singer—Hope something—her voice, the words, that slide on the guitar are all magical. But if you ever see videos of her performing live, she just seems so vulnerable and in the moment. So present. Her eyes are closed for a period of time, as she feels the music, and then…when she opens her eyes and looks at the camera, you're possessed. Like a mythical siren…"Don't look her in the eyes." (I think with sirens, you're not suppose to "hear" them, but you get the idea.) She was just SO...authentic. (I've always struggled with authenticity. I worry too much what other people think.) Her unearthly voice always drew me in and that, combined with such evocative lyrics, kept me spellbound. I had such a crush on her.

Twenty-two years ago, I was at a bar in LA with Keiren, where he and his server friends met up after work. If servers went to a place after work, those are the "cool" joints. That's where I first met Sophie. She was working as a bartender. I pointed out Sophie to Keiren.

"Look at her...behind the bar."

Sophie served up a drink and had long dark hair that she flipped out of her face, as she gave a smile and the drink to a patron.

I immediately melted. "She looks like that lead singer in Mazzy Star."

Keiren agreed, "Oh, wow, you're right."

I'm telling you, I couldn't move. It felt as though my heart stopped beating and the blood emptied out of my body and none of my nerves would work. Sure, she was beautiful...physically attractive. But it was the way she interacted with people. I would see her smile, and I would see her give guys a look like "Don't mess with me"...she seemed to have a BS meter, and then she'd give them a playful nod. She absolutely controlled the room.

To this day I have no idea how I mustered the courage to walk up to her, or how my body physically made it there, but I did, and I ordered a Jack and Coke.

"Easy-peasy," she said.

"I've never been here before."

"Yeah, I've never seen you around."

I think I stared at her too long. "I'll come back every night now."

I knew I was giving myself away, but I didn't care.

"What's your name?"

"Max."

"I'm Sophie."

"Yeah, I know."

"How'd you know?"

But I didn't know. I just didn't know what to say and that's what came out.

"I don't know actually. I was just trying to come up with

something to keep the conversation going."

She gave a little laugh.

"May I be honest with you?"

"Please, Max." She had already given me my drink.

"I should've ordered a more complicated drink."

"Why's that?"

"So, I could talk to you longer."

And she laughed again.

"Actually…"

Other people were waiting to order…but Sophie didn't look bothered. She was listening to me. They could wait, and I was falling even harder because of it.

"Actually…the honest thing I wanted to tell you is…"

There was a sigh from an impatient patron behind me.

"You're the coolest person I've ever laid eyes on."

"You don't know me, Max."

"Well, like I said, I'm coming back every night."

"Ohh, that's too bad…"

I gave her a look.

"Tonight's my last night."

"No."

"Yeah."

"You're messing with me."

"I'm not. I start a new job in a couple of days."

My head dropped.

The patron behind sighed again, even louder.

"Please, sir, don't be mad. I'm falling in love." I spoke in a boyish British accent, a la Tiny Tim, but the patron wasn't amused. Sophie laughed. In fact, she kind of doubled over behind the bar. I caught her funny bone, and I noticed she wiped a small tear from her eyes from the laughter.

"Wanna start a tab?"

And I gave her my credit card.

"This will ensure I come back."

And I walked back over to Keiren and his friends.

While Keiren and his friends were doing shots and making fun of the people they had served that day, I was trying to figure out how I could ask Sophie out. Every time I looked over at her, she was laughing, pouring, mixing, listening…all at the same time. She seemed light years ahead of me and so out of my league. But I did feel something there… between us.

The hours were moving and some of Keiren's friends had left. Keiren, himself, was getting tired and was ready to head out. I had made my way back to Sophie to order more drinks. To be honest, whenever anyone wanted another drink, I offered to get it. That was an expensive night. But it gave me a chance to talk to Sophie some more. I learned that she was going on to be a production assistant at some entertainment company. This was the start of her amazing climb as a producer in reality television. She learned that I was an actor slowly making my way in Hollywood. I made her laugh some more, and at one point she pulled me aside to tell me a joke.

"What did the limestone say to the geologist?"

"I don't know, what?"

"Stop taking me for granite."

"Knock knock." I said.

"Who's there?"

"Interrupting Cow—"

And I swear, before I finished the word "cow" she screamed "Moooo!"

God, I liked her a lot.

So, now it was late, and I kept wanting to ask her out…but my insecurities got the best of me. I mean, I had dated before and even had some longer relationships, but there were other times it didn't go so well. I had asked Sherrie Hughes out for homecoming our junior year, and she told me that she was waiting for a better offer. And another time I asked a woman out at a bar right after college, and all she said was "Eww" and walked away. So, it was the asking out part that got me all nervous.

Finally, as an attempt to stop Keiren from leaving, I drew on a bar napkin.

WILL YOU GO OUT WITH ME? CHECK THIS BOX FOR YES AND THIS BOX FOR NO. And I asked Keiren to walk up and give it to her.

I was on pins and needles. I was shaking. I watched him hand the napkin to Sophie, and I saw her laugh. And it was the laugh I absolutely loved. The laugh I would do anything for. The laugh I would compromise my own best interests to see. The laugh I would die for. I saw it for the first time. Those huge brown eyes squinting shut and her shoulders shaking. She pulled out a pen from a Mason jar and jotted down her answer. Honestly, I didn't know if she was checking "YES" or "NO," because she kept writing. So, the fear in me created a story in which she wrote something like OH MAX, YOU'RE SO SWEET, BUT I'M SEEING SOMEONE.

Keiren walked back over and handed me the napkin. "Here. I'm tired. I'm going to bed."

I read the note, and she checked YES and wrote down her number with "I'm free tomorrow, wanna hang out?"

I screamed and grabbed Keiren and gave him a big ole bear hug and then ran around the bar screaming some more. Everyone stopped to look at me, but I could only see Sophie...she was smiling...oh that smile...and she was happy.

20

You Don't Know Who People Really Are

"Fade Into You" had long finished as I continued to drive towards town. And that's when I saw him...I saw the guy again...the one from before who was running in jeans. It was kind of near the same spot where I saw him before. As I passed, I wondered *what should I do? Should I help him? Does he even need help?* I decided to pull over to the shoulder and find out what was going on.

I got out of the Jeep and waved to the gentlemen. He slowed down as he approached me. This was going to be awkward only because I was going to have to get right up to him for him to hear me. I'm sure he didn't want me pulling over, getting out, and then getting right up in his face. *Where's that damn dry erase board?* I decided to point to my throat, and he, like so many others, looked inquisitively at me. I tried to get out some words, all the while still pointing at my throat.

"My throat."

"Sorry?"

"I can't really speak."

He had no idea what I was saying.

"Are you choking?"

Now he seemed concerned.

I shook my head fiercely and muttered "No."

He got closer, and so I leaned in.

"Everything okay?" I whispered.

"With me? Shoot, yeah. Cold as hell. But yeah."

I managed to say "Good," but I don't think he heard me.

"I'm more worried about you." The jogger said.

And I waved my hands in front of me in hopes of signaling that I was fine. I started to get back into my car, but his voiced stopped me.

"I'll take a ride into town, if you're heading that way."

I looked at him and gestured for him to get in and off we went.

"Wow, heat. Damn. That's nice. Thank you."

I nodded and drove. A Neil Diamond song was now playing on the radio. "Cracklin' Rosie," and I instinctively turned it off. I guess I thought the jogger would think that it was nerdy and old and would judge me. (Like I said…I care too much what people think.)

"Why you turning off Neil?" The jogger asked and turned the radio back on. He joined in.

He sang right along with the radio at first but then started to pause as the words seemed to escape him. He did that thing that people do where you chime in at the end of each line, as if you're brain finally remembers what it has stored in long term memory. And he kept a very steady, rhythmic snap going with his right hand. I noticed he snapped with his thumb and index finger. *How is he making such a strong snap like that?* I looked up from his snap and he smiled. He was enjoying himself. Yeah, why did I turn it off? I love Neil Diamond.

It then got quiet when he didn't know the words at all. The snapping stopped and he mumble-hummed for a bit, and then the song played in the background as we drove. I wanted to say something, but I knew I really should rest my throat. I struggled with the awkward silence. So occasionally I would glance over to him and smile, and then I nodded to the rhythm of the music, which had to have made the awkwardness even worse.

"I'm Brian."

I whispered, "Max."

"Matt?"

"Max."

"Nice to meet you, Matt. Thanks for the lift."

I wanted to correct him, but I also didn't, so…he called me Matt the rest of the way.

"I'm guessing you don't see a lot of black dudes around here." He stated or asked; I couldn't tell. Brian continued. "I mean, I haven't seen any. Just me."

I didn't know how to answer. Brian wasn't wrong. It was a very homogenous area. LA is very diverse, which made this area stand out even more to me.

"You don't say much do you, Matt."

"Um—"

"That's okay."

"Uh, no, it's—it's my voice."

"Oh. Okay."

"Yeah."

"Your voice?"

I nodded.

"You hurt it or something."

I nodded again.

"Gotcha. Well, it's all good. I can talk for both of us."

But it got quiet again.

"It sure is cold out there."

I nodded.

"You think I'd be used to it. I grew up in Baldwin."

I nodded again.

"You know it?"

And, again, I nodded. Baldwin is a village about an hour or so north of my brother's place. For the longest time, I didn't know why, but in a very rural county in northern Michigan, Baldwin had its fair share of black residents. Baldwin is a small place, like so many towns around that area. It has, maybe, 1000 people. I was researching it one time, because I thought I'd write a screenplay while I waited for my agent to call about auditions and thought of writing some version of *Romeo and Juliet*. I thought it would make for a great setting—*Romeo and Juliet* set in a small logging town in the 1880s in which half of the population was white and half was black. I thought that was an interesting idea. Baldwin actually is more like three quarter white and a quarter black, but still, that struck me as a big percentage. I mean, look it up on a map, it's in the middle of nowhere. I went to elementary, junior high and high school not too far from there, and we had one black student my entire time there. And here is this village with around 250 black residents. I thought it was cool, but it was a mystery to me for awhile, because any time I researched it, the internet would talk about Idlewild, Michigan, which was a resort town for blacks during segregation known as Black Eden. I would google "Black Rural Town Northern Michigan" and only get Idlewild. Why didn't they have any information on Baldwin? Finally, I pulled Idlewild up on a map and noticed it was only five minutes from Baldwin. Now it all made sense. But isn't it interesting we were never taught about Black Eden back in school, a school just one county over. And the only reason I knew about Baldwin is because we played them in basketball, and their team looked a lot different than ours. I thought the segregation, that lasted well into the 20th century, would be perfect for the Montagues and Capulets. When I sent it to my agent for him to read, he told me the story was overdone.

"You alright?"

Ha, Brian pulled me out of my trance, thinking about Baldwin. I wanted to tell him what I was thinking about, but my throat was too tired, so I just smiled.

"It's cold as balls around here. That's why I was running."

I whispered, "I saw you a few days ago as well."

Brian nodded, but I don't think he understood me. "I've been seeing this girl. She's pretty sweet. But I think she's with someone else, because she don't let me hang around."

I grinned.

"You from around here?"

"Not really," I whispered. "Visiting my brother."

"Oh…you know a girl named Crystal?"

Well, only one…And she was with Mitch the other night.

"Crystal Gingrich? She married?"

And that's the same Crystal. But they weren't married. And judging from the other night, they weren't even an item. But who the hell knows what Crystal was telling Brian.

I managed to say, "I don't think so." I wanted to say, "But I don't know her that well," but again my throat.

Brian started telling me about himself, and I was struck immediately by how he seemed to roll with the punches that life threw at him. He told me that he had a basketball scholarship to Wyoming but blew out his knee his freshman year. Instead of heading back to his hometown, he moved to Grand Rapids and attended community college while working a couple of jobs.

"I figured if I went back to Baldwin, I'd never leave. Shoot, I don't know what I would've done…plowed driveways in the winter? What about the summer? Mowed lawns, I suppose. Man, no. I went and stayed with my cousin."

One of his jobs was delivering pizzas.

"I delivered pizzas to my own apartment complex one night. The complex I lived in with my cousin. It was shaped like a horseshoe, U-shaped, so it had a courtyard. Man, I got mugged there. I was about to ring the bell to the east entrance and felt something hard on my temple. Dude was hiding in the shrubs...literally."

I gave him a startled look.

"Yeah! Scared the shit out of me. I said, as calmly as I could, 'Man, this is my first delivery of the night. I don't got no money.' I was like 'Check my pockets." And right behind the guy with the gun came another dude who did check my pockets. Let's just say 'Thank God I wasn't lying,' 'cause I think they would've shot me....You ever have a gun pulled on you, Matt?"

I shook my head.

"Shit's scary. Scary as hell. I'm not wired for no shit like that."

"What happened?" I whispered.

"They were pissed. They started pacing and looking around, arguing with one another. 'What a' we gonna do?' 'Man, chill. Lemme think!' 'Do we shoot 'em?' 'Bro, shut up!' And then the guy with the gun put it up against my head again and said, 'Give me the pizza'."

A laughed escaped and hurt my throat a little.

"I shit you not. Those dudes stole four large pizzas and ran the hell away."

I shook my head.

"That wasn't the first time I was mugged either. Some crazy shit has happened to me. Hell, I lived in that complex, right? Some weird dude would set our cars on fire. The ones on the street next to the complex. Same time every week. You'd be asleep and hear a car alarm or the smashing of a window and poof, these flames engulfed like a Ford Escort or Plymouth Sundance at 4 a.m. every Tuesday morning. Like clockwork for three weeks. Needless to say, it wasn't hard for the police to catch him the fourth time. He wound up throwing the...whatchamacallit ... Molotov Cocktail at the police...so they shot him."

Whoa.

"That's nothin'. Our maintenance guy...you know, for the complex? Yeah, he was murdered in my basement...where we did laundry. My cousin found him."

I couldn't believe it.

"It turns out that the apartment manager, this lady...She had been seeing the maintenance guy. You know, sleeping with him. I mean, why not, right? You both work there. You're both lonely. Makes perfect sense to me. But see, she had just broken up with her fiancé not long before that. So now the police are looking for the fiancé. Get this…he turns up dead."

Brian had some stories…

"Yeah. Dead. They found the fiancé in his car, parked on some street in the city, shot in the head. But wait…Gets better. The police go ahead and write it up as a suicide, but…"

He paused for dramatic affect.

"They didn't find no gun. Shot himself in the head but there's no gun? How does that make sense? It don't. My cousin said they told him that some homeless guy must've come by and taken the gun before the police found the fiancé…"

I could feel Brian looking at me, seeing if I had a reaction. I just shook my head.

"Yeah. Hard to believe, right? Here's what I think. I think the fiancé shot the maintenance guy, and then the apartment manager lady went out and shot the fiancé. That's what I think I mean, I have no idea what happened, but damn…she was a nut. Man, I would walk into the courtyard on my way to my cousin's apartment, and see, she had this nice first floor apartment on the other side, right next to the main gate. You had to walk by her place when you walked in, and the land lady had these big bay windows. And there she stood, right there behind those windows staring out at you. Uh-huh, AND…She had this cat that she held. Always holdin' that cat. And she would slowly stroke its back."

He demonstrated with some mime work, and I smiled. *This was the best ride into town I've ever had.*

"I tried, Matt. I tried not to look. I would tell myself, 'Walk straight ahead, motherfucker. Do not look at that crazy bitch'."

And he demonstrated that as well.

"But damn, you know, sometimes you can't help yourself, and I would look. And brother, she would just be staring at me…Oh, and she had these big, huge glasses that she wore, and I remember her having long, silver grey hair. Like, I didn't know if she was sixty-five or like a thirty-five-year-old, female Steve Martin."

Man, I wish I could laugh. Brian was cracking me up. He went on telling me how he got an associate degree in business and started selling insurance.

"I got accused of sexual harassment though. I'm telling you, Matt, I didn't do shit. I didn't. Swear to God. I was working with this lady, and she was always flirting. And you know, I would joke with her, but we didn't do anything. She would text me memes and what not…pretty inappropriate stuff. Like pornographic. But I was cool. I just thought of her as a friend. But then…she starts dating the office manager. And I knew shit was about to hit the fan when she told me that she told Steve… that's the manager…about "us." And I'm like "us?" There is no "us." And she's like, 'Oh I know, I'm just messin' with him.' And I'm like 'Don't. Don't do that. I like my job.' See, she was playing mind games with Steve; it was just her nature, I guess. Kept things lively for her, I suppose. Well, sure as shit, I get called into the office, and they start showing me memes that Ashley—yeah, she was an Ashley—they started showing me memes that Ashley showed ME! And I told them that. I was like 'Nah, I didn't send those to her.' And they tell me 'Well, she's already filed a complaint with corporate.' See, Steve was about to break up with her, and while they were dating, he promised her a promotion…" It was quiet for a moment.

"I mean, you can do the math."

A "yeah" came out of my mouth. Followed by a "damn."

"So, she tells Steve that she's going to go above him and complain that he puts up with a toxic work environment, and you get the idea…I'm apparently the toxic work environment. And I didn't do shit, Matt! So, I ended up back in Baldwin. Be with my mom. She's been ill. Oh, right here is fine."

And he motioned for me to pull over and drop him off.

"You know what's hilarious? I heard she wound up being Steve's boss, and she fired him."

I smiled and looked around.

"Where's your car?" I whispered.

"Ah…don't have one. It broke down last summer. Maybe I'll see you around. I find myself down here quite a bit lately to see that Crystal girl," he said with a wink and then got out of the Jeep.

I had to ask…"How do you get back and forth?"

"Is the fuckin' you're gettin' worth the fuckin' you're gettin'?"

Brian must've seen the confusion on my face. He continued, "It's an old saying. I figure it out. Walk, hitch hike. Sometimes someone I know helps out. You know…"

Wow, Crystal must be something else in the sack. *That's a ways away,* I thought. Crystal may not have lived right around here but close enough for me to see Brian twice now...and her with Mitch.

Brian pulled out his wallet. "Here, let me give you some money..."

But I waved him off.

"...For gas."

And I waved even more emphatically, and softly said, "It was my pleasure. If you ever need—"

"Thanks, Matt. That was a fun ride."

"I barely said anything."

"I know," and he winked one more time and shut the door. And he walked out of sight. I sat there for a moment hoping that we'd cross paths again...And to think the first time I saw him, I was apprehensive about helping him out. If I'm being honest, I might be cautious the next time I see anyone walking on the side of the road. I mean, you don't know who people really are or what they're capable of...even if you think you know them...so especially strangers. I saw some *20/20* or *Dateline* episode where this old lady kept murdering her husbands. The picture of the old lady looked like this sweet, innocent, white haired woman who wanted to cook you a nice hot meal and hear all about your day—not some psychopath that had no measure of right and wrong. Hell, if I remember correctly, the first husband had a life insurance policy, but the next two didn't. So, she just killed for the joy of it. Crazy world, man.

And then there was this guy who delivered food on a sitcom I recurred on. I think I did like five episodes during its six-year run. The guy—I forget his name—would show up during the shoot with a special meal to keep the cast and crew energized during the long night of filming—fixings for tacos, platters of burgers and hot dogs, or even one time, he had five twelve-foot subs that he cut up so that everyone could have some.

Anyway, I had run into him the first time I was on the show, and he was a fan of some of my other work, namely *Men in the Blue.* I didn't usually run into people who knew my resume, so it was flattering to hear that. He was an interesting dude. He was an art teacher trying to become a set designer and used this time to stay close to the goings on in the industry...at least that's what he told me.

He also had a huge scar around his left eye. Whatever happened to him, not only left his socket and cheek mangled with scar tissue but also forced him to wear a glass eye in his left eye socket. The problem was—and by "problem" I mean for an over-thinker like myself—was that his right eye—or "good" eye—was what some people call "lazy." It would drift when he talked. (Strabismus, I think it's called. A friend back in grade school had surgery to correct it.) So, he had a glass eye AND a lazy eye.

I would listen to him (and I always ran into him whenever I was on the show), and I kept thinking *Don't look at his glass eye, that's rude.* So, I would look at his lazy eye and then tell myself the exact same thing regarding that eye. Needless to say, I had no idea where to look. So, I just kept popping back and forth from the glass eye to the lazy eye when I looked at him. I must've looked ridiculous. I would wonder if he knew that people were overthinking like that when he spoke to them. I mean, I couldn't have been the only one. But whether he knew or not, it didn't seem to bother him at all, and I appreciated that he wasn't as base as I was.

But then, years after that show was cancelled, and I stopped running into him, Sophie had the local evening news on, and his mugshot came up. I mean, it was definitely him…I don't imagine he had a doppelgänger given how I described him. And wouldn't you know it, he had been arrested for child trafficking. He was accused of luring certain students to study at this remote desert "art" camp in the summer. The camp apparently got busted and all of these cameras were discovered hidden in the bathrooms and cabins. I never found out what happened regarding the accusations, but it goes to show that, just when you think you know someone…you don't.

Then there was that one time in Detroit when I was in that production of *Twelfth Night* with my friend, Brandon, I mentioned before. I was walking to the theatre, and a guy approached me dressed in scrubs. He said that he was a medical student and was in a real jam. He was trying to get to Grand Rapids, and he blew a tire in his Chevy Citation. He needed to see his ailing mother across the state and could I help him out. He tried to assure me that this wasn't a scam and that he was in a dire situation. I felt bad for the guy. I didn't have much money at all back then. In fact, there was a running joke during the production of *Twelfth Night* of who could get to the bank first to cash their check because the theatre was broke, and the producer was always trying to find a corporation or a benefactor who could donate enough money that week to cover expenses…and there was never enough to pay everybody and keep the lights on. I reached in my pocket and counted…$43. That's all the money I had for two weeks. Rent was covered and we had boxes of mac n' cheese and ramen, so I gave him $25 figuring $18 would see me through until next payday. (Young, dumb, and broke.)

The next week I was walking to the theatre and the same guy in the same scrubs approached me with the exact same story. I felt naive and foolish. I was gullable and believed his sob story. I interrupted his spiel and said, "Man, you have the shittiest luck with tires."

"Beg your pardon?"

"You told me this exact same story last week."

And he hustled away. The fact that he played dress up to look the part angered me as I walked into the theatre. Of course, Brandon was in the dressing room and was quick to give me his take after I told him what happened.

"Would you have given him any money if he was obviously homeless?"

"I'd like to think so. Help him out a little bit."

"But not twenty five dollars."

"Hell no. But he lied."

"He was hustling. Trying to make as much as he could in as short amount a time as possible. I imagine he went the old route and just asked people and got tired of getting nickels and dimes. Or flat out ignored or rejected."

"Yeah, but he lied."

"We all lie, brother."

All of those old stories raced through my mind as I approached a red light in town. I glanced over to my right and in the other lane was a nicely well-dressed, older gentleman sitting in a very nice car. He had to be in his late seventies, but he had a full head of white hair, which was mullet-esque. His car had a beige leather interior which I thought bounced off his charcoal grey exterior rather nicely. I think I took all of this in so quickly because I was a little surprised that there would be someone in Greenville with "Fuck You" money. (That was Sophie's phrase for the uber rich in LA.)

I usually turn back towards the road because either I don't want to make eye contact when I do look into another car, or I don't want to be sitting at a green light and make people behind me wait. But I kept staring at the old guy and wouldn't you know it, he put his right thumb up to his right nostril and picked inside the front part of his nose hole. He then, as God as my witness, placed that same thumb in his mouth. I quickly turned away, refusing to believe what I just saw, (The light was still red) but I couldn't resist and looked at him once more. And sure as shit, the old dude put that same thumb back into the same right nostril and, yes, then proceeded to put it in his mouth again. I almost threw up. I don't know why. It was too much of a juxtaposition for me. I guess I make too many assumptions in life, and I made the assumption that this guy was all class. And then to see him eat some salty snot or boogs at his age and presumed wealth was just too much.

But what does that say about me? I bet I'd be the one to give an accused murderer the benefit of the doubt if she wound up being a successful super model or hall of fame athlete. That's terrible. People get to behave how they want to, as long as they're not hurting someone else. And it wasn't the first time I've seen some weird happenings through another person's car window—I saw a twenty-some snort a line of coke off the dashboard while stuck in traffic in LA; I've seen a head come up from a guy's crotch like you might see in an old, bad eighties comedy, and I've actually seen a woman driving AND breast feeding her baby. (Our eyes actually met, and she looked at me like I was a disgusting pervert. Excuse me, Lady, you're breastfeeding your infant while driving!!!) This may serve as a reminder for everyone that just because you're trapped in your car at a red light in Greenville or rush hour on the 405, you're not alone. The outside world can see you. Those aren't walls you're sitting behind. They're actually fairly large windows. But it also serves as a reminder to me to not prejudge strangers. I assume I know what they're all about, how they'll behave, how much money they have, and quite frankly, I have no idea.

21

Remember That One Time?

My favorite memory…

It was a Saturday. I was napping on the couch. I was alone at the house. Sophie was away on location in Santa Fe producing a new cooking show. It was a concept show where contestants had to hang out in the back of restaurants at night, waiting to see what the cooks were throwing out. The contestants would gather up that food and then had to reimagine the "leftovers" and create a new dish.

Graeme was at a seventh-grade camp at Joshua Tree for the weekend, and Bree had a sleepover with a friend at Disneyland.

I had fallen asleep watching college football early in the afternoon. I had just wrapped a guest spot the night before that went really well. It was a pilot starring Cedric the Entertainer. He was terrific. I had hoped that pilot got the green light and got picked up, not just because I wanted the opportunity to maybe film another episode, but also because it was really funny. It was a multi-camera comedy with a live studio audience at a time when studios weren't producing many of those because they thought they had become passé. Single camera comedies were the trend, but the cast of this one was terrific, the script was hilarious, and I thought it had a real shot.

Anyway, the kids weren't getting back until Sunday, and Sophie was to be gone for another week. So, I figured I'd take the day and basically do nothing except watch football and have a few beers.

Something tickled my lips. That's what stirred me from my nap. And then it happened again, and my eyes slowly opened from my sleep.

A blurred image hovered in front of me as my eyes tried to focus. It was Sophie's smiling face, and she leaned down again and gave me another kiss.

I was frozen or paralyzed or…I don't know what. I just know I didn't want that moment to ever end. All I could manage was a smile. But it was a big ass smile.

She kissed me once more and gently grabbed my cheeks with both her hands.

"Remember that one time you loved me? That was right now," she whispered ever so gently with her face so close to mine.

Please, God, let this last forever.

"I kissed you nine times. You must have been sleeping hard."

"Why aren't you in Santa Fe?"

"Two of the contestants got into a huge fight on the kitchen set, and they shut down production."

"Wow."

"Yeah, like a fight fight. There was blood. Probably assault charges and lawsuits."

I tried to say "whoa," but it wasn't so much a "whoa" as much as I just blew air out of my mouth. Sophie chuckled, "You smell like beer."

"I started a little early."

"Looks like I better catch up." And she took a swig from my bottle and lay on top of me and kissed me again. She then spread out her arms and legs and put her full weight on me.

"I'm a rock." She said. I had played "Rock" with the kids when they grew up, and they hated it. I also called it "Warm Blanket"…any reason to squish them with my body weight and have them laugh and beg me to get off of them.

"How are you not grimacing in pain?" She asked. Sophie thought she was heavy. I never thought that. In truth, she wasn't.

"Sophie, you are the most beautiful woman I've ever laid eyes on." She always gave me the smallest smiles of gratitude and this was no exception. I think she thought I was being polite. I don't think she ever believed me. So, I would always follow it up with a "I'm dead serious. I don't think any woman I've ever run into is as beautiful as you are." And I meant it. I've always meant it. I guess because I've worked with very attractive actors and models, that somehow, she thought that I was only being nice or kind or trying to say the "right" thing. But it was the right thing, because it was the god's honest truth.

She kissed me again, this time sticking her tongue in my mouth. "Now I taste like beer too."

I was helpless in that moment. I remember it so clearly. I just wanted to keep looking at her. Again…and again…her eyes. Those big brown eyes…shit.

That's my favorite memory. I guess that would have been eight or nine years ago. What a fantastic day that was.

Maybe the birth of my kids should be my favorite memory, but Graeme's birth was just stress. Period. That's all I remember. And I spent Bree's birth managing my mom. My mom begged me to be in the delivery room with Sophie and me.

"Please, honey, I've never been to a live birth before."

"What do you mean, mom? You were there for Nate's and mine, weren't you?"

"Oh, you smartie…you know what I mean."

"No, I really don't. If you want, you can take my spot." To which, Sophie gave me a nasty look.

I made a deal with my mom that she could be in there with us, but she had to run the camcorder. That was a big mistake. I don't know how many times I had to show my mom how to record…I still think she was just trying to get out of doing it.

Anyway, when it came time for Bree to come out, my mom sprung into action. She started recording. Apparently, she had one of her eyes looking into the viewfinder and one of her eyes looking at Sophie, and it was messing with her vision. My mom couldn't tell what was going on. When we watched the video later, my mom has this very clear shot of Sophie's vagina, but when Bree's head started to show, the camera tilts down and records the tiled floor, and you can hear my mom exclaim, "Oh my Lord, would you look at that!" My mom wanted a better look and simply let her arm fall, which made the camera tilt and record the ground.

22

He Was a Somebody.
He Did Do Something.

"Hey, Asshole!"

I was just about to open the door to head into Jack's Café when I turned to see where the voice was coming from. In the street, stopped, sat an S-10 pickup. The passenger window, which was cracked, was now descending, and I tried to get a better view of the driver. "Yep, It's me!"

The brightness of the winter sun cast a huge shadow inside the small truck, and I couldn't tell who it was, though the voice was oddly familiar. Was it an old high school friend being playful? Perhaps someone else I knew long ago, who thought they could act this familiar with me even though we hadn't seen one another in years.

"How's the cart stealing business, you prick?!"

As I started to put the voice to the memory and recall who it was, a loud honk interrupted my train of thought. There were cars piling up behind the old man in his truck, unable to pass and continue on with their day. Not willing to budge, the old man tried to wave the cars to move around him. I heard a faint voice cry out from two cars behind, "We can't! You're in the middle of the street!"

"There's plenty of space!" The old man charged back.

"You're blocking the damn road!"

"Oh, give me a break!" I thought this would be the perfect opportunity to slink inside the diner but for some reason I stayed put. And a new honk blasted from a few vehicles behind the action.

"Move, your ass!"

"Hey, don't blame me!" The old man yelled back. "Blame this, douchebag!" And he went from yelling outside his driver's side window at the stopped cars to pointing at me through his open passenger window.

A big black truck, about four vehicles back in the blockade, quickly pulled out and squeezed past the other stopped cars, who were unwilling to chance it. However, as the driver of the truck tried to slowly maneuver past the old man in his S-10, an oncoming sportscar, if you would call a Ford Probe that, came racing down from the other way. Brakes squealed loudly as the old late-eighties model car came to a stop just inches before hitting the black truck.

"Now look what you've done!" I noticed the old man staring straight at me as he continued and yelled out straight in my direction, "What's your goddamn problem?!"

By this time the driver of the black truck had gotten out of his vehicle. He was a giant, barrel-chested man, who for whatever reason was shirtless—bare chested—on a rather cold December day. I remember my head tilting like an inquisitive dog as I took in the scene. It was difficult to tell where his chest stopped, and his belly started. All of it was enormous. His fat rolls hung over his jeans like the smallest of micro-miniskirts and managed to hide his crotch and derriere. *That's a well lived life of beef, potatoes and beer. Lots and lots of beer. God bless ya.*

At first, the big guy marched towards the Probe, but that driver was already backing up. As the Probe spun around and headed off in the other direction, the huge guy started towards the old man in the S-10. This got the old guy's attention, and I could make out the motion of him throwing his shift lever that was mounted on the steering column into "drive." The giant was clearly looking for a fight, but the old man managed to evade him and drive off. Still, I was able to hear the old man yell out, "Once an asshole, always an asshole!" I knew that was directed at me. In order to leave no doubt, I faintly heard, "My cart!" as his little truck turned right at the next block and disappeared.

The big fella returned to his black truck, and the stopped cars started to move and get on their way. I still stood there, and I could see some of the drivers glare at me and shake their heads. Some made it a point to roll down their passenger side windows, so that I would see their animosity. Me being me, I gave them each a little wave and a smile, and then I walked into Jack's Cafe for a bite to eat.

As I sat in the booth, the same booth I occupied the previous time, I noticed, lo and behold, Sue and Pat were sitting in their exact same seats. I checked my phone, and it turned out that it was around the same time I had sat next to them on the first occasion. I made a mental note of the time in case I was ever in need of some good, local gossip. Well, on this particular day, I was, once again, in for it.

"They found him dead."

"No."

"Yep."

"No!"

"You can keep saying 'no,' Pat, but it's the truth."

As I sat beside the two women, my heart started to pound. The drive with Brian had taken my mind off everything else including the whole fiasco involving Kirk, Janice, and Gary. I don't know if it was Andy's suspicion about the circumstances involved in Gary's disappearance, but to think of him winding up dead still made my head rattle. I mean, I assumed Gary had to get away from that fight with Kirk, and yeah, maybe he felt he couldn't go back to his house, or an urgent care, but maybe he would end up at a bar just to numb the pain. After that, depending on if he was in trouble with the authorities, he would end up at a relative's house or some dive motel on the side of the road…at least that's what I assumed.

And now to hear Sue say, "They found him dead?" Well, I didn't know what to think so I just tried my best to listen in on their conversation.

"It's such a shame, ya know?"

"Oh my, yes."

"From what people say, he changed."

"Well, yeah, he didn't look very good to be honest."

Listening in, I couldn't believe just how "small" this town was. I mean, everyone seemed to know what Gary was going through, and yet for me, there were so many holes in his story.

"He was drinking more and more."

"Well, obviously," said Sue.

"What do you mean?"

"Everyone's saying that's what killed him."

"How would they know?"

"I don't know. How they found him, I guess."

"May I take your order, sir?"

I didn't hear the server's voice at first…Or rather, I was so focused on Pat and Sue's conversation, that I only heard a faint garbled sound. I felt a tap on my shoulder, and when I turned to look, a face appeared only six inches from my own. He slowed down his speech to over enunciate and shout every word.

"May I take your order?"

I looked up, and it was the same pimpled faced, young man from the last time. I whispered, "I'm not deaf."

He looked so confused…his head tilted as he studied me, but he didn't move his face back. He was way too close.

"Sorry, another minute?"

He slowly stepped back and then walked away. I couldn't wait for him to go, so I could get back to Pat and Sue's conversation.

"What's that report called?"

"What report?"

"The report report. You know, the thing where they see if you had drugs or—"

"Toxicology?"

"Toxi…Toxi—"

"Toxicology."

"That's it. Toxilogicly."

"Toxicology."

"Yeah, that. Those take awhile."

"Sure. But like I said, I think it's how they found him."

"And how was that?"

"I don't know. It just happened, right?"

"And that's my point, Sue."

"What's that?"

"People don't know, so they're jumping to conclusions."

"That's what they do when they don't know."

"Well, I think it's wrong."

"How do you think he died?"

"I don't know. Tell you truth, I don't really care—"

"No?"

"I don't. I'm just sad he died."

"Did you know him?"

"No. No, I didn't. But it almost felt like we did, ya know?"

"I guess."

"I mean, we all rooted for him throughout the years."

"I suppose."

"And then with what happened recently."

"What?"

"You know, Sue, at the park. The Christmas concert."

"The Christmas…"

"Where everyone was laughing at him. Making fun."

"Oh yeah, right. I heard about that."

Wait…

"You don't think that had anything to do with his—"

"People are awful nowadays."

"People have always been awful, Pat."

Wait…

"I know, but with social media—"

"Yeah."

"I heard that people posted video of that night and were just down right cruel in the captions."

"Oh no."

"Yeah. People say or post whatever they want and they hide behind a fake name and a picture of a frog—"

"A frog?"

"I don't know. It's just not them, that's all, so they say whatever they want. And it's evil."

Wait! They aren't talking about Gary. They're talking about Mickey. Mickey's dead?

"Ready to order?"

Damn, had it been a minute already?

"Um…could I just start with a tea, please?"

"What's that?"

My voice was still barely a whisper, and I certainly didn't want to strain it again, so I just pointed to the Lipton logo on the menu.

"You got it."

"Why do people hate others for being successful, Sue?"

"I don't know, Pat."

"Everyone made fun of Mickey for having a hit song."

"Well, I think it's because he ONLY had that one song."

"No, he had that duet with Anne Murray."

"You know what I mean, Pat."

"But still. How many people have even just one hit song, you know?"

"I know."

"People are mean."

"They're just jealous."

"Exactly. But now Mickey's dead."

There was a brief silence, and I wondered if it was quiet so that it could really sink in.

"Let's just say," Pat's voice was now garbled from food in her mouth, so I think they had just taken that time to take a bite. Still, she continued. "Let's just say it was the drink. That the drink killed him. He probably only drank to hide the pain…"

"That's what people say. That he was depressed about his career, about people talkin'…about being a 'somebody' and then a 'nobody'."

"That's just it, Sue. He was a somebody. He did do something. And then, poof…it's not enough for some people?"

"Yeah."

"But it is enough, you know?"

"Sure."

"No, I mean it."

"No, I know. But it is a 'What have you done for me lately' kind of world."

"Yeah."

"It is."

"But, he did do something, Sue."

"I know…A long time ago."

"And then he tried something else, you know, later…with Ann Murray."

"Sure."

"Did you know, that night, the other night, in the park…Did you know he sang a new song?"

"I didn't."

"Walter and I were there."

"Oh."

"And people just…left. They walked off. It was actually a really beautiful song."

"I bet."

"Sort of…Simple. But pretty."

"Mmm-hmm."

"Still, what have these people done?"

"Who."

"The—the—any of those that walked away. That night."

"I don't know."

"Exactly."

"Yeah."

"I don't know."

"Me neither."

And then the young man brought me my tea and just stood there waiting to take my order. I pointed to the Cobb salad, because, again, I didn't want to speak.

"Dressing?"

I whispered "House."

"Sorry."

"House," a little louder, and I must've made a face, because it hurt my throat.

"Tossed or on the side."

You bastard. "Tossed."

"Sorry."

"Tossed!"

"Okie dokie."

And he finally left.

My dad always told me that deaths, especially celebrities, always happened in threes. I remember back in the '80s Rock Hudson died, and my dad said, "Now watch, there will be two more." And it seemed like the next week both Orson Welles and Yul Brynner passed. "See? Told ya." But it all seemed pretty arbitrary to me. I remember one time James Cagney died…in like, March, and my dad said "Be on the lookout. Two more are coming." And then in late November of that year, Cary Grant and Scatman Crothers both passed, and my dad was like "See? Told ya?" *November? Eight months apart?* But then, in what I thought would really throw a wrench in my dad's theory, Dezi Arnaz passed away early December. When I asked him if that makes four, he covered and said "Nope. Just means two more will be dying here soon." And wouldn't you know it, my dad was waiting for me when I got home from school one day and he asked, "Did you hear?"

"No, what?"

"Otto Preminger died."

I didn't know who that was back then but would learn of him later in college.

"Oh."

"One more."

And just before the year ended, he tracked me down right after Christmas and said, "Sad news." He said it with a big smile though.

"What?"

"Elsa Lanchester died."

"Who?"

"C'mon. Elsa Lanchester. *Bride of Frankenstein*? *Witness for the Prosecution*? She was amazing."

I was, like, ten at the time. So no, that one didn't count for me. But my dad couldn't lose. So, he bent the rules to fit the game, so that he could always win.

I sat there and thought about Mickey. I recalled a time when I was working and had a modicum of celebrity in the area. I had come back to participate in a fundraiser that my sister-in-law had put together for the local hospital. It was like karaoke but with a live band. They pulled in some local big wigs like the mayor and the owner of the Buick dealership in town, and we sang our favorite tunes in hopes of raising some money for play areas in a newly renovated children's wing. I remember the dealership owner being drunk as a skunk singing "Taking Care of Business." I forget what the mayor sang but it was Rat-packy...probably "My Way" or "Fly me to the Moon," something like that. I got with the band and rehearsed a mash up, which was alot of fun. We started with the Doobie Brothers' "Long Train Running," and right in the middle of it, we cut to Heavy D and The Boys' "Now That We Found Love." The two songs blended nicely together and it turned out great. Even the older folks got a charge out of it.

And then there was Mickey. If I remember right, I think the mayor originally wanted to sing Mickey's hit song, but Mickey wouldn't have it. He was extremely protective and always worried people would purposefully sing it "wrong" as a way to make fun of it...I guess, kind of like that bearded singer at the Fat Cat. The mayor surely would have been respectful, but even if the mayor gave it his best shot but sang out of key, Mickey (or so I had heard) would worry that people would laugh, and the song would become a mockery. So...Mickey agreed to sing it. And as a bonus, since that year's Ms. Michigan was from the area, and her special talent was singing, Mickey agreed to do the Anne Murray duet as a second song. From what the band told me when I rehearsed with them, Mickey was a bonafide diva—a big ole prima-donna that got angry at the base and drums for going too fast and kept correcting the piano for dragging. They told me they wound up rehearsing with Mickey for five and a half hours. As a comparison, I rehearsed with the band for forty minutes, and we were messing with the music a little bit. The audience was polite with Mickey, but even back then, you could tell they were tiring of him. It was the same one or two songs whenever he made an appearance. And he was very demanding. He had to perform last, like he was the headliner. And he also made sort of a big deal upon his arrival, which I remember at the fundraiser, took attention away from a children's choir who were singing "Imagine." As he made his entrance, he walked through the crowd mouth kissing the female guests, like Richard Dawson on *Family Feud*. The children's choir got off the beat and started singing over one another because their choir leader got distracted by the reaction in the crowd to Mickey's behavior.

There, in Jack's Café, as I sat there and ate my Cobb salad and drank my tea, I couldn't help but smile with appreciation at Mickey's life. The ups and the downs. The cringey moments. I imagined him smiling when he first had that hit, thrilled. It was a full life. And sitting there, I no longer wanted to listen to Pat and Sue; I just wanted to think about Mickey and imagine that full, yet somewhat complicated, existence he must have had being a local celebrity in the middle of nowhere.

My phone buzzed, and it pulled me out of my thoughts.

I miss you dad

Wow, it was Graeme. I can't remember the last time I got a text from him like that. Honestly, I don't know if I ever got a text from Graeme like that.

I miss you too, son. Everything okay?

We do that as parents, don't we? Something seems out of the blue, and we worry something's wrong instead of our kids simply expressing their love.

Oh yeah all good. Making you a playlist

Oh, cool. Another playlist. I hope that's not read as sarcastic. I genuinely enjoyed Bree's playlist. I'm sure I wouldn't know the songs Graeme would send me either, but that's what made me look forward to them...something to expand my musical horizons, and more importantly…something from my kids.

Send me one

I texted back: *One what?*

Duh make me a playlist

Graeme knew my musical tastes. It's mostly classic rock. I mean, I like all sorts of music…country, blues, hip hop, even pop. Hell, I secretly love filthy ass rap songs like that "My Neck, My Back" tune. Love it. Missy Elliot too. She and Biggie could always get away with it. People seemed to love whatever they put out. Dirtier the better. "Want That Old Thing Back" by Biggie and Ralph Tresvant is so damn good.

It'll prolly be classic rock.

Cool

That's a pretty broad genre.

Dad

Yeah?

Don't overthink it

I tried not to. This was a big deal. My son wanted some music recommendations…from me. This was an absolute first.

Okay…just one question? What kind of mood are you in? I mean, I could send some real bangers of rock or I could send you some nice peaceful jams.

Dad

Yeah?

Just send me something you like and why you like it

Got it. Love you!

You too

I put my phone down. *Oh, wow, what do I send?* You can't go wrong with rock. You can play it for all occasions. I had this screenplay… another one I wrote during my gaps in acting gigs. It was actually based on true events that surrounded one of my uncles, who was a black sheep type. And it was another script with a Shakespearean spin; this time… *MacBeth*. It was set in the early 80s, in the rural north during winter. It all revolved around a snowmobile club. The idea of a no-name snowmobile club that the rest of the country could care less about, going to war with one another in an attempt to run and control things, really piqued my interest…and the fact that it was all pretty much true was fascinating to me.

My agent disagreed. He said it was too specific and nobody would buy it. I still love the idea. It feels kind of Coen Brothers-esque.

And I had some great jams in the script for inspiration. During the opening snowmobile montage I had, of course, "The Boys are Back in Town" by Thin Lizzy. King Harvest's "Dancing in the Moonlight" was used in another montage. I set the witches as strippers at a local topless club outside of town. For their scenes I had "One of These Nights" and "Black Magic Woman," as they seduced the lead character. During an intimate scene between the MacBeth character and Lady MacBeth, I had in mind "So Into You" (That's a damn sexy song) by Atlantic Rhythm Section. And then I had written a bunch of fight and chase scenes with songs like "War Pigs," "Good Times Bad Times," "Strange Brew," and "Run to the Hills." In my mind, the credits had to be "Midnight Rider" by the Allman Brothers.

But those were all specific to that script. I started throwing together some music in my app…

"Still The One" by Orleans

"Let Your Love Flow" by Bellamy Brothers

"End Of The Line" by Traveling Wilburys

"Spirit in the Sky" by Norman Greenbaum

"Joy to the World" by Three Dog Night

But then I stopped. I was compiling these because I thought they'd put Graeme in a good mood…but they weren't necessarily my all-time faves. He wanted me to express myself, so I gave it some thought and started creating a whole new playlist, then shared what I had created.

"You Make Loving fun" by Fleetwood Mac

"Southern Cross" by Crosby Stills and Nash

"Down the Line" by Gerry Rafferty

"Into the Mystic" by Van Morrison

"Night Moves" by Bob Seger

"American Girl" by Tom Petty and The Heartbreakers

"We Just disagree" by Dave Mason

"Purple Rain" by Prince and the Revolution

"These Days" by Jackson Brown

"Wish You Were Here" by Pink Floyd

Then I started working on why I really liked those particular songs. The truth is each one of those songs has a killer line or two that has stuck with me throughout my life. Instead of telling Graeme the lyrics in each piece, I texted…

When you give it a listen, let me know if you can spot my favorite lines from each one. They all have some gut punches in them. Good and bad.

I hit "send" and sat there staring into space, no longer hungry. I couldn't hear Pat and Sue, so I assumed they had left, and I hadn't even noticed. I kept thinking of Mickey. The stoics call it "Memento Mori"… "Remember you must die." I had a friend who thought it was morbid, but I've learned it's anything but. We have a shelf life. Yes, we will die… so we should live. Really live. I sat there with such mixed feelings. I was feeling a little fragile at the thought of Mickey's passing. But I also felt alive, excitedly alive, after Graeme reached out to me. I couldn't wait to hear back from him with the playlist he promised. I so wanted to dive into it and hear music that was new to my ears. I wanted to hold Sophie and apologize, or maybe not even waste time apologizing…just hold her and not let her go. To feel her embrace and for that to be enough. I kept waiting for her to tell me why she wanted the separation, and instead I should have been communicating with her about all the things I was feeling. I should have already told her so much…but it lay deep within me in such a cavernous sleep, wrestled awake only now by the inspiration of Graeme's texts mixed with the vulnerability of Mickey's death.

I was looking for something more from Sophie because I lacked something in myself. Maybe I demanded that she be my foundation. But the truth is, I needed to build my own foundation…for me. We all do. And if I had built that for myself, then she could just be who she was… Is. Which is more than enough…it's plenty. I wanted to tell her all these things, and yet, I also wanted to stop analyzing the whole marriage and just…be. Just be with her. Just be together.

My phone buzzed again. It was Graeme.

is there a good gut punch

Oh yeah there is, I thought to myself but didn't text. Then I closed my eyes and started to hear those favorite lines of mine in each of those songs. It didn't take long for that warm, excited inspiration I was feeling to turn into a small state of panic. My eyes opened brightly as I started to overthink. My anxiety started to override my brain and alert it that Graeme would read into those songs and lyrics and think that I was being manipulative about Sophie's and my separation. That I was trying to get him on my side. That I was pressuring him to choose. I know, it sounds crazy. I know. I've done that so many times in my life. I jump three steps ahead of any situation trying to figure out if something I've said or done might get me in trouble, especially after experiencing a safe, warm feeling—like waiting for the other shoe to drop. I think it's just what I learned to do as a kid, as a way of protecting myself, and I've never been able to stop doing it.

In a bit of a frenzy, I quickly texted Graeme.

I don't ever want to burden you or Bree with this separation stuff. That was never my intention sending you those lyrics to mean something coded about your mother and me.

I sat there...anguish started marching up my spine.

My phone hummed.

What? I haven't even listened to the playlist I have no idea what you're talking about

I felt like an idiot. In my dire need to convince him that I didn't want to burden him, I actually wound up burdening him with my made-up dread and angst.

Once again, my phone vibrated...

Also, dad? I know you wouldn't do that. And you're not a burden. Love you.

Relieved, I typed...*I love you too.*

How'd you like that punctuation? Graeme replied and sent a"wink" emoji.

And I sent back...*wow that was pretty darn good way to go so proud of you*

My brother, Nate, once told me that it's inevitable...we give our kids a load of bricks to carry when they set off on their own. Depending on how we parent, it might be a small sack or an enormous one...but we will give them something—stress, trauma, damage—that they will have to take with them and figure out. I fear I gave them unnecessary worry of things that weren't real but imagined, and as I sat there shaking my head, I knew it was time. It was time to change those entrenched habits. To end the self-sabotage and...just live life a little bit.

"How about that ride along?"

I looked up and there was Andy, standing next to my table inside Jack's Cafe.

"Oh," or a sound similar to that came softly out of my mouth. Truth is I wanted to get back and reach out to Sophie, although I wasn't sure she would be around to talk in the middle of the day. And quite frankly, I wasn't sure how much of a voice I would have if I got the chance to tell her everything I was feeling.

"C'mon. It'll be fun."

I whispered, "I, uh, just have to pay."

"Already took care of it."

I muttered a thank you, but I don't think he heard me. Hopefully my nod of appreciation was enough. Truth is I was trying to put off the ride along until I was heading back to California, and then I could tell Andy that I ran out of time and couldn't do it this trip. It's not that I didn't want to do a ride-along...no, the more I had thought about it, it's that I didn't want to do a ride-along with Andy. Not much had changed with him, I realized. He was an okay guy. He just overshared and wouldn't shut up. Plus, he was set in his ways, he was arrogant, but he was always arrogant...and having a badge and being the big boss man around these parts didn't help.

23

You Never Get Used to That Sort of Thing

As we settled into his patrol vehicle, Andy said, "Make yourself at home, big guy." I always wondered why people called me big guy. Yes, I was overweight. By government standards, one could even make an argument that I was obese. At 5'9" I think my weight should be around 180 pounds. And I was a little under 210. So, yeah, thirty pounds overweight. But "big guy?" It's not like I was 6'4", 300. Now that to me would warrant a "big guy." Maybe I'm too sensitive about it.

He pulled out of the parking lot and off we went.

"Man, I do not know what is going on around here. I mean, it's usually slow. Maybe a break in here or there or a domestic dispute, even some meth busts…but nothing deadly."

I gave him an inquisitive look.

"I've had two calls for DOAs these past couple of days."

Two? Oh, God, did Gary turn up?

"Two?" My voice was soft but healing and coming back.

"Well, I assume you heard about Mickey…"

"Yeah."

"Yeah. Poor guy. Drank himself to death."

Oh, so that was true? "How do you know?"

"Awful, really. Nobody had heard from him since around the time of that Christmas concert, you know?"

No, I didn't.

"Well, it appears he drank himself to death, because his neighbor called—he had been living in a senior apartment sort of situation—and well, a neighbor called complaining about a smell."

I grimaced.

"Yeah...I know. I can tell you, you never get used to that sort of thing. Anyway...there were bottles of booze around his body. One was still in his lap in the chair where we found him."

I was disgusted. Not just at the thought that Mickey had died alone, but I couldn't help but think that he DID hear the audience that night making fun and ridiculing his hit song...ridiculing him. He DID hear it, and it sent him over the edge. That was the final straw, I thought. So many straws. So many times, hearing offhanded remarks. I felt miserable, sitting there, riding along with Andy. *Why do people have to be assholes?*

"And then..." Andy continued.

Oh right, there were two dead people. That snapped me out of my melancholy trance.

"And then we found a guy off the side of the road yesterday. Hit and run."

"Really." My heart started beating faster, and I wasn't sure why.

"Yeah. He went flying. He landed in a corn field."

I didn't need to know that.

"That's terrible."

Oh, my heart. I had to ask but didn't want to...but I had to...but really, really didn't want to...

"Was he black?" I finally asked.

Yeah, how'd you know?"

Oh, God.

I couldn't believe it.

"You okay?"

Oh, God.

I stared out my window.

"Hey, Max. How'd you know?"

"I didn't. I took a guess."

"Oh."

"Hoped I was wrong."

"Weird guess."

Should I go into it with Andy? "Did you catch who did it?"

"Uh, no. Doubt we ever will."

Bullshit. "Wait—what?"

"It happened in the middle of nowhere, Max."

"Yeah, but—"

"Max, how the hell are we supposed to know who did it?"

"Well…"

"I mean, it's not like it happened in town. There are no cameras or shit like that. Hell, there's not even a house for a quarter mile from where he was hit."

"Maybe they saw something."

"Quarter mile away? They weren't even home."

"Did you ask?"

"Of course, we asked. I mean, we tried. Nobody was there. Probably still on vacation."

"But maybe they were there when it happened and then left."

"Relax, man."

"No. I mean, maybe they saw something."

"Max…"

"You have to go back, Andy."

"Dude—"

"No! Don't fuckin' 'dude' me."

"Whoa!"

"A guy is dead, Andy. I mean…fuck."

"I know, Max. I was there. Chill, man."

"I knew him, Andy. I knew him. Brian. That's his name."

"Is it?"

"I picked him up—I don't know—yesterday, I think. I drove him into—Wait. What do you mean 'is it'? You haven't ID'ed the body?"

"No, there was nothing on him."

"That's bullshit, Andy!"

My throat started to hurt again.

"Dude—Seriously, chill."

"Brian pulled out his wallet when I dropped him off. Offered to pay for gas." My throat started hurting again.

"Then maybe it's not your friend, Brian."

"How many black guys are around here?"

"I don't know. That sounds kind of racist."

"What? Racist? What?!"

"I'm just saying, Max. Maybe it's someone else."

"Well, let's go identify him. I can tell if it's—"

And that's when Andy's radio crackled loudly. I could only hear gibberish and numbers and codes that I didn't understand.

"Okay, here we go."

And Andy forced a hard U-turn and began driving faster, as he responded in code back to dispatch.

"What's going on?" I asked.

"Some sort of fight or dispute just outside town."

Andy's phone buzzed inside one of his pockets, and he shimmied around and dug it out. He looked at it.

"Oh shit."

"What?"

"It's Gary."

Oh, wow.

"And Mitch…McCoy." And Andy stepped his foot harder on the gas.

Whoa, that's weird.

"Wait…" I couldn't help but ask, "What about Brian?"

"Max!" Andy was now agitated. "If it is your friend, he's not going anywhere."

I hated Andy for saying it like that.

We drove in silence, and I sat there wishing I was anywhere else but there. I wanted to be somewhere where I could call Sophie and use what voice I had to tell her I'm sorry. I didn't want to just say I'm sorry so that we could get back together. I wanted the "I'm sorry" to spark a deeper discussion…one in which we would both express what we were feeling about ourselves and each other. I wanted her to know what she already knew…that I had been feeling insecure for a long time now. I had thought work would lead to more work. "Work begats work," my agent would say when he wanted me to do a guest spot on a kid's show. "You never know who might be there watching you and remember you for something else." In my experience, you work that one day, and that's it. But, he's right in some ways, because you just never know. But I had started feeling sorry for myself, and I stopped putting myself out there. I resented that getting work wasn't getting easier, and in fact, as I got older, it seemed to be getting harder. I started to judge the auditions that were coming in. Did I half ass the small ones? Was I too desperate auditioning for series regular roles and pushed too hard?

All of this put pressure on my marriage. When I wasn't working, I couldn't wait for Sophie to get home, so that we could be together and do something. But she was tired…I've said that before, I know. But as I sat there with Andy, I had clarity. It's as if these clouds of excuses and pain and fear were all moving east or west, but in some direction, and they were flying by. And in my head, it was brighter. The sun was shining, and I so desperately wanted Sophie to see this side of me. I wanted to tell her "You be you." That's it in a nutshell. You want to work? Work. You want to sleep? Sleep. Have something trivial on TV while you prep for the work you have the next day. Make the countless number of phone calls you need to make. I remember her asking me "We're in the same room right now. Isn't that enough, Max?" And I told her "No. I want more. I want more of you." But I remember when I first laid eyes on her. We were in the same room…and it was enough…It was more than enough. She was working then, but still had time to talk. She was working now, but still had time to talk. She never changed. I changed. Or maybe she changed as well, and I just didn't adapt.

When I proposed to her, she told me that she sort of anticipated that we would just be partners. She thought our career paths were so sporadic and unreliable. I remember she said "Yes," but it was hesitant, it was a hesitant "yes." Maybe because she was pregnant with Graeme. Or did she know? Did she know that she would just keep working…going from one job to another, but I would have countless days of "down time" and knew I would be the type to fall apart?

Then we had the kids, and it was easy to pour my attention into them. Hell, I loved it. So, when I wasn't working, I'd just spend my time raising them. I was their dad. It was my favorite role ever. But then they grew up and needed me less. My influence waned as they spent more time away from home than in it.

I became…what's the best word here…

Lonely.

I was lonely. Sophie worked, the kids were getting older, and my friends had moved away. I was lonely. I just wanted to tell Sophie that. I was lonely, and I relied on her to remedy it. I didn't put pressure on the kids. I didn't put pressure on my friends or my agent. Only Sophie…and it became too much for her to bear.

Suddenly images of Mickey and Brian and Mitch and Michelle and all these people around this town raced through my mind. I saw Pat and Sue. Did it ease their loneliness by being inseparable? I overheard them talk about so many people around town but only once heard a word about one of their husbands. And yet, I remember seeing wedding rings on both of them. You're married for what I assumed was a good deal of time, and the times I overheard you talk, nothing—absolutely nothing about your husbands…other than "Walter was there with me that night."

Kirk and Janice. They seemed like they were so into one another that first night I saw them at dinner with Gary and Michelle. They were constantly touching and grabbing and leaning into one another when they laughed. And yet both were accused of cheating on one another. Was it all performative?

Mitch and Crystal. Crystal and Brian. Three lonely people that found some sort of connection to ease that pain inside. Crystal seemed at ease with Mitch until Mitch crossed the line, as though they had some unspoken agreement about just what their relationship was…and Mitch seemed to violate that contract. Brian didn't seem to violate anything. He was out for a good time, as was Crystal. So, I guess they were cool. Would Brian be cool if he knew about Mitch? Did he know about Mitch. Maybe Brian had someone else beside Crystal. So, again, maybe they…were cool. Or maybe they weren't. I have no idea really.

Our loneliness is like a pool of water that keeps filling up and it will either overflow and become unbearable or it finds an outlet and the water level drops. Some of these folks seemed to have found their outlet…or maybe I just thought that, and for the others, the water level just became too high.

For me, that was Gary. He couldn't find an outlet. Maybe Mitch couldn't either. And now we were on our way towards them…towards the water overflowing. Why Gary…and Mitch? That made no sense to me. Gary and Kirk, sure. I couldn't wrap my head around it.

"We're here. You stay put!" Andy giving me an order like that was a sure-fire way of me getting out of the vehicle…But I waited for him to leave first.

When we arrived, I could see a fenced in area which enclosed a bunch of parked cars ranging from fender benders to being completely mangled and totaled. But then I heard yelling, and saw Andy give pursuit. That's when I hopped out of the car to get a closer look. I kept hearing Mitch's and Gary's voices but couldn't see where they were through all the parked vehicles. I kept moving to get a better look, and then they appeared. The fence was like a cage, and peripherally, I could see Andy, walking outside the perimeter, searching for a way in, while there in the near distance, were Mitch and Gary shoving one another back and forth.

It was like a stupid middle school fight or something out of the NBA where no one really wanted to throw a punch.

"Gary, I said go home. I already called the cops."

"Fuck you, you worthless piece of fuck!"

Gary seemed drunk or desperate. Both states looked the same to me. I heard Andy yell to make his presence felt. But neither man seemed to hear him.

"Gary, I don't want to hurt you."

"Mitch, you're a dumb fuck you know that?"

"Gary...leave!"

The two were squaring off. Mitch looked annoyed more than anything. He had on his security uniform; the one from the bar a few nights ago. I guessed this was the place he watched. I remembered seeing a story on the news when I first got to my brother's about guys hopping the fences at area body shops and stealing catalytic converters and other parts.

Gary seemed to have some sort of bad intention, though I couldn't figure out what it was. Why would he be messing with Mitch?

"Gary, get out of here!"

And I heard Andy again yell at them to stop.

"Everyone thinks you're a fucking fraud, Mitch."

"Gary..."

"Given so much and did so little! You're a fucking failure!"

And I saw Mitch's posture rise, and his chest puffed out...like some sort of animal threatened and contemplating an attack. Gary, for some reason, needed to poke the bear. I saw firsthand guys try to do that with Mitch, and Mitch found a way to remain calm. But even from a distance, his eyes changed. They had a sort of fire in them...right at that moment.

And sure enough, before Andy could get any closer, Mitch launched himself at Gary and tackled him. The two tussled and kept rolling over on top of one another, trying to gain an advantage. Right when it looked like Mitch might actually subdue Gary, that's when I saw it. Gary managed to pull out what looked like some sort of knife, and he jabbed it into Mitch's thigh. Mitch grabbed his thigh, which allowed Gary to start to get out from under him. And that's when Gary stabbed him again, and I saw the blade pierce Mitch's side.

I wanted to scream but couldn't.

Where the hell was Andy? I couldn't get eyes on him.

Gary rolled on top of Mitch and stabbed him with short jabs that I think went into Mitch's left arm. But then somehow, as Gary pulled the knife back to then again plunge into Mitch's body, Mitch grabbed the knife—the blade actually—and squeezed. He squeezed it so hard that Gary couldn't free the blade from Mitch's grasp. That's when I saw blood starting to appear and flow from all around Mitch's fingers, clenched so tightly to the sharp metal. With his free hand, Mitch was then able to grab something from his holster on his right side, and he shoved it into Gary's stomach.

Was that a gun? Oh, God!

Everything was now happening at lightning speed, and my head started to spin. I heard a buzz and saw Gary's body convulse. I now saw Andy, and he drew his weapon.

"Mitch, stop. Don't make me shoot!"

Andy had appeared behind them, just inside the fenced in the area which now seemed like a prison yard.

Mitch was now out from under Gary, and jolted Gary's limp body again with another round from what was now clearly a taser.

I saw Andy raise his weapon and could see from his vantage point that he now had a clear shot.

Oh God, no!

What the fuck?!

What the fuck?!

I could only hear the thoughts screaming in my head, and as Andy's finger went to the trigger of his piece…I yelled out as loudly as I could.

"MITCH!!! STOP!!!"

I don't think I've ever yelled that loud in my life. Not on stage. Not on the field coaching my son. Never.

And Mitch stopped. He turned and looked in my direction which pulled the taser away from Gary's seemingly lifeless body.

I went to speak again, as Mitch and I made eye contact…but absolutely no sound would come out. Mitch must've seen my eyes look towards Andy, because he turned back, just in time to see Andy lower his weapon and holster it. Andy spoke into his walkie and rushed over to Gary and Mitch.

Mitch dropped to ground, trying to hold some of his wounds. Both he and Gary lay there, and soon I would hear sirens approach.

24

A Lie That Would Destroy Lives

What a long night. It seemed like there was endless processing, and because I was now a witness, I had to stay at the station and give a statement. Of course, my voice was completely shot again, so I had to write everything out, which took longer. I learned that both Gary and Mitch would survive. Surely, Andy and the other officers would spend weeks trying to figure out "why," but given everything that I experienced while I was here, I thought I had it pretty much figured out.

In a nutshell, both men were tired of the losses they seemed to take over the course of their lives. For Gary, you would need a bit more information:

As I sat at a desk at the station, I noticed Kirk and Janice walk in. Kirk and Janice. The couple that rubbed my sister-in-law the wrong way? The couple who sat with Gary and Michelle in that booth, which felt like a month ago with all that had happened. The couple who told Andy that Gary had attacked them on Christmas morning, and they retaliated in self-defense. Sitting there at the station was the first time I had seen Janice not look like, well...Janice. The night at the restaurant and even that late afternoon in the back room at Big Boy having a heart to heart with Michelle, Janice looked like an Instagram model. Her face was always perfectly constructed, and there seemed to be a determined effort to get her cleavage to blossom out of her tight fitted tops. But now, her makeup was smeared all over her face from crying, and she was wearing what seemed to be an old crewneck of Kirk's. It was large and unshapely, hanging well past her ass; and she clutched it, like it was some sort of security blanket. Kirk's shoulders were super tense. I thought that maybe he was impersonating a body builder. It was not unlike him to exaggerate his toughness and swagger, but of course, this was neither the time nor place, and I quickly realized he was dealing with something really stressful. Andy pulled them inside a room, and I could see Janice crying through a window. Kirk was pacing. Before the door closed, I saw Kirk violently punch the wall with his hand and let out a loud, angry moan.

If that wasn't peculiar enough, I saw a man, who in many ways resembled Kirk, led into the police station in handcuffs. This happened after Kirk and Janice were in with Andy for some time. The door to Andy's office opened as the dude in handcuffs was led down the hall. To my great surprise, Kirk leapt out of Andy's office and tackled the handcuffed man. Kirk got in several jabs to the back of the man's head before being pulled off of him, and I got a clear picture of Kirk's rage and what he must have done to Gary's face back on Christmas morning. When officers pulled Kirk away from the man, I noticed that both his hands were limp, and I assumed he broke his right hand punching the wall in Andy's office and now broke his left hand punching the back of this man's cranium.

Andy told me later that the handcuffed man was Ray, Kirk's brother, and that Ray was being arrested for sexual assault of a minor. It turns out, as Andy would continue to explain to me, that Janice had made up Gary's affair with the high school student. She made the whole thing up. In fact, it was Gary who walked in on Janice and Ray at school. Janice and Ray had snuck into a custodial closet at the high school, where all three were teachers. Apparently, Janice and Ray, Kirk's brother, had been having an affair over the course of the school year. I remembered Pat and Sue's gossip session where Sue quoted her friend Dottie talking about Kirk suspecting Janice of sleeping with his brother, and Janice pivoted and focused on Kirk's infidelity with Brittany, the young worker at the gym.

In her interview with Andy at the station, Janice swore to him that that particular time in the closet, Janice was calling off the affair with Ray, and that Ray had gotten controlling and demanding and pulled her into him when Gary opened the door. Janice was breaking up with Ray, because she found the picture of the naked high school student on Ray's phone. Janice had promised Gary that she was going to tell Kirk, that she had been miserable and ashamed, and that she was hoping Kirk would forgive her...She just wanted to tell him herself. So, when Gary threatened to tell Kirk, Janice panicked and told Michelle that it was Gary who was having the affair with the high school student. And, I imagined, she had told Kirk that same lie as well. For what it's worth, Andy added that, given all the lies, Kirk didn't remotely buy Janice's story—that she was breaking up with Ray in that moment when Gary walked in on her and his brother in the janitor's closet.

"She's bullshitting."

"I'm not."

"More lies."

"No."

"Goddammit, stop! You just got caught is all."

Those were the words that Andy later told me as he reenacted what was said in that room at the station. He also added that Kirk was going to file for divorce and seek full custody of the kids.

Again, that, in a nutshell, was what Andy told me. I have no idea what was actually said. Andy was one to add flair and hyperbole to make himself come across as a great storyteller, but I believed all of the essentials. It made sense to me, and I had no reason to doubt him. I don't think it was his place to tell me these things. I just think Andy enjoyed being in the know and having the power to do and say what he wanted. But when he told me this, an image of Michelle popped into my mind, and I saw Janice and Michelle sitting in that Big Boy, however many days ago. I recalled that moment when Janice told Michelle that Gary had been having an affair with the student and the visual that stuck with me was when she gave Michelle a sympathetic smile. That smile, it occurred to me, wasn't sympathetic at all, but rather diabolical. It was a smile of getting away with a lie. A lie that would destroy lives.

I surmised that Michelle didn't need a whole lot of convincing because Gary was unhappy in their marriage. Both felt isolated and ignored, I imagined. Maybe Gary was waiting for Michelle to initiate intimacy with him, and when that didn't happen, he turned to watching the porn on his phone—Michelle had brought that up at the restaurant in front of Kirk and Janice...embarrassing him. He resented her for not wanting him in the way he wanted her to want him.

He resented her for not wanting him in the way he wanted her to want him. Oh God...Sophie...Oh God.

But maybe Michelle wanted Gary to want and desire her and waited for Gary to come closer, and when he didn't, she resentfully rolled over and pretended to fall asleep...and when she overheard the sounds of sex coming from Gary's phone, perhaps she not only felt unloved, but that Gary was…in her mind…cheating. Perhaps this created a perfect storm… one in which, when thinking of Janice's conversation with Michelle at Big Boy, was set up by Michelle's eagerness to believe a dramatic lie—that Gary was sleeping with someone else, and that someone was a minor—rather than the boring truth that they stopped working at their relationship and simply fell out of love with one another. I don't know.

Damn, Sophie. What have we done?

Once Michelle kicked him out, Gary was lost and lost control, and that turned into a course of action that would get him arrested for attempted murder. And Mitch was never the intended target. Gary was just waiting for an opportunity to explode. I mean, nobody believed him regarding his fidelity…especially his wife.

Janice had ruined someone else's life in an attempt to protect herself. Was she really ever going to tell Kirk about the affair with his brother? According to Andy, Janice only confessed to Kirk once she got wind of the incident at the auto body shop. Perhaps she was always lying and never intended to tell Kirk, let alone end the affair. Not that Kirk was a hero. Nobody was going to feel sorry for Kirk. Hell, everyone knew, or was convinced, that Kirk was cheating on Janice with Brittany from the gym. Was Janice just retaliating…by doubling down with Ray and making Kirk hurt even more than the pain she felt? *What a mess we make of things.*

In any case, I suppose once Gary was kicked out of his home, he thought it was only a matter of time that the awful, egregious accusations would make their way to the authorities. He would not only be fired from his job, but he would also be facing charges of having sex with a minor… all for something he, in fact, did not do. He lost control and had nothing left to lose especially after confronting Kirk and Janice on Christmas day. To me, Gary spent his time taking too many metaphorical and literal punches and was now looking to deliver some shots of his own.

Mitch told Andy from his hospital room that Gary just sort of snuck up on him, and that he really didn't know Gary all that well and had no idea why he came after him. That's why I think Gary went looking for someone, anyone, to unleash all of his pent-up anger. Gary knew of Janice's affair, but she turned the tables on him and convinced Michelle that Gary was the one who had been cheating. And when he went to confront Janice, Kirk got the better of him and beat him to a bloody pulp. Angry and ashamed, Gary went looking for a fight, and he found Mitch. He would have gone after any man at that moment, and Mitch just happened to be there when Gary became irrational. Or maybe…if he could take down the former football hero, the local legend, the one so many others seemed to want to mess with, then he could get back his manhood, his lost masculinity…the tiniest bit of dignity perhaps. That's what I think was going through Gary's mind, and you won't convince me otherwise.

And as for Mitch? Mitch was doing his best to ignore his disappointments…to blur and bury the past. He tried to bury it with the drink and the drugs, but he couldn't push them far enough down, and his regrets stayed close to the surface. Mitch thought he had failed in life. But…he found a way to live with it. It's when Gary reminded him of his worst fear…that everyone else thought he indeed was a failure… that constant repetitive droning he continued to hear from so many other people, that Mitch finally broke, was triggered, and he unleashed his bubbling rage on Gary. Perhaps too, Mitch was sick of being the target of all the empty, dark souls looking to challenge him and fulfill some fleeting expectation of their false masculinity they never lived up to… guys like Gary or the little drunk cowboy, and whomever else. I don't think Mitch would have stopped tasing Gary. I think he would have killed him. And…I think Mitch would have never forgiven himself for that.

That's why I screamed. Mitch wasn't a bad dude. He was a good guy, who simply had a story. I wish he could have owned all the events of his life—the good and the bad—and toasted himself. Hell, he lived out some adventures, but he could never get beyond the expectations others had of him. That immediately struck a nerve inside of me. I had been driven over the last several years by self-pity. I wanted to work more but didn't. I wanted the kids to want to be with me, but they were growing up. I wanted Sophie to want me. But yet, I had lived and experienced, just like Mitch…just like Mickey. And here I was admiring these two for having the bravery to risk—risk winning AND losing. I didn't think any less of them. Hell, I thought more of them. So, why wasn't I willing to give myself that same sort of grace? I think those answers tried to emerge when I went up north on Christmas Day. And I knew right at that moment, thinking about Mitch and all the others, that I had some work to do on myself. I had to learn to give myself a break.

Oh God, Soph.

And Andy? Well, Andy had a mess to clean up, and I think it thrilled him. He was in charge, and he loved it. His first order of business was to yell at me. "What the hell do you think you were doing?! I told you to keep your ass in the car! You could've gotten killed, Max! This is the real world…not some actor's bullshit! You're not a real cop, asshole!"

He just kept yelling, and there wasn't anything I could do about it, because, of course, I couldn't talk. Of course, after his tirade he asked…

"Well?"

And I couldn't respond.

You don't have anything to say for yourself?"

I pointed at my throat for what felt like the hundredth time, and he finally said, "What? Are you not able to speak?"

I just sat there, shaking my head. All my assumptions about my high school friend were true…Andy was so self-obsessed, he simply lacked awareness of others. It's just who he was. And in that moment, I finally accepted that. Right then, my disdain for Andy diminished. Those years of pent-up agitation and resentment seemed to fade away. Suddenly there was no anger, but there was also no pity. There…was…well, nothing.

"I need to make a quick stop. You don't mind do you?"

I did mind. I just wanted to get back to my brother's car.

"I ordered some food from Jack's Café. I'm frickin' starvin'."

Andy pulled into the parking lot, and I debated on whether or not to just stay put, but I decided to follow him inside…not sure why. While we waited for the host (the one with the interesting lisp) to get Andy's order, I took a peek into the seating area, and I noticed Sue…but not Pat. Sue was sitting across who I assumed was her husband. They looked like they were around the same age and looked comfortable enough with one another. Too comfortable, really, because they both sat in stone cold silence, taking bites of food, looking out into the distance while they chewed, and occasionally looking at their phones. When they did, almost simultaneously, look at their phones, it made me think to look at mine. When I did, I was surprised to see a text from Sophie. I immediately opened my phone to read the message.

Do you have time to talk, Max?

Shit. Shit! Oh, man. There's nothing I wanted to do more than talk to her. I had given her the space she said she needed, so I only occasionally texted. Hell, I didn't even tell her about my voice.

I quickly texted back: *Yesyes. I can'ttalkright now but I want to.* I pressed send and read what I texted. I had texted so fast, so hurriedly, that it came out a garbled mess. I thought about correcting what I texted with a new text, but Andy interrupted my thought.

"Got my order. You ready?" I instinctively started following him back out to the car. "Oops. Didn't think to ask if you wanted anything."

I didn't answer, Andy. Not so much because I literally couldn't, but because I was thinking about Sophie and getting in contact with her…and then Sue and her husband…if it was her husband. It struck me, as I got back into Andy's vehicle, that Sue seemed to have way more fun with Pat. I thought of those times when Sophie and I sat in silence. When times were rough like they had been lately, those were unhealthy, awful silences…like punishing one another. Those were nothing like earlier in our relationship where we could sit in one another's company and simply be content doing what we were doing.

When Andy dropped me back off at my brother's car, he confessed that he was about to shoot. He was looking to stop the scuffle between Gary and Mitch and was looking to take down the aggressor. He never saw Gary stab Mitch, because he was trying to find a way into the yard, and the automobiles masked his vision of the fight. So, he assumed Mitch just lost it and was looking to kill Gary. Andy told me that he almost pulled the trigger with his gun pointing square at Mitch's chest just before my scream. But unbeknownst to me I had positioned myself directly behind Mitch, outside the fence, taking away Andy's clean shot.

As I walked to my brother's Jeep, Andy called out to me.

"Max?"

I turned and looked at him.

"You remember back in high school…I had that Mustang, and you were still riding the bus, because you didn't have—well…and you asked if you could ride to school with me?"

I did remember but couldn't respond, so I just waited for him to continue.

"And I agreed but only if you gave me gas money, because…"

It got quiet for a moment.

"Because I told you your weight was hurting the gas mileage I was getting?"

He paused. I guessed because he was checking to see if I remembered…

"That was a real dick move…"

Was he about to apologize?

It was awkwardly quiet again.

"But kind of funny when you think about it now, huh?"

And he gave out a nervous chuckle. No apology was coming, I thought. And so, I opened the door to my brother's Jeep. "Max?"

Oh, for the love of God what?!

Andy was shaking just a little bit.

"I've never shot anyone before. I don't know what I would've felt, um, gone through, you know, if I would've shot him…Mitch, I mean."

Wow…I think Andy was trying to say, "thank you."

I nodded my head, managed a half smile, and gave him a half-assed wave goodbye. I got in my brother's car and drove off.

25

Do You Think We Could Give It Another Go?

That drive back to my brother's felt like an hour. I couldn't wait to get back to his place and reach out to Sophie. I didn't want to do it while driving. I wanted to be home, at least my brother's home, start a fire, have a glass of wine, and tell my wife all that I had been feeling. Of course, I would have rather called her, so she could hear my voice. That was the plan, but Mitch, Gary, Andy…or rather, life, had other ideas.

When I did get back to the house, I poured out my soul to Sophie. I explained why I couldn't call. I even tried to tell her briefly about Mitch and Gary. I must've come across as a psycho because I just kept sending these long texts en bulk telling her about everything I was going through, and the things I discovered about our relationship, and how high maintenance I had become, and how I burdened her with my pain, and how I didn't let her just simply be herself, and that she didn't need to be anyone else, and that, while it takes two, I was the one who was hurting our marriage.

I looked back at the text thread, and I wondered how she could ever get through it all. I mean, there's only so much room when you text, and for her to read everything that I sent, she would have to scroll and scroll, and scroll some more.

I finally texted…

Sophie…

I'm really sorry.

I felt tears welling up, and it made it a little tough to see. I don't know why I didn't just wipe them away.

You are the same woman I fell in love with 22 years ago. I don't want anyone else. I don't want you to be anyone else. I want you.

The tears built up in my eyes like a dam and began to cascade down my cheeks. I just let them…and I waited. Realizing there was a shit ton for her to read, I drank the rest of my glass of wine and poured another one. I drank that one as well waiting for her to respond.

I couldn't wait any longer and texted again…

Do you think we could give it another go?

And I poured another glass.

Finally, she texted back…

Max

I didn't type anything back. I mean, do I type "yes?" or was she about to send some super long text herself? So, I just waited.

Max

Why did she type Max twice? Yes? I wondered. And waited.

I'm seeing someone.

Fuck.

My phone vibrated again.

I'm heading back to LA. We can talk more there.

Fuck.

Of course she's seeing someone.

I couldn't help but laugh. Even though my stomach lurched, my chest seized, my shoulders tightened, and my neck disappeared.

Life, man.

Fuck.

26

Beware of Thy Guests You Entertain…

I have no idea why, but I wasn't anxious or numb. I had just been metaphorically flayed, and my tissue and organs were completely exposed, and yet I felt…nothing. What I actually thought about, or rather who, was Mitch. He was in the hospital, and I hadn't seen him, and I wanted to. I wanted to see him before I left. Maybe I was repressing everything or needed a distraction. I have no idea. But I grabbed a couple pieces of paper, a pen, and my brother's keys and left.

At the hospital, I approached Mitch's room. It was dark, and he was asleep. I didn't want to wake or bother him, so I jotted down a quick note, folded it, and stealthily placed it on a table near his bed. I looked at him for a few minutes. He seemed at peace. Like maybe he was healing.

So, I left. And drove back to my brother's. It was time to leave Michigan.

My brother and his family were almost home. In between Nate's text messages to me, I booked a flight. Nate had told me to just leave Chad, that the old dog would be fine until they got back. So, I ordered a Lyft, and packed up what little I brought with me. He then added a peculiar question in his text message to me:

What did you do to Richard Bell?

Who?

Mara's boss's uncle.

I again typed, *Who?*

Mara's principal at the school texted her and told her that you were trying to steal from his uncle.

I have no idea what you're talking about.

Apparently, you stole his shopping cart?

Ho. Ly. Shit. I thought that. I didn't text it. I just texted back a laughing emoji, even though I didn't feel much like laughing…or smiling. Then I texted…

Sophie's seeing someone. And I stared at my phone for a minute. My brother would either immediately text back an emotional reaction in order to protect me (Something along the lines of calling Sophie a name that American women, in particular, cannot stand, but the British use all the time), or he wouldn't know how to respond and wouldn't answer my text for a couple of days. The longer I waited for a reply, the more I knew it would be the latter.

I washed up some dishes I had used—primarily wine glasses and coffee mugs, wiped down the counters, and managed some general straightening up.

My phone buzzed, and it was a text from my mom…*Merry Christmas, my baby Max. Sorry it took so long to text back. Your Aunt Rosemary took me to some casino resort. Or resort casino. I don't know what they're called, but it was a lot of fun. Your Aunt Rosemary spoils me. It's nice to be loved out here.*

If you knew my mom, you would know she simply didn't know how to communicate without being passive-aggressive. That text was code, and only Nate and I knew how to decipher it. She was trying to say that her sons don't give her the attention she feels she's entitled to and had to seek it out from someone else. And the time it took for her to text me back was once again punishment for not loving her like she thought her son should love. Meaning, she was waiting to be invited for Christmas, and the invitation didn't come. It didn't matter that I was going through what now seemed inevitably like a divorce. She deserved to be invited for Christmas, even if she turned down the invitation. *It's nice to be loved out here.* Whenever I confronted her about this behavior, she got very defensive, even hurt, and denied it. But yet, she continued to do it. Hence, the text I had just received. She wasn't changing. And if I let it continue to bother me, then I guess I wasn't changing either. I managed a smile as I reread the text and thought of all the memories from my youth that came rushing back on this trip. It was time to give my mom a break and let her be who she is…she had been through enough, and it was time to bury my resentment and frustration…and just love her. Hell, that's really all I want. It's really all any of us want…to be loved. I suddenly heard the frictional sound of tires cutting through impacted snow. My ride was here.

I struggled a bit to drag my roller bag through the snow towards the running car parked behind my brother's truck.

"Max?!" A voice shouted but I barely heard it with the winter wind. Still, I looked up before getting into my ride. It was Evelyn. She was crossing the street and feebly walking towards me. I left my bag by the trunk of the car hire and jogged over to meet her so that she didn't struggle to walk all the way to me. Meeting at the edge of my brother's driveway, her gloved hands grabbed ahold of my bare ones. This affection surprised me, though I didn't resist. Her grip was firm and confident but not blustery like a car salesman.

She didn't speak right away. That seemed her way. She looked deep into my eyes.

"Max, I'm old. I think the most fun you can have at my age is to simply tell the truth. So many people avoid it throughout life. And then some of us realize we don't have a whole lot of time left, and so...you just say it how you see it. You don't lie to save feelings. At least I don't."

Even if I could talk, I wouldn't know how to answer that, so I just kept looking at her. Contrary to our first encounter in which I constantly avoided eye contact with Evelyn, this time I lacked the energy to do so, and so I stared back into her eyes...and listened.

"My husband, Simon, he was a doctor. I don't know if your brother ever told you that."

I don't think Nate knew that actually.

"All his life. A doctor. Worked right up until he died, really. Last part of his doctor life was spent around here locally...at an urgent care. But for a long time, Simon, basically, WAS the doctor up in Reed City. Years ago...when he was younger. Thirty-five years. General practitioner. So, that meant he had all sorts of patients. Everyone in that town came to see my husband. Physicals, the flu, emphysema, broken bones, hunting accidents, gynecology, bunyons, you name it."

I now wondered where she was going with this. I didn't move. I wasn't antsy like before. Any pull to leave the conversation was only felt out of consideration for my driver, who was waiting on me. But *hey, I paid for the ride so...he can wait.*

"Max, there was this one time towards the end of his work up there when Simon...well...how do I put this? He couldn't urinate. Strictures. In his urethra. He went to see a urologist, who asked if he had experienced physical trauma to that area. You know, like, did he get hit there? There was also the possibility of an STD." Evelyn gave a small chuckle at that notion.

It turns out, Max, that stress...stress caused the urethra to constrict. You see, Simon had carried the weight of that entire community on his shoulders. They all came to see HIM. And, of course, they all came to see him with something wrong...something that was ailing them. They came to him worried...and my husband comforted them. They came to him broken...and he fixed them. As best he could. But it came with a cost."

I heard the sound of the driver's window lowering. Still, the only move I made was giving a little smile to assure Evelyn that I was listening.

"Max?" She gripped my hands a little tighter. "I'm a therapist. Was. I was a therapist. Long since retired. Anyway. I'm going to say this... well...because I can.

She paused.

"I find it highly unlikely that taking a log to your throat would make you lose your voice."

She took another moment.

"No doubt you experienced physical trauma. A deep contusion, I imagine. But I feel inclined to let you know that I think—this is just my humble opinion mind you—but I think...you are experiencing a psychogenic voice disorder. A laryngitis, if you will, caused by stress."

Her smile was not one of comfort or kindness. It was a smile that asked, "Okay?"

"Safe travels." And she gave my hands a sort of double shake and let go. She then looked both ways and crossed the road. When she was at the top of her driveway, she looked back and said, "Kind of a lot to lay on you...just maybe something to think about. Be good to yourself, Max." She turned and slowly made her way back to her home. I just stood there watching her, thinking about what she had said.

Hmmm.

Hmmm.

ERRN-ERRN. The faintest beep came from the Lyft, as if the driver was trying to be as polite as possible. I did, after all, need to get to the airport. My luggage was still waiting for me by the Lyft driver's car and when I got closer, I heard the pop of the trunk and it opened up a bit.

I swung my bag into the boot and slammed it shut.

Inside, a tiny, grey-haired man with an obnoxious goatee sat in the driver's seat. "Pancho and Lefty" was playing on the radio. I noticed it was Townes Van Zandt's original, not Willie Nelson's and Merle Haggard's cover. (It's much more melancholy.) The driver gave an obligatory greeting, and I pointed at my throat…once again.

The car headed towards Greenville past woods and fields, and I just sat there silently looking out the window, watching life move past me at 35 miles per hour. It reminded me of when I was a kid, stuck in the back seat, long before cell phones occupied our time, and I would just sit back there and watch the trees and round bales of hay sitting strategically in random fields and imagine being anywhere but there. I thought about what I wrote Mitch…

HEY MITCH, HOPE YOU HEAL UP NICELY. NOT MY BUSINESS, SO FORGIVE ME. BUT I THINK IT MIGHT BE TIME TO GO SEE THAT DAUGHTER OF YOURS. YOU GOT A LOT OF LIFE YET TO LIVE, MY FRIEND. MAX

I focused once again on the woods. A poem rushed at me from somewhere deep. A poem I had written—well, not actually "written"—I never did write it down. More like a structure of words that I kept repeating as a kid, an eleven year old, alone…seemingly always alone at that age, repeating the same thing over and over again, like eleven year olds can do (or at least I did…for countless hours). An eleven year old, who spent hours after school in woods just like these that I was seeing. I could only recall parts of the poem. It was epic when I was a kid, and I committed to memorizing what I had created. But riding in that back seat, I could only recall pieces of it.

I know these woods all too well
With its thick patches of light
And its caves of darkness.
I've dwelled far deep
Asking these trees to keep my secrets.
Asking to hold me in their branches.
Something, something…
Standing there in my loneliness
My emptiness
I became majesty. I morphed into light.

There was a large chunk in the middle, I could not recall. *How the*

hell did it go? Oh well. I do remember parts...of it.
  I know these woods all too well
  As I stumble back towards the house I cannot call it a home
  I look back. Tell me to stay
  Tell me to lie in your leaves
  The end...I remember the end...
  I wish the woods would adopt me.
  Would call me "son."
  Would strip its birch bark and envelope me.
  Bend its poplar arms around my waist and lift me up.
  An eleven year old shouldn't have these thoughts, I thought.
  "Maybe next time I'll be better."
  "What's that now?"

The old man's voice snapped me out of my trance. I noticed both my cheeks were wet. As I wiped them dry, the old man spoke again. "What's that you say...I missed it." I didn't realize that I had aired my pain; I had spoken my thoughts...Well, spoken as much as someone who can't speak...speaks. I can't imagine what he heard had much volume to it...more like an involuntary wheeze in one's throat...or a barely mumbled sigh. I tried to offer a smile, which I hoped conveyed that I didn't feel much like explaining myself, and then I turned to look back out the window.

Maybe next time I'll be better. And I saw Sophie's face...neither smile nor pity nor...anything. *Damn it...*I wiped my cheeks again.

The woods disappeared and now town buildings trudged past my view. As the Lyft entered Greenville, I saw the attractive woman again. The one with the cheekbones and long winter coat. She was walking on the sidewalk. I rolled down my window. I wanted to yell out to her. I still wondered if she would remember me from that quick exchange at the café. But, again and again, I had no voice. Plus, she would probably see it as a cat call, and I didn't want to be that guy.

There was this moment when I lived in Detroit walking down Woodward...I'll never forget it. I had to decide whether or not to make the big move to LA or stay in Detroit. In Detroit I was getting cast fairly regularly in plays and was given the chance to play some terrific roles. Fewer people but also fewer opportunities. What would Los Angeles be like? I had no idea. This voice stopped me.

  "You okay, son?"

It was an older gentleman with a spotty beard, wearing a cap which didn't hold in much of his greying, woolly, shaggy hair. He was leaning up against a stone half-wall which divided the broken sidewalk and a beautifully manicured lawn leading to an old Baptist church. Next to him, sitting on the half-wall, was another gentleman cloaked in an old army jacket. The presumed buddy sat and rocked back and forth with his eyes closed, muttering Bible verses.

"For God shall bring every work into judgment. Whether it be good or whether it be evil."

"Sorry?" I've always had a habit of making people repeat themselves. Sometimes I even know what they said, but I guess my brain needs some time to process it. Maybe it's some sort of stalling technique. It's a bad habit. But in this case, I wasn't sure if the man leaning against the wall was talking to me. Besides, the bible verse kind of got in the way and split my focus.

"I said are you okay?" The man was definitely asking me this question, and as I was about to answer, another bible verse was murmured from the other guy.

"The Lord loveth judgment, and forsaketh not his saints, but the seed of the wicked shall be cut off."

Wow, this guy must be a lot of fun to hang out with. I focused on the army jacket dude. His eyes were closed as he continuously rocked his upper body, squeezing himself with his folded arms. I then realized I hadn't answered the other man's question.

"Oh, yeah…" I was about to give my usual answer that I was fine. But this time I stopped myself and said, "Actually, I'm not sure what to do."

And he replied, "Nobody does. And yet, ya gotta make choice." And he smiled at me. It was such a warm smile, and his piercing eyes held so much kindness. It stopped me cold…in my tracks.

Nobody does. And yet, ya gotta make a choice. The next two words that came into my conscious thought were…*Los Angeles.*

I nodded and walked past him only to turn around and say, "Thank you." To which he gave me such an empathetic nod. Then, his friend opened his eyes, and my heart raced a bit when I noticed he had no pupils and barely any observable irises. A strong white glaze coated his entire corneas. Perhaps my heart skipped a beat because I was not used to seeing something like this, but honestly, I think a tickle ran up my spine because it felt like the blind man was looking right at me when he said, "Beware of thy guests you entertain for thereby some have entertained angels unaware."

And there I was again…frozen. Honestly, I couldn't move. I could only stand there and watch the man in the cap help his friend off the ledge of the half-wall and proceed to walk in the opposite direction until they disappeared into the fog of the city, which was really just steam coming from the sewer grates on Woodward Avenue.

So, when I saw the attractive woman for a third time on my trip, I recalled that last line from that man from Detroit. I wondered *Has this been my angel.* And then…As luck would have it, the attractive woman's head looked up before we passed her, and our eyes met. I gave a half smile and a slight wave. Without hesitation, she flipped me off and kept walking.

I guess not.

And as my ride slowly crept along, Mary Ellen suddenly appeared in my mind. The one who rambled on in her quaint, cool, cluttered shop, where I had seen that attractive woman for the second time. I quickly recalled much of what Mary Ellen told me about relationships and attachments and how people change, and dang, she had some—what would Graeme call them?—"Bangers." She was dropping some knowledge, and I never really took the time to let what she said sink in.

"Forgiveness turns regret into experience." Those were her words. And they rang in my head like an old, famous song lyric you wind up repeating all day long.

Mary Ellen had a past, and she just rolled with it. Or rather, she forgave herself where and when she needed to…she didn't cling to that past or allow it to cling to her. She talked of ghosts…memories that hadn't seemed to affect her self-love or weigh her down. And if there were demons from way back when? Well, it seems she befriended them. She didn't cast blame and seemed to have no space for remorse. Thinking of Mary Ellen brought back visuals of the old couple sitting next to one another, laughing in that booth at Big Boy. And then I remembered the couple with the noodle that ended with a kiss and an obvious proposal. People living their lives. *Damn, Mary Ellen…Thank you. I think you may have been that angel I entertained. That is, if I hadn't met Evelyn.* Evelyn. If there can be only one…one angel…I knew sitting there, reflecting on my trip, that Evelyn was the one.

The Lyft pulled up to the stop light at Washington and Lafayette, and would you believe, the same short square of a man with his shopping bag and wearing the bright red stocking cap with the poofy ball on the top was once again walking against traffic. Cars started honking, and I couldn't help but wonder if, for some of the cars, this was a recurrence. The honking got louder, and I assumed people were getting tired of this man's schtick. As he gave his quick wave to each honk he heard, I saw someone run over to the man and help him finish crossing the street. My eyes grew in amazement when I realized the man helping him was Brian!

I tapped the driver incessantly, and he turned back and looked at me. I motioned for him to pull over, and he confusedly did so.

I hopped out of the car, and you wouldn't believe it, but now it was I who was stopping traffic, and there was a new round of honking. It was a cacophony of car horns and screaming voices coming from every direction. I met up with Brian and the man at the street corner, and I gave Brian a huge embrace. He was taken aback a bit, even when he realized it was me.

"Matt?"

As soon as we broke from the hug, I quickly reached for scrap paper in my pocket and something to write with.

"Thank you." The square of a man looked at Brian, and he hugged him as well. "No one has ever helped me before." The man, maybe in his forties, seemed to have down syndrome from my quick observation. "I can get home from here."

"You sure?" Brian asked. And the man gave Brian another hug and walked away.

I gave my newly written note to Brian, and he read it.

I THOUGHT YOU WERE DEAD.

Brian looked confused, and I pointed to my throat, hoping somebody in this town would finally realize or remember that I couldn't speak. I took back the paper and wrote as fast as I could. When I handed it to Brian, he read it aloud, trying to understand my handwriting.

"I heard there was a hit and run and thought it was you." He then looked up at me. "Oh yeah, I heard about that. God awful. Nope, not me, Matt."

I was thrilled and then a sadness pierced my heart thinking that someone did die, and that somebody was a somebody to someone.

But I was happy that it wasn't Brian.

"Sir?!" We both turned and saw my Lyft driver standing outside his car waiting for me. "Your flight!"

"You leaving?"

I nodded.

"Time to go home, huh?" And he offered his hand…and I shook it.

Back in the Lyft, my phone buzzed. It was Graeme's playlist. I opened the app and took a quick glance at some of the songs…

"worldstar money (interlude)" by Joji

"Riot!" by Earl Sweatshirt

"Empty" by Kevin Abstract

"Outside" by Kota the Friend

"Ginger" by BROCKHAMPTON

"Unhealthy" by Bakar

"Some" by Steve Lacy

"TOGETHER" by Amine'

"16" by Baby Keem

"Solo" by Samsa

Yeah, I hadn't heard of any of these guys. I looked up at the title of the playlist…DIFFVIBE…and noticed that it was three hours and nineteen minutes. Gratitude erupted inside of me at the thought that Graeme would spend this much time assembling something like this for me.

At the gate at the airport, I walked down the bridgeway to board my plane, remembering what Brian had asked, "Time to go home, huh?"

No…no it wasn't.

It was time to get livin'. First stop: England…and surprise my friend, Danny.

LARRY JOE CAMPBELL is an actor and author living in Los Angeles. His first professional gig was back in the summer of 1991 as a part of Central Michigan University's professional Summer Theatre. He spent two summers performing as a member of CMUST, and it had a lasting impact on him. So much so, that in 2007, Larry Joe started the Summer Theatre Endowment to help ensure that future CMU students get to experience the Summer Theatre Program. Larry Joe graduated from CMU in 1992 with a BAA in Broadcast and Cinematic Arts & Theatre and Interpretation...learning under the tutelage of Steve Berglund, Jill Taft-Kaufman, Tim Connors, and Denny Bettisworth. He also holds an MA in Theatre from Wayne State University ('98). Larry Joe is a former member of the internship program at the Boarshead Theatre (which was run by the legendary John Peakes) in Lansing, Michigan, and is a proud alum of The Second City in Detroit ('96-99).

Larry Joe made his way out to Los Angeles in the winter of 1999 thanks to Bob Saget and Dave Coulier, who told their manager about Larry Joe and fellow SC actor, Eric Black. Ray Reo and Peter Safran signed Larry Joe and Eric, and the two moved from Michigan to Los Angeles.

Larry Joe got his start in Los Angeles with the pilot *The Trouble with Normal* created by Victor Fresco and starring David Krumholtz, Jon Cryer, Brad Raider, and Paget Brewster. Around this time he also appeared in *Friends, Stark Raving Mad, Suddenly Susan,* and the *Geena Davis Show* before landing the role of Andy on *According to Jim*, starring Jim Belushi, Courtney Thorne-Smith, and Kimberly Williams-Paisley. *According to Jim* would run from 2001 to 2008 for 182 episodes...of which, Larry Joe got to direct nine. During this time, he appeared in the films: *Wedding Crashers, Jimminy Glick in LaLawood, Showtime,* and *Drive Thru.*

Larry Joe continued to work with Jim Belushi on *Growing Belushi* and continues to tour with Jim along with Joshua Funk and Megan Grano in *Jim Belushi and the Board of Comedy.*

After *According to Jim*, Larry Joe made appearances in *Weeds, Killers, Hall Pass, Rules of Engagement, Pacific Rim, R.I.P.D., Last Man Standing, The Goldbergs, Key and Peele, Detroiters, American Vandal, The Orville,* and *Mom* to name a few. He also enjoyed stints on Disney shows *Good Luck Charlie, I Didn't Do It, Dog with a Blog,* and *Best Friends Whenever,* as well the Northern Michigan independent franchise *Dogman,* written and directed by Richard Brauer.

Larry Joe is currently recurring in Fox's *Animal Control* in the role of Carl.

All told, Larry Joe has appeared in over 70 television and film productions during his professional career. It was during this time that Larry Joe self-published a children's book entitled *The Castle Messengers,* which was based on a made-up children's game he and his kids played while they were growing up. The book is illustrated by his brothers, Danny and Gary Campbell.

When he is not acting and writing, Larry Joe enjoys coaching football. He's been a high school football coach for the past 9 years. He also enjoys teaching, walking, music, philosophy, and art.

Larry Joe has been married for over 27 years to his wife, Peggy, who is a middle school teacher. They have five adult children: Gabriella, Nathan, Madelyn, Max, and Lydia.

www.ingramcontent.com/pod-product-compliance
Lightning Source LLC
Chambersburg PA
CBHW031058020726
47495CB00007B/1948